the
PORTALIS
RUNES

BERRYTREE
PUBLISHING

THE PORTALIS RUNES

To Angela,

Happy Reading!

Alice Brogan

A. G. BROGAN

-For my Grandparents, John, Rita & Gerry-
I carry you in my heart.

♦ ACKNOWLEDGMENTS ♦

Thank you ...

To my Mother, for fiercely backing me, always.

To my Husband, for your unwavering support, even when I thought writing a novel was beyond me.

To my Children, my inspirations and proudest joys.

To Pete, my rational and stoic adviser.

To my Nan Maureen, your faith in me always gives me courage.

To my Father, for your quiet and consistent praise.

To Clare, for showing me what it means to persist against the odds.

To Spiffing Publishing, my guides through the world of self-publishing.

Finally to you, the booklovers, for reading and supporting my novel.

◆ 1 ◆

Aria

I scrambled, weightless and desperate, arms outstretched and reaching, *reaching*, for what I did not know. I was startled awake before my freefalling body met the earth, and pressed a hand to my erratic heart, reminding myself all the while that the ordeal was simply a dream, despite my intense reaction. After a moment, I shook my head, cleared the unsettling vision from my mind and dressed for another day on my grandfather's farm. Our own little piece of paradise nestled harmlessly within the vast Kingdom of Arckus.

The farmhouse already smelt of old oak and cooked meats, so I decided to leave my room and break my fast. I left my comfortable chambers reluctantly, littered as it was with all the memorabilia I had collected as a small child, from glass pebbles to dried flowers that hung softly around the small window frame and creating, as they had for many years, feelings of warmth and nostalgia, whenever I gazed upon them. Thick rugs kept the room at a comfortable temperature throughout the year and I found myself digging my toes into the soft fibres, before donning my socks and worn boots. Reaching the vaulted hall, I pouted unhappily as small scatterings of dust danced through the subtle rays of light that streamed from the taller windows. The thought of having to clean those windows in a sennight's time was not a pleasant one, but as this was once a grand home, fit for a lord, it maintained some eccentricities of its previous owners and that included the awkwardly perched windows. Arriving at the kitchens, I spied a man who sat proudly at the large wooden table and despite exuding the presence of a great nobleman, once he saw me, I was greeted with nothing but a warm and humble smile, nearly hidden completely by a thick, silver moustache.

"Aria my girl, grab some breakfast and sit with me, we have much to discuss about the upcoming harvest and I wish to be organised before the festival in three weeks' time."

The harvest festival. It was one of the most joyous occasions on our calendar, barring the winter solstice of course, and celebrated the end of a plentiful summer. Sadly we had not seen one of those for some time, but thankfully it had not dampened the mood about the farm, nor the village.

"Yes Grandfather," I replied enthusiastically, eager to grab what was currently simmering over the impressive kitchen stove. I'd always admired the beautiful and intricate carvings in the surrounding brickwork, but did not tarry for long. Hurrying my booted feet along the flagstone floor, I grabbed my bowl, filled it with a spoonful of rabbit stew, some freshly baked bread and sent a smile to Wendy our cook as I passed, before heading back to the table.

"You will be placed in charge of calculating the number of wheat sacks harvested this year, Aria. This is your chance to prove yourself."

I grinned up from my bowl of stew at my grandfather, the salty goodness now dripping down my chin in an unladylike manner, but this did not dull my excitement. Of course, I had been arguing my case for a few years now, but since turning ten and eight a sennight ago, Grandfather had taken to including me in the farm's affairs, as finding a husband was not currently my main concern. A sentiment which he remained uncommonly supportive of, despite Wendy's chagrin.

"Of course Grandfather, I shan't let you down. I will go and speak with Geoffrey post-haste, once I have finished my meal and head to the market with Wendy this afternoon, if she needs any assistance?" Geoffrey was our main labourer and farm hand. Stocky and stubborn, he was built for hard work in the fields.

"That is a very sound idea and yes, you have my permission to accompany Wendy to the market this afternoon, but do not dally, for I expect dinner to be on time." He smirked knowingly and eyed Wendy from across the room, whose face was the picture of innocence. On occasion, we were distracted by the wares in the market town, so I could not fault Grandfather for his comment. "I will also be meeting with some merchants this afternoon, so please prepare the hall before you leave, and make sure to provide a few sweet treats for our guests, Wendy."

Wendy smiled at my grandfather, her slightly greying, warm-brown hair and plump features gazed at him fondly. "Yes Sir, I shall prepare a tray now especially. Will they be attending dinner tonight?"

"No Wendy, our business should be concluded by then," he replied smoothly, by which time I had moved from the table and began washing my bowl and spoon, eager to complete my tasks for the day so I could venture to the market. With a wave and a smile at them both, I left quickly through the kitchen door, intending to catch up to Geoffrey before he ventured out into the fields for the remainder of the day.

Thankfully I caught sight of our senior farmhand just past the kitchen gardens, the smell of lavender and sage soothing, while he spoke with Berta our housemaid.

"Geoffrey! Berta!" I called eagerly and waved my hand in the air to gain their attention before heading closer.

"You really must stop shouting like that Miss Aria, it's not very ladylike," Geoffrey chided at my approach and I rolled my eyes. They all knew I was no court lady and Grandfather did not bring me up to be such, just a strong woman, capable of running her own home, *if* the occasion ever arose.

I smiled placatingly at Geoffrey's frown, his flat nose taking up a large portion of his chiselled face. He would have been appealing to the eye, were it not for his shaggy blond hair.

"Yes, yes Geoffrey, I won't raise my voice again …" and his frown softened, "unless you are a fair distance away, or I fear you will ride off."

The man shook his head despairingly, before huffing, "Well, what can I help you with, Miss Aria?"

"I must speak with both of you," I said, then explained, "Geoffrey, Grandfather has put me in charge of counting the wheat stores this year and I would like to liaise with you and your plans for the harvest."

He nodded easily. "Of course. I will finish my tasks for today, but shall we meet in the kitchens midday on the morrow to discuss our plan of action?"

I nodded my agreement and turned uneasily. "Berta?" A thin, dark, brow arched slightly, her tall and slender frame now rather imposing, but I continued nonetheless. "Grandfather wishes that I help arrange the hall for his meeting this afternoon, if you are agreeable?"

"Of course, Miss Aria," Berta conceded to my relief. "I would be glad of the help, but no dallying. I expect your work to be swift and impeccable." I grimaced inwardly, hoping I was up to the task and even though some of the maids called her a shrew for her dark hair, sharp features and even sharper tongue, I knew she was just a perfectionist and if it served Grandfather well, I could put up with a comment or two.

We left for the market just after our midday meal and the trip did not come soon enough. Berta, upon hearing of the wealthy merchants' impending visit, was even more viper-like in her manners today. Her standards seemed almost untenable. The silverware was polished until it gleamed and the sweet treats made by Wendy left the whole house with a watering mouth. Unhappy about missing such treats, but glad to be away from Berta, I turned in my seat as we slowly left the farmhouse grounds. The horse and cart were our current means of transportation, which rumbled lazily down the dirt and gravel road, surrounded on both sides by thick grassy meadows that drew your eye to the property.

Sitting alone yet proud, the farmhouse did look rather striking from afar, but not in the conventional sense, as to many eyes, it appeared to be a mismatch of designs. Thick stone brickwork drew the eye up to a clay-tiled roof on the right and a low-slung, neatly thatched one on the left. Clutching the building grew a picturesque, lavender-shaded wisteria which hung around the proud oak front door and up to the small first-floor windows. Wendy once explained what an oddity it was, that they flourished at this time of year and that their fragrant blooms seemed to last longer on our property. I however chose not to dwell on the thought and simply admired their beauty for what it was, before the splendid picture of our home faded slowly from view.

We reached the treelined market town of Great Barrington, which was bordered on three sides by a gentle babbling brook and edged with patches of fluffy white grasses, dotted sporadically about the area. On the eastern side sat a charming willow tree, that many of the town residents used for shade to enjoy their luncheons during the stifling summer season. Not in need of any great bridges with which to cross, special attention was still paid to the decorative woodwork along its walkways. It had four bridges in all, in and out of the town. We passed over the bridge from the western side of the village, intent on heading straight for the main market street and despite it being little more than a glorified dirt road, the market still carried an air of excitement which was difficult to replicate. The bustling stalls that lined the main thoroughfare smelled of baked goods, leather and even newly forged steel. The surrounding, and dare I say wonky in appearance, stone and thatched properties which were crammed into the space, lent the area a humble air during one of the busiest times of the year. People milled about enthusiastically while they prepared for the harvest festival, each having their own jobs to do and taking enjoyment in the work it entailed. It was also a proud moment for the vendors and provided ample opportunity for their wares and skills to shine.

"I have made an order with Monroe the spice merchant, Aria, which I will collect first. I would ask you to see Mrs Schiffer and retrieve the rolls of material for our new festival dresses that I plan to sew."

Despite being distracted by the market stalls and their many wares, I turned as Wendy addressed me, her face flushed and eager to start haggling a good price as usual. "I'd be more than happy to Wendy, have you agreed a price for the fabric already?" I smiled slyly, knowing she would have already bartered fiercely.

"One silver piece for the fabric, Aria, and do not let Mrs Schiffer persuade you into buying more. I've checked the amount of fabric myself before placing the order."

After passing me the silver coin, we agreed to meet outside the fabric shop in a few turns of the dial, before I left Wendy and hurried to speak to Mrs Schiffer. Her stall wasn't far, but I found it difficult to remain on course with all the interesting trinkets and food on offer, until a familiar voice distracted me.

"Why Miss Aria, how nice to see you on this fine day."

Harold the jeweller greeted me with a mischievous smile. Over forty years of age, he sported long, unclean hair and a missing tooth, but you could still see he must have been handsome in his youth, despite the years not being kind.

"Good day Harold, did you find anything interesting on your travels?"

"Curious you should ask," he replied innocently and I smirked, knowing he only wished to gloat about his new and exotic finds, all the while hoping for a sale. Despite his lack of success thus far, Harold still pulled out a dainty silver necklace from the back of his stall, a small emerald dangling from its centre and reflecting the autumn sunshine.

I gasped, not at the fine piece, but upon recognising the familiar symbol etched into the back setting. A symbol akin to the one carved upon my grandfather's fireplace. Eager to view it closer, I asked Harold if I could hold it. His lips tilted up into a smirk, likely thinking he had made a sale following my loud gasp and purred, "Of course my dear, take a closer look."

My fingers closed around the pendant and I could

have sworn the etching glowed, when suddenly, it vanished.

"THIEF!" Harold roared, while all I could do was gape and blink in shock, at a complete loss for words. I did nothing as the market guards stormed over to Harold's stall at speed and grabbed my arms.

"State the events, Sir," one of the guards addressed Harold, his hold on my upper arm not in the least bit gentle.

"This young harlot just stole one of my rare necklaces!"

"Stole?!" I shouted above Harold's rantings. "I stole *nothing*! I was holding it right in front of your eyes, as plain as day! Surely if I stole it, I wouldn't stand here and await my own arrest!" I fumed at the turn of events, yet stalled my overzealous reaction and remembered my grandfather's advice to remain calm and control my temper. I took a deep breath and thought rationally, even as they began dragging me to the market dungeon for further questioning, but it wasn't long before my nerves overshadowed all thought and my feet began to shuffle in protest along the dirt road.

We reached the building that was little more than a glorified horse stable and before they could shove me past its gloomy threshold I spat, "I wish for you to retrieve my chaperone Wendy from Monroe the spice merchant immediately!" I glared at the guard holding my left arm in a vice-like grip and while they continued to ignore my protests, I was ushered down the damp stone steps and shoved into a right-hand cell in the centre of the dim room. I staggered to maintain my balance while the door closed abruptly behind me and all there was left to do was to scowl at the unaffected guards who hastily left. I counted six cells in all, pressed to the outer walls on either side of the building. The one opposite mine was also occupied, but I didn't care to spy its occupants. It smelt foul and of all manner of bodily fluids; with nothing but a shallow hole in the floor with which to relieve oneself, I had to curtail the impulse to wretch.

Time passed and the ever-growing silence left me feeling dejected and fearful that the guards had ignored my request, until I heard vicious shouting above ground and my hope began to rise.

"Miss Aria?!" It was Wendy's hysterical voice.

"Aria, you say?" came a lecherous rumble from across the room. "Pretty name, for a pretty girl." Although I had yet to see his face, the man's thick accent made my skin crawl. I tried to ignore him, in favour of listening to the conversation outside but frustratingly I could only hear it in part.

"… Jacoby Torvel will be here post-haste, she is not to be addressed until her guardian is present …" I hadn't heard my grandfather's name for a while, Wendy's final words of authority the last I heard before a guard re-entered the room. Distracted by my circumstances, I barely registered the guard's droll voice as he told me I would remain here until my guardian arrived. Soon after, he stalked away once more and I was left with nothing but my confused thoughts and an unnerving stranger for company.

Perched on a low stool and fearing to sit on the filth-ridden floor, I should have felt alone and yet my attention was elsewhere. Diverted by the gaze of the other prisoner, that I could feel boring into my cell like a physical presence and forcing a shiver from my body. Determined not to be intimidated, I ignored him and thought back to the events that caused my current situation. The necklace. Beautiful, yes, but where did it go? I'd searched my person several times while in my cell, to be sure my mind wasn't playing tricks on me and found *nothing*. It just disappeared, but how? And what was that glow?

"Pretty girl, how did you end up in 'ere?" I grimaced as his oily voice interrupted my thoughts, but I remained adamant that the leery man bathed in shadow would not affect me. "I can help get you out if you like?" he added and I glanced up from where I sat. The man now shifted forward in his cell, his boots rattling the dust and rocks at his feet, while his long, dirty fingers coiled around the bars. Soon after, his face was pressed between them and I could finally witness his unfortunate visage.

He could not have been older than five and twenty. Dark eyes that I dared not stare into for long and what skin I could see was covered in grime. His smile was lecherous and revealed two missing teeth. I could only scowl when he insisted on sneering further, "But such a feat would come at a cost, pretty girl," and the wretch proceeded to look up and down my body.

I retorted, "Keep your thoughts to yourself, you dirty ass rat, and don't address me again. If you wish to escape, flee as far away from me as your legs will carry you and I will not care one wit!" My response was very unladylike, but I felt it appropriate given the current company.

"Such a temper," he replied, but did not say another word. The silence was interrupted a few dials later by a commotion outside.

"Where is my granddaughter?!" I recognised the roaring voice of my grandfather immediately. A roar which had frightened me a time or two as a young girl and I almost felt pity for the guards who were on the receiving end of his wrath. *Almost.*

"On what grounds do you hold her? I demand to see her at once!" I jumped up from my seat and headed to the bars, afraid to grip their soiled surface despite my desperation, and heard the strong gaited steps of Grandfather echo down the stairs, followed by the two market guards. Grandfather grimaced at his surroundings once he entered the darkened room and scowled when he caught sight of the other smirking prisoner, before walking straight to me. His eyes were relieved, that much I could tell, before his questions began.

"Aria, what happened?" And I rushed to reply.

"Harold the jeweller accused me of stealing, Grandfather, but I was right in front of him, the necklace it just … just disappeared and there is *nothing* on my person. I don't understand what has happened?!" The last of my words ended on a confused sob and my grandfather turned to glare at the guards.

"Is this true? She was arrested, despite there being nothing on her person?! You will release her at once before I have this taken further and have you both dismissed for incompetence!" With that tone, I knew Grandfather was not to be argued with.

"We must investigate these incidences, Sir," the guard on the left conceded, now appearing uncomfortable in his heavy chain-mailed armour, while he hastily moved to open my cell. I ran into my grandfather's arms and despite his less than stocky build, I had never felt safer. He glared at the guards as we left the dungeon and again I felt the eyes of the other prisoner on my back. We headed to our cart at the far end of the now quiet market street and greeted Geoffrey quickly in the low twilight, before making our way home in silence. Unsure of what to say, I looked up at my grandfather with concern, the jostling of the cart uncomfortable in our haste, but instead of his usual complaints, he simply stared pensively ahead the entire journey home.

♦ 2 ♦

Vylnor

In the darkest hour of night, unbeknown to the eyes of the mortals, the prisoner in cell three smirked at the events that had unfolded, while his mind repeatedly turned over the name *Aria Torvel.*

Broken out of his musings, the rotund guard rapped on his bars with his sword, in some pathetic attempt to intimidate him.

"Do not look so pleased." His beady eyes narrowed. "You will be charged on the morrow, most likely to hang from the noose."

Unruffled by the guard's words and with his cold grin still in place, the prisoner instead mumbled *"arvemnico,"* and his mortal disguise faded slowly into a cloud of black smoke. The guard's stunned eyes widened; his trembling sword drawn protectively as he took a step away from the bars.

And with an inky voice born of cold calculation, the prisoner murmured, "I cannot have a fool such as you spoil my plans." His dark magic clung to the guard like a second skin and dragged him across the worlds, desperate screams of terror echoing from his lips, before they were both summoned into the unmerciful realm of Oromos and the suffering that lay waiting within it.

Aria

The events at the market seemed to have been forgotten by the household for the time being, although I was taken off guard by the huge and awkwardly prolonged hug from Berta the following morning. Grandfather had taken more time to compose himself, as he was rather abrupt the following two days after sending Geoffrey out to find that weasel Harold and wring his neck. Sadly, Geoffrey had no such luck in locating him. Instead, I focused on the tasks Grandfather had given me over the next couple of weeks and was pleased by his praise, when we had counted and stored all this year's wheat sacks in record time. Not our most profitable year, but enough that we could sell some of our stores and livestock and still provide for the household over the winter period.

It was now only a few days until the harvest festival and even though what occurred that day still baffled me, I chose not to dwell on it for too long. Wendy and I had a few hours that afternoon with which to finish our dresses for the gathering and I looked forward to spending time with her. Currently perched in one of the ornate dining chairs within the hall, Wendy held up the material we had bought from Mrs Schiffer, a rich blue that reminded me of the darkest depths of the ocean, and proudly commented that it matched my eyes. Ignoring the slight chill from the lofty space, I simply rolled said eyes and remained pleased by my modest boat-necked design, with long sleeves and no train.

I refused to be one of those ladies who were asked to dance, only to have some poor fool continuously treading on her dress. The cut would also ensure Grandfather's approval and I would have no unwanted attention directed my way, like that prisoner in the market cell.

I shuddered at the memory, Wendy's voice clearing my thoughts as she spoke. "Will you accept any invitations to dance this year, Miss Aria, as I know that Thomas Fjorman asked you on a couple of occasions at the last festival?"

I internally cringed and looked up at Wendy from where I was sewing the cuff on my dress, my face failing to hide my disgust. "I doubt it, Wendy, and especially from him." Pursing my lips I added irritably, "He called me 'carrot freckles' when I was younger and you and I both know I never had that shade of colouring!"

"Oh, well you cannot blame him for that, he was a young lad and probably fond of you even then," Wendy chortled, eyes glazed and her mind undoubtedly depicting some mock romantic notion. I, however, did not accept that explanation at all and decided not to voice that I thought he had the manners of a fox and the face of a toad.

My afternoon with Wendy flew by, as did the next couple of days until it was the evening of the festival. The farmhouse was a buzz of excitement while everyone dressed and readied for the festival in town. Wendy had just finished pinning my braids into a soft up-do, when Berta rapped on my bedroom door.

"Your grandfather is ready and waiting downstairs for you, Miss Aria."

I grinned and stood, while Wendy offered her hand and gently spun me in a circle.

"You look beautiful Miss Aria, your grandfather will be fighting off offers for your hand, mark my words!" she squeaked excitedly, while I tried not to let the revulsion show on my face.

I certainly had no plans to be married off and hoped to prove useful enough to Grandfather and this farm that I wouldn't need to be, unless I chose to, of course. Ignoring her comments, I replied tactfully, "I will see you there shortly, Wendy, and we can fill our stomachs with those sugared candies from Gilroy's stall."

My mouth was salivating at the thought alone and I smiled before leaving Wendy and Berta behind. They would be bringing spiced wine and fruit pies along with Geoffrey in tow a few dials later. So, skipping down the stone staircase, I saw Grandfather waiting patiently by the front entrance. He looked regal for a man in his sixties, wearing a deep burgundy tunic and matching hose with black, knee-high boots. We weren't the richest farm in Great Barrington, but Grandfather would always make sure the household looked presentable on special occasions. It was a time for celebration and morale he would say, and after witnessing the jovial faces of his workers and our friends, I couldn't help but agree.

"Ah there's my beautiful girl," he smiled warmly

and grabbed my hand, tucking it in the crook of his arm as we made our way to the cart. I suddenly blurted, "I forgot, I must fetch my cloak!"

Now the fall season was in full swing, the nights had become chilly and I did not want some man with less than honourable intentions to offer me his cloak.

"That's quite alright my dear, I had a new one made for you." And stepping up to the cart, Grandfather presented me with a large wooden box. With tentative hands I traced the smooth grains of wood along its surface, stunned; he had already paid for my new dress and now this. I opened it up and lifted out the most beautiful deep-green cloak with a brown fur trim and remained speechless. With tears in my eyes, I turned to my grandfather and watched him hand the empty box to a farmhand, before throwing my arms around his shoulders.

"Now that's enough of that," he said gruffly. "You have worked hard my girl and I would have you rewarded as my other employees." Although we both knew he would never have had something so thoughtful and expensive made for his farmhands.

"This is perfect, I cannot thank you enough!" I let go of Grandfather and gave him my biggest smile while he awkwardly waved away my gratitude. "No need, just keep working hard, Aria. Now let's get going before all those sugared candies are gone." With lighter hearts, we both climbed into the cart and headed off to the festival, ready and thankful to experience one of the year's greatest delights.

Vylnor

Deep in the mountain fortress of Oromos, an ancient evil was stirring. The screams of the guard he had stolen from Great Barrington repulsed Vylnor, *"pathetic"* being his only remark while he stalked the oppressive halls and headed towards his Master's residence. Vylnor remained satisfied by this new development, but his Master was brutal and power hungry, so he would be wise to tread carefully when delivering his news.

Reaching the Master's domain, he entered a great towering room bathed almost entirely in shadow. Small torches which usually flickered violently now remained motionless and caused the shadows along the rock-covered walls to halt their positions. The sight was eerie, as though the darkness also sought to avoid his Master's attentions.

The eastern side of the mountain had been carved wide open to the harsh and freezing elements. It was cold yet still. So very, very *still*. Despite the sounds of the wind howling through the vast mountain scape. A gale so vicious, it could cut even its flying brethren from the skies if provoked, and for centuries none had dared to climb the winds so high. Vylnor knew this meant his Master was calm, lethally so, and he spoke quickly into the waiting silence. "Master, I bring news from the Mortal Realm."

Vylnor dropped to his knees, his forehead pressed harshly into the icy rock to demonstrate his submission.

"Do not delay then ssservant, or your life may be the

pricccce," came a rasped and hollow reply from the dark. Gaze still fixed to the mountain floor, Vylnor continued quickly, "I may have found a lead to the Portalis, Master." Silence reigned while Vylnor braced himself against the floor and prepared to be struck down by his Master's power.

"If what you sssay is true ssservant, do not dare disssappoint me." Vylnor welcomed his Master's merciless hiss of dismissal, while the wretched presence slowly faded from the room.

Standing swiftly, he turned to leave. Vylnor's calculating mind plotting in earnest until an invasive darkness began to writhe within his chest. It was cold, barren and lifeless. And a stark reminder from his Master that should he fail in this task, Vylnor's life, nay his very *soul*, would be the price.

Aria

The festival was located on the outer edges of Great Barrington and sat to the north of where the market was usually held. Occupying the area were but a small cluster of timber-framed buildings which made up the central square and I was especially grateful for the festival's rural location, for I did not wish to revisit the market again for some time. It drew up too many questions, questions I had no answers to and only served as a reminder of my unfortunate incarceration.

Today however, the air was thick with happiness and cheer and I was excited to walk around the many colourful stalls and establishments that littered a recently cropped field. The food vendors in particular.

We left the cart with a stable hand and Grandfather slipped him a copper coin to ensure he looked after the horses, before we strode towards the field. My enthusiasm grew quickly at the luring torchlights and delectable smells, until I practically dragged Grandfather alongside me.

"Hold up, Aria my girl, these legs don't move quite as quickly as they used to!" he huffed good-naturedly and tugged his arm away when we reached the first stall, where the blacksmith Armand was selling his most interesting wares.

The outer face of the narrow tent was decorated in a myriad of horseshoes, locks and keys, the metal jingling sweetly as it was hit by the soft autumn breeze, but it was the weapons that quickly drew my eye. They always fascinated me. Grandfather had his own collection stored in his chambers and yet he would never let me pick one up, nor would he speak of them, but I caught him practising a time or two as a child. Despite his intriguing stance, however, he did not wish for me to be completely useless in a scuffle should the occasion arise, so I was taught basic defensive techniques, in the event I should need to flee a pursuer and summon Grandfather of course.

A small, ornate dagger caught my eye at the back of the stall, its slightly arched blade artfully decorated with etchings of dancing flames. I did not dare ask to view it closer, afraid Grandfather would not approve, so instead

I turned to leave.

"I would like to see that dagger," came Grandfather's even voice to my left, which halted all movement. Amazed, I spun around and saw he pointed to the same dagger I was previously perusing.

"Of course, Sir," and Armand promptly retrieved the dagger and set it in my grandfather's hand.

"Where was it forged?" he questioned and eyed the blade curiously.

"I am not certain, Sir. This was a purchase from a merchant and rumoured to have been forged in Elavon, one of the few left behind in battles past I would assume. I have been using it as a study piece, for it is finely made despite its foreign heritage ... perfect for say, a young lady." The blacksmith waved in my direction, while I distractedly rolled the name *Elavon* around my mind and tried to place it within the Arckus Kingdom. I failed quickly to do so, given my lack of travel experience and knowledge of maps. In the end, I could only surmise that it was a place of interest, if it were a foreign study piece for Armand and made a mental note to question Grandfather about it at another time.

After handling the blade for a moment or two, even I began to grow bored, until Grandfather said unexpectedly, "What is your price?"

A little taken back, I stared open mouthed, quite thinking I must have looked like a large catfish.

"For you Sir, three silver coins," and I gasped, knowing that was far too expensive.

"I will give you one silver and five coppers, no more.

The leather strap needs renewing and there is a small indent on the back edge of the handle. I will take a sheath as well."

After a short pause and clicking his tongue several times, Armand conceded and Grandfather quickly paid for the dagger before ushering me away to the next stall. Unsure of what to say, I remained quiet until I heard Grandfather huff beside me. "Well, aren't you going to take it?" I looked down at his freshly polished boots and chewed my bottom lip.

"Am I allowed to take it, or is this a test?" I finally looked up and arched an eyebrow at my grandfather who laughed in response. "No my dear, but I am aware that as you get older, I cannot stay by your side forever. So give this old man a bit of peace and keep this on your person at all times."

"But …" I stuttered, "what changed your mind?"

"As I said," and he spoke slowly as if addressing a child, "I cannot protect you all the time, so this will suffice if the occasion ever arises, which I hope it does not." I took the blade from my grandfather and tucked it into my belt, its weight comfortable, and I grinned proudly.

"There now, go enjoy the festival. By the looks of things, Wendy has just finished setting out her refreshments, so you can meet with her while I go and speak to Monroe."

Waving to Grandfather's back, I walked briskly towards Wendy in the hopes I would not catch any unwanted attention before I reached her. No such luck accompanied me this evening however, for Thomas Fjorman's lanky form stepped around Mrs Birkshore's vibrant hat stall and intercepted me.

"Aria, how lovely you look this evening," he purred and eyed the neckline of my dress beneath the clasp of my cloak. I failed to hide my cringe, but remained relieved at my forethought to sew the dress into a more modest fashion.

"Thank you, Thomas, but if you would excuse me, I am just on my way to meet Wendy." And would rather avoid his beady eyes and dreary conversation, I thought, but chose not to say aloud.

Attempting to weave around him, Thomas caught my forearm with his sharp grip. Shocked, I stilled and looked up to see him smirking.

"Come now Aria, you have been avoiding me for some time and I would like to get to know my future wife before our wedding."

I stared wide-eyed in disbelief and tried to rein in my temper, while he attempted to coax me around the back of Mrs Birkshore's stall without drawing too much attention. Knowing my grandfather wouldn't want me to cause a scene, I followed genially until we were out of sight of the main crowd. I turned to Thomas with a false smile fixed on my face and hissed, "Listen here you little weasel, the next time you address me so, manners be damned, I will not be so kind as to decline your offer in private, but in front of the whole town."

His grip tightened on my arm during my little

speech, when it fortunately began to loosen. Naively thinking that was the end of it, I looked towards the festival lights and shrugged off his arm, intent on leaving the little swine, when the back of his other hand connected sharply with my left cheek. My head snapped to the side and he grabbed my chin roughly until our faces were uncomfortably close, the smell of his stale breath nauseating.

"You think you have a say in this, little bitch, well, let me make this easy for you." He stuck his toad-like face right up to mine until we were nose to nose, his spittle landing next to my mouth during his speech. I felt my skin crawl. "I have arranged for certain townspeople to catch us in an uncompromising position in a moment or two and to save your reputation, your grandfather will have no other choice but to grant me permission to marry you."

I responded meekly, saying nothing, while his arms moved carelessly from their current positions and his smile morphed into something akin to triumph. I knew then that if I did not act now, I may never have another chance, so I struck my right knee in between his legs causing him to cry out a string of curses and hunch over.

"You bitch!"

Afraid the attack wouldn't stop him for long and remembering what my grandfather taught me – *'strike while they are weak, Aria'* – I threw a right hook across his face and Thomas's form crumpled to the ground.

I clasped my hand gingerly and gritted my teeth, wondering if I had broken or just bruised the bones, before quickly deciding to run and spun towards the festival crowd. Unfortunately I spotted a few of Thomas's supporters heading in our direction, so instead sped towards the far end of the field. Seeing that no one was following me, I rushed into an open tent attached to a caravan and hoped frantically that I could hide there for a moment or two, or at least until I could locate someone familiar and more importantly *safe*.

"Everything alright my dear?" I jumped at the elderly voice that came from behind me and scrambled to sound amiable.

"I apologise, but would you mind if I stayed here a dial or two. I am trying to avoid some unwanted company and would be happy to peruse your wares in the meantime if you would allow?" I sent a beseeching stare at the elderly woman, whose large nose dwarfed her deeply wrinkled face. My attention was soon drawn to her piercing, ice-blue eyes and the colourful scarf wrapped around her grey hair, while I awaited her response. Hoping for understanding, I was surprised by the huff of laughter she sent my way instead.

"No wares to purchase here I'm afraid, knowledge is what I seek." A knowing look crossed her features. I stood there uselessly and unsure of what to say, before I decided to shrug in agreement, highly doubtful that she would receive any information of import from myself and hoped the elderly woman wouldn't be too disappointed when that turned out to be the case. She smiled back with her crooked teeth on show and gestured for me to take a seat on one of the small stools in her caravan, towards the back of the tent.

"Forgive me, but I did not ask your name?" I questioned while taking a seat.

"I did not ask for yours either my dear, but all in good time." Sitting opposite me, she moved to a small trunk on her left and grabbed an ornate hand mirror. "Have a look in this my dear and tell me what you see." I stared at my reflection for several moments and told her this was all I saw. Clearly disappointed, she frowned and replied irritably, "Do not lie to me dear, what … do … you … see?"

Again I stared at my reflection for some time before glaring back at her, thinking she was a lunatic rather than some sort of wise woman and then repeated, "I see nothing but my own reflection."

Her expression turned thoughtful at this and I got the impression she believed my response this time. I heard a "hmmm" as she placed the mirror back into the trunk and proceeded to pull out another. This one slightly larger and more rectangular in shape, also gilded in silver. Again the mirror was placed before my face and she looked at me expectantly. After several tedious moments nothing happened and she now offered a look of surprise, before standing and moving into what looked like her private chambers.

"Here I keep my rarest collections child," she murmured, whilst rummaging through what sounded like one chest after another.

Head in my unhurt hand and smarting cheek now having dulled somewhat, I was later caught staring around her caravan, eyeing the odd implements, nameless books and trinkets, when she finally exited her bedroom. "Try this one, my dear."

I looked at her sceptically and muttered, "I think I should be going now," when her face morphed into displeasure.

"You cannot leave if a gracious host has not yet dismissed you and you asked to stay here for a short time, did you not?"

Sighing I told her, "Fine, but this is the last mirror, I must get back to my family." She nodded before taking a seat opposite yet again and held up a small oval mirror. I inhaled sharply, the etching around the frame sadly familiar, and twisted my hands in my lap to calm my otherwise fraying nerves.

"You recognise these I see," the old woman said smirking and, not wanting her to jump to conclusions, I explained. "I could not tell you what it is, only that I have seen something akin to these symbols before." This time she gave me the mirror and before I could refuse, the markings began to glow.

♦ 3 ♦

Eron

Erondriel remained one of the most highly decorated Generals of the last seven centuries in Elavon. His reputation was impeccable, not only based on his skill and war strategy, but most importantly because of his loyalty to his people. Only he and a handful of elven Elders were in charge of protecting their kin and home world. And what a beautiful home it was.

Named by the ancestors of a fallen star, Elavon was created as a sanctuary for all those who wished to remain in the Light and forgo the darkness of Oromos. His protection and that of the elven armies extended to all creatures who wished to live peacefully and maintain a natural balance by using resources that their own realms provided.

"Excuse me, General Erondriel?" Very aware he was being addressed, Eron could not look away from the beautiful landscape that was his home. Standing on the parapets of the imposing elven training fortress bearing the title 'Locksnight', he gazed out at the uninhibited beauty of the surrounding forest. Its great cedaris trees, decorated in rows of fine, deep-green needles that saw fit to blanket the floors of the forests, were nearly as tall as the council tower itself. Their height so great, one would have thought they were created as pillars to bear the weight of the skies.

The weather was balmy near the Citadel, it changed with the seasons of course, but never to extremes. It was neither too fresh in spring, too stifling in summer, too wet in autumn or too cool in winter. It was what Eron considered to be perfect. However, should you decide to venture further than the capital, the smaller outer colonies experienced different weather systems entirely. The north being cooler throughout the year, the south warmer, the east lush and green with the rains, while the west clung onto the colours of autumn.

Turning to face his former student and longstanding friend, Eron spoke easily. "So formal today, Rendon, is it serious?"

With bated breath, Rendon looked directly into his silver eyes. "A Portalis artefact has been discovered in the great library" and Eron's previously tranquil thoughts abruptly stopped. He inhaled sharply and hissed between his teeth, "You are sure old friend, this is not a mistake?" Eron fervently hoped Rendon would deny what he feared or at least provide a plausible explanation, but instead he responded with dire surety.

"No mistake Eron, we may need to prepare for war."

Eron exited the barracks and edged through the golden Locksnight gate, ignoring its slow yawn open in favour of pace and tucked himself tightly against his steed's neck.

Warriors and civilians alike glanced at him curiously as he cantered past, but he paid them no heed, eager as he was to head further into the city.

Eron expected an event such as this to occur, but given that the four-hundred-year delay between a new Portalis emergence had passed almost two decades prior, he had naively hoped the realms would not have to face this threat yet again. A fool's hope, he realised upon reaching the great library of Elavon half an hour later. The imposing cylindrical building that was built by the hands of their ancestors stood prominently above the city, the scatterings of silver ivy across its surface depicting glimmers of starlight. Its small gardens were protected by rows of living fences that bloomed with sweet-smelling flowers across the seasons, only adding to its charm. It was a place of warmth, a place of history and more importantly, a place of learning for any and all of Elavon's citizens, but in this moment, Eron looked at the building with apprehension.

Astride his famed warhorse Argenti, whose hooves nervously clicked against the cobbled floor, Eron suppressed his concern to instead openly admire the illustrious Citadel spread out before him. The familiar view of arched and domed rooftops tiled in clay littered with silver ores, helped to settle his mind as they glistened under the midday sun. Golden pathways which spread like roots from the library's matching platform were meticulously paved in spiralling patterns that mimicked the Elavon sea and reflected Eron's own scattered thoughts perfectly. Being a master of the water element, he found certain similarities with it often and used the picture it presented now to calm himself, before facing this next trial.

He jumped swiftly from Argenti and stilled, before pressing his face into the horse's silver mane and whispered earnestly, "I hope this is not what I fear my old friend, and if so, I will it that I and my kin have the courage to face this torment once more, for the sake of a brighter future."

His friend shuffled and nudged Eron towards his destination. So stepping away quickly, the First General of Elavon stiffened his spine and left to face the elven Elders, his loyalty forever remaining with them and his people, no matter how grave the outcome.

Sitting at least three storeys high, Eron walked through the arched wooden doors of the great library gilded with the words *"knowledge above all"* and spotted the three elven Elders and two Generals awaiting his arrival in the centre of the vast room. The former wore their signature embellished robes and the latter their warriors garb. They all stood uneasily and fidgeted around an aged wooden table, carved of the finest cedaris wood. The furniture had clearly been used and loved by the library for many centuries, given the occasional notch and scratch which marred its surface, but what was once a piece used in the aid of learning, would now become a meeting place for the discussion of war.

Eron needed a distraction from the ominous thought and glanced at the row upon row of scrolls and books that littered the walls, inhaling the smell of aged parchment which predominantly floated about the room, before greeting the three Elders in turn with a small bow.

"Elder Petriel *(ancient knowledge)*, Elder Florel *(earth and healing)*, Elder Kalor *(light and flame)*, for light and peace." He pressed his fist over his heart after echoing the small prayer and turned to his two other Generals. "It has been some time Havrel and Talos, I am sad to see we are not meeting under more joyous circumstances."

Both Generals grimaced. "Indeed Erondriel, but now that we are all here, shall we find out if what our second-in-command has told us is true?" This came from Havrel, the Second General of Elavon. A master of earth, he was a giant of a male and matched by his long dark hair and bronze eyes. Usually level-headed, Havrel's demeanour was like the very earth beneath their feet, but under times of great duress, his emotions could easily fray and shift, akin to the ground tremors of the north. The elf remained stubborn in his quest for success, or in this case answers, while he shuffled impatiently awaiting a reply.

"Let us all take a seat," gestured Florel, her warm brown hair fastened in a set of beautiful long braids that complemented her delicate face and vivid green eyes.

Turning to the rows of scrolls and books in the ancient library, Petriel called forward one of the librarians, who held a small item wrapped in a piece of purple silk. "I would also have you bring the twin mirror with you," the blonde Elder added and Florel gasped.

"You think that necessary at this time, Petriel?"

"Unfortunately Lady Florel, I have a feeling we may need it." Despite his decisive reply, the male seemed nervous while he peered keenly down his sharp nose at the item covered in silk, which now sat idly in the middle of the table, as though it might combust at any moment.

Two librarians followed, bringing with them an average-sized table mirror, again covered by a fine cloth, and placed this next to the other artefact facing the Elders and Generals. Removing both coverings, the two librarians stepped back hastily, their teal cloaks rustling about their bodies while the attention of six powerful elves was placed on the two objects before them.

Both items were scored with similar but an unmatching pattern of runes that could be activated only by a Portalis. The singular being capable of ending the Three Realms as they knew it.

Taking a deep breath, Kalor, with his short red hair and golden eyes, addressed the group. "As you can see, there is no mistake as to what the necklace is. A Portalis artefact to be sure, wouldn't you say Petriel?" This was confirmed by a short and serious nod.

"It must have laid undiscovered for some time," the male Elder mused.

"How is that possible?!" came the disbelieving outburst from Talos, Elavon's Third General and master of lightning and air. His temper was quick and hot but just as quick to cool, while he pulled irritably on his black and silver loose braid, clearly displeased with this new information, as were they all.

A few muttered curses echoed around the table,

much to Florel's displeasure, which were quickly cut short by the sharp and sudden glow of the twin mirror. The drawing of blades sounded quickly and all members were on their feet in moments. Six of Elavon's most formidable beings stood tensely, unwilling to take their eyes off the mirror for fear of what it may show, or more dangerously, *who* it may bring through.

The picture grew clear in the time of a breath, when auburn hair and blue eyes as rich as sapphires greeted them. "A *mortal?*" hissed Havrel and Eron could not take his eyes from her confused face and worried expression. As the First General, Eron thought he knew fear, had been in enough battles to see and taste it. But nothing frightened him more than hearing the words from a foreign evil across the worlds, addressing the pretty, worried mortal with a malicious cackle, "Oh my dear, the Master will be pleased I found you."

Aria

Jolted out of my daze into the mirror and the beautiful people which it contained, I narrowed my gaze at the old woman across from me.

"Master? I do not understand your meaning?" And before I received a reply, she launched herself at me, hands outstretched in what looked like, *claws*?! Grasping the mirror like a shield, I threw it at the old banshee flying towards me. This appeared to have done the trick, as a look of panic crossed her face and stopped her advance, while she chose instead to dive towards the mirror and squealed, "FOOLISH MORTAL!" Despite her age, she deftly caught the mirror and rolled, moments before it could shatter upon the floor.

Recognising a distraction when I saw one, I fled through the caravan and towards the front of the tent. "*Entwinor!*" came a shout from behind me and a rope which had lain harmlessly on the ground suddenly darted up to wrap around my arms and legs. I cried out, falling harshly to the floor and unfortunately my face was the only body part available to break the fall. Stars filled my vision while a pair of hasty feet headed towards me. Panicked and with limited options, I tried to reach the small dagger my grandfather had gifted me and just as my fingers grazed the handle, I was roughly pulled over onto my back. Maniacal black eyes and a smile bearing a row of rotten teeth greeted me. Her claws punctured my shoulders and I bit my lip to stop myself from crying out.

"Do not run again little girl, for I am unlikely to be so obliging a second time," she sneered. Her long grey hair had now fallen from the confines of its scarf and into a stringy halo around her head.

With gritted teeth I managed, "What do you want from me?" And she smiled slyly, eyes overly pleasant and claws sinking further into my shoulders.

"Oh my dear, it is not what I want, but what my Master will obtain and I can tell you now, his methods are not pleasant." I looked around frantically trying to think of an escape and she began to chant, "Dark spirits move, open my path ..." when she was abruptly cut off by the word "*diminous!*"

The old woman flew off me and through the wall of her linen caravan, which crumpled in her wake, and after a few moments of uneasy silence, I presumed she would not be rising again. One problem dealt with, I turned my head to nervously gauge this other new threat and was shocked when I caught the unlikely hazel eyes of Monroe the spice merchant.

Monroe ran towards me, concern etched across his face.

"Aria, are you hurt?!" He drew a long dagger from his belt, before cutting the rope free from around my arms and legs, eyeing my undoubtedly bruised face with worry. "Can you stand?"

"Yyyes, Monroe? Is that really you?" Perhaps I had hit my head harder than I first thought.

"Indeed Miss Aria, but we shall talk soon, I would have you back with your grandfather and in a place of safety first." He put his arm gently around my back, lifting the hood of my now muddied cloak and led me quietly out of the tent.

We skirted the edges of the festival and any gazes that landed our way conveniently turned in the other direction. It was likely Monroe's doing I deduced, now highly suspicious of the man, but I remained grateful for his aide and when we reached Grandfather's cart, Monroe swiftly placed me onto the back seat. His next orders were firm and so unlike his usually friendly demeanour.

"Stay here while I retrieve your grandfather, I will not be long. Do not leave for any reason, Aria, am I understood?"

I nodded quickly before he left and nervously awaited the arrival of my grandfather. I did not realise until he appeared, that I was shaking. The events of this evening suddenly taking their toll, while Grandfather proceeded to call my name worriedly several times on his approach. He hopped onto the cart and immediately put his arms around me and for that I was grateful, as I could not find the words to articulate how I felt. Instead, a small sob escaped my lips which halted any further conversation. Despite his obvious curiosity, Grandfather did not question me further and instead, briskly ordered Monroe to take us home.

Vylnor

Walking past the crumpled mess that was Mirell the old crone and eyeing the recently vacated festival, Vylnor clicked his tongue in disappointment. He'd heard her chant just before it was abruptly cut off and frustratingly, he could not locate the hag in time to assist. Whatever she had discovered must have been worth the trip, due to the volumes of magic he could sense scattered about the area. Someone had made sure this scene wouldn't be discovered anytime soon, going by the invisibility veil that currently shimmered around the caravan and the unconscious servant within it. Keen to retrieve answers and destroy any evidence of dark magic, Vylnor raised his left arm and spoke "*infernous*," igniting the hidden scene before him with a sphere of molten flame. He turned Mirell over with his boot, from where she currently laid face down in the dirt a few feet away from the blaze and pulled some amadine salts from his person. Not only did they wake the unconscious or freshly deceased, but also lent them a loose tongue.

Vylnor grabbed her by the chin, the lax skin wrinkling under his harsh hold and placed the crushed salts briefly under her nose. Startled, she awoke with snapping jaws and he shoved her to the ground.

"Calm yourself servant, before I pull out your teeth!" Her eyes soon focused.

"Lord Vylnor?!" she cawed in panic and quickly settled into a crouched position, face pressed to the earth.

"Explain your failure and be quick about it," he barked to a flinching Mirell, who spilled her knowledge eagerly and paused only for a brief breath.

"The mage was unexpected my Lord, but if you would be gracious enough to give me the opportunity, I will finish what I started."

But that was not the only reason for Vylnor's foul mood and his eyes narrowed on her viciously. "You kept an artefact from the Master?"

Her pale eyes widened before she began to tremble uncontrollably and stutter, "I thought it useless, its power slumbering …"

"And now his enemies have it?!" His servant recoiled at Vylnor's violent roar of disgust, until he took a calming breath and hissed, "Your incompetence is astounding, but your discovery will keep you from the clutches of Oromos for now." He would just have to retrieve the item himself, he mused, and thought of the new study piece before adding, "Return home, servant, and prepare your crafters. Should you fail again, I will let the Baromorph devour your rancid flesh."

She scrambled to follow his orders, while Vylnor considered the implications of a mage acting in such close quarters. His next meeting would be interesting indeed.

Eron

The picture in the mirror abruptly disappeared leaving Erondriel fearful for the mortal girl's fate and this spurred on his next actions. "Petriel, can we locate any active Portalis runes to the Mortal Realm?"

Petriel gaped at Eron. "You cannot be serious Eron, to amass a force at such short notice?"

Eron cut him off before he could continue. "I do not need to, I will go myself to secure the girl and confirm what we suspect."

Florel turned. "You would do this alone, Erondriel?"

He nodded, certain of his next task.

"Then we shall aid in whatever way we can," and the Lady of Elavon addressed the group.

"Erondriel will secure the mortal's safety, for if she is the Portalis, we will need her in order to secure victory in the coming battles. In the meantime, our duty as Elders is to guard our current portals. They now all pose a threat to our world and should she fall into the hands of Oromos, Elavon will be in great danger."

Meeting their gazes individually, Florel imposed

the gravity of the situation on each of the Elders and Generals in the room. "Erondriel, the closest runes are within the Verouse fountain and if the portals have been activated, we will need to move swiftly. This task will not be easy First General, for we cannot be certain of her position, but I am confident they exit through to the Arckus Kingdom. I will pray for the Light to aid us this day and hope it will bring you close to her current location. Petriel, I will need you to research and allocate each possible portal on our maps of Elavon and their corresponding locations within the other realms. Even ones from the First Age. Talos, Havrel and Kalor prepare our armies, they will be moved to these locations as rapidly as the Locksnight bird flies."

With that, the room dispersed in haste. Eron ran to Argenti and mounted with a swift jump on his back before racing to the Verouse fountain. His mind was fraught with the possible obstacles he may encounter, but still he remained determined to reach the Mortal Realm and sent a small prayer to Anala, that he would reach the girl before it was too late.

Aria

We arrived home promptly, Monroe having pushed the horses hard to do so. Grandfather helped me from the cart and into the kitchens, while I sat myself gingerly in a chair by the large fireplace. I flinched upon noticing the carvings. Just seeing them only served to heighten my fear, as my imagination conjured up all manner of ghoulish monsters and their devilish eyes fixed upon me. Unfortunately, Monroe noticed the small movement and sent a concerned frown my way which I chose to ignore in favour of silence for the time being.

"Monroe." Grandfather spoke and drew his gaze thankfully elsewhere. "Will you please take the cart back to the festival and collect the rest of the household, I should not like them gallivanting, unaware of the dangers in the area."

The spice merchant tilted his head thoughtfully and nodded. "I shall not be long, please await my return before we speak on tonight's events."

Grandfather grunted his agreement and went to peruse the medicinal cabinets in the kitchen, while Monroe swiftly took his leave of us. He pulled out bottle after bottle of herbs and tinctures, his frustration steadily growing before he burst out, "Ruddy jars and not one label!" and slammed the cupboard doors shut. I decided to remain quiet and watched curiously as Grandfather paced up and down the kitchen. Every now and then he glanced my way, his hawk-like nose either wrinkled in displeasure or his nostrils flared in anger. I was both relieved and worried when I heard the cart rumble back down the pathway towards our house a few dials later.

The front door opened, followed by Monroe's commands. "Geoffrey and Berta please coordinate to ensure the farmhouse is secure, using as many of the farmhands as needed. Wendy, come with me to the kitchens, I will need you and your healing herbs."

I turned as they entered the room, Wendy's sharp

gasp echoed about the vaulted space when she cried, "Miss Aria?!" She ran to me, arms enclosing my sore shoulders while she held me steadfast for a moment or two, before turning raging eyes onto the other members of our group.

Monroe sighed, "Can you please fix a poultice for her head, Wendy, and any other injuries she may have?"

With pursed lips, Wendy reluctantly let go of me and headed to the same cupboard Grandfather had recently been grumbling at. She realised quite quickly someone had been rearranging her stock and sent a scowl Grandfather's way. After a few moments, Wendy approached me with a damp cloth covered in a poultice of herbs and smelling vaguely of rotten weeds, before placing it over the bruise across my right cheek and forehead.

"Thank you," I said gratefully, despite the initial sting, when to my surprise Monroe requested she leave the room.

That statement was met by a pair of scathing blue eyes and Monroe's hands waved placatingly. "We need to discuss this evening's events; it will not take long Wendy, and you can tuck her safely in bed within the next hour."

Seemingly satisfied she left the room, not before letting out a long and exasperated huff, until I was left to face the two men alone, their gazes expectant, while I struggled to decide where I should start.

"Sodding hags! I'm surprised you didn't burn her unconscious bag of bones and send them back to

Oromos, Monroe!" Grandfather was in quite a state since I revealed what had happened tonight and I was equally baffled about his apparent casualness for otherworldly beings. Clearly upset, his usual composure slipped while his rant continued. "And that Thomas Fjorman is on my bloody list! I will have him strung up by his man parts in Great Barrington square, you mark my words!"

I looked for Monroe's reaction and caught him cringing while he stood at the far end of the kitchen table, his short grey hair now ruffled, speaking of his distress. "Calm down Jacoby," and he eventually smirked, "all in good time."

Worryingly, his demeanour had shifted into something more sinister and I could only cringe in response. At least this seemed to pacify Grandfather somewhat and I wondered if they had exacted revenge of a similar nature before, but thought it best not to ask. Meanwhile, Monroe continued, "I couldn't very well create a raging inferno in the middle of the festival now, could I? The hag was incapacitated and I didn't return empty-handed," he said and nodded to the far corner of the kitchen.

I recoiled. "Is that …?!"

"Yes Aria, it's the mirror from your tale. I thought it may come in use. We could always contact the elves with it again, if you are agreeable Jacoby, and ask for some additional protection for young Aria here. And I wouldn't mind gazing upon the beautiful Florel for a moment or two either." Monroe smiled to himself looking wistful. My gaze, however, was fixed to Grandfather in surprise.

Turning my tone serious, I addressed him with as much respect as I could muster, given my rattled state. "Grandfather, what are you keeping from me? The idea of Oromos hags and elves does not ruffle you at all?"

For the first time in my life, my grandfather looked uncomfortable and dare I say, nervous. This did nothing for my anxiety, as I waited uneasily for his reply. A dial passed and the silence stretched painfully while the two men looked to each other conspiratorially, until my patience ran its course and I snapped. "You will tell me the truth!"

Both men winced and Grandfather frowned, until I added more subtly, "I deserve to know."

He glanced at Monroe who nodded his support, before drawing in a deep breath. His reply was something I never expected, nor ever dreamed of, when he said regretfully, "I am not your grandfather, Aria."

♦ 4 ♦

Aria

Stunned silence. That was what filled the room. I paused a moment and drew the poultice from my face before whispering in disbelief, "What did you say?"

I wanted desperately for Grandfather to refute his last words, but to my devastation he replied gruffly, "Please do not make me repeat it again, my girl." His face was crestfallen and must have mirrored my own.

My emotions were in turmoil. Confusion. Shock. Anger. Hurt. I felt them all, my world threatening to crumble around me, until I composed myself enough to stutter, "But, why would you *lie* about something like that?"

He slammed his fist on the table and I tensed. "Because I have a duty and that duty is to protect these worlds and the creatures that reside within them!"

Angry at his response I argued back, "You think *that* is an excuse?! How dare you! I trusted you! Loved you! And all this time you were keeping secrets from me!" Tears poured from my eyes, wetting my whitened knuckles currently clenched in my lap and all I could do was remind myself to breathe.

Clearing his throat, Monroe took advantage of the lull in conversation and walked around the far side of the table. "He is not angry with you, Aria, but with the cards that were dealt by higher powers. We are all pawns in one way or another, to be moved around the table at will."

My grandfather's, or rather *Jacoby's*, glistening eyes met mine. "You are my family, Aria, by blood or not and I have loved you ever since your tiny fingers wrapped around mine nearly twenty years ago, when you were passed into my care."

The revelation was too much and the whole room began to spin. Thoughts and feelings surfaced which made me doubt not only the people I trusted most in this world, but *myself*. Who were we, if we did not understand the very foundations of our lives and where we came from? Was Aria a lie? The life I had lived for eighteen years certainly seemed so in that moment and with each affronting question, I felt as though my very mind was being stretched too thin, until suddenly something *snapped* inside of me. Monroe spun to the carvings which now glowed painfully bright against the kitchen fireplace, when three dark shadows rapidly shot through at ferocious speed and landed menacingly at the back of the room.

Black smoke immediately encircled us and Grandfather roared, "Monroe to Aria! *To Aria!*"

In the same moment, I heard steel being drawn, before he barked a second command. "Close that portal!"

Clasped at the shoulder, I was dragged from my seat towards the fireplace by an ominous looking Monroe, his instructions short. "Place your hands upon the carvings and whisper *sigillum*. Do not stop no matter what you hear!" He shoved me forward towards the fireplace and my blood went cold at the words that rumbled across my path.

"Aria, pretty name for a pretty girl."

My eyes widened painfully as Monroe called "*aclarium!*" And cleared the smoke in a matter of moments, finally exposing our new enemy, whose appearance was not at all what I expected.

Standing two heads taller, with hair as black as midnight that fell to his chest, my eyes nervously followed its silky dark path up to an unfamiliar but cruel gaze. Set into an unnaturally pale face, I was caught by a set of irises that at first glance appeared black, but upon closer inspection were in fact a deep green. His full lips twitched at my blatant perusal and revealed a pair of sharpened canines.

"Aria!" Grandfather cried from the far side of the room and charged recklessly, straight for my assailant who simultaneously frowned and raised his clawed hand in the air.

Realising our enemy planned to retaliate, I hissed angrily, "You will not harm him!" and threw myself forward, arms outstretched and intending to delay his attack, but with no notion how. Yet I could feel within my very bones that if I allowed this creature to harm what was most precious to me, I was not sure I would survive the aftermath. Before my hands could meet his leather armoured chest however, a strange energy pushed forth from my palms and flung my imposing enemy through the back wall of the farmhouse. The resounding rumbles of fallen rock was the only proof of my assault, while I stood motionless and gawped at a pair of hands that no longer felt my own.

Unwilling to question my luck, I spun on my toes and pressed my palms to the fireplace before shouting, "*sigillum!*" Unsure if it would work, I was pleased when the carvings yet again began to glow golden and the shimmering veil within the hearth receded into the stone. Not waiting another moment, I headed towards Grandfather who was now backing away from an armed ghost swathed in a cloak of shadow and now hovered threateningly above the flagstones.

"Stay back Aria!" he commanded harshly and I paused my advance before he griped, "Monroe assist, darn you man!" Grandfather seemed rather put out that Monroe was not helping and yet the man appeared rather occupied to my eyes, currently slashing a bright sword at his opponent.

"Getting old Jacoby I see, where are those sword skills from thirty years ago?!" he jibed and with a scorching gaze, Grandfather cut back, "Those went along with my back a decade ago, you cheeky swine!"

Sadly I couldn't appreciate the banter, as still advancing at a rapid rate was the shadowed monster. Although not particularly large, it looked deadly and cold, as though it was slowly sucking the warmth and light from the room. Chuckling at the most inopportune time, Monroe instructed "Shield your eyes!" With barely enough time to do so, he spoke the word *"illumenti!"* and a piercing light exploded from the mage. I winced, a brightness flashing behind my eyelids that was akin to staring at the sun under the summer skies. I imagined the whole farmhouse was shining like a beacon, that could be witnessed as far as the Ingoreen Mountains to the north of the Kingdom.

The spell was quickly followed by a piercing howl from the two shadow creatures and, under the wavering glow, I peered cautiously to see their strange unearthly bodies beginning to warp, fade and eventually perish.

The light gradually dimmed and I opened my eyes fully to find what looked like two black scorch marks, marring the stones like a scar.

"More warning next time, you buffoon Monroe, I nearly added blindness to my list of ailments!"

Monroe laughed and walked jovially towards us whilst sheathing his sword and I paused, my gaze fixed on him, for he was no longer the person I had grown to know. Still with hooded hazel eyes and a thick but straight nose, he appeared much younger, no more than thirty years of age and with a build to match. His grey hair completely replaced by shoulder-length brown locks and smooth skin and I spluttered, "Monroe?! You … your *face* … your *hair*?!" while waving my arms frantically up and down his new façade, until he sent me a wicked grin in return.

"Ah my lovely Aria, this is my actual form. The chores of being a mage you see, a rarity to this world. Long-lived and particularly handsome." He winked and began to spin languidly in a circle like a show pony. "As you can guess, I could not very well allow my enemies to know of my skill, so I had to age ungracefully, as to match your grandfather here."

I looked at Grandfather and could see his cheeks were turning an unflattering shade of puce.

"The audacity, you arrogant rat! I'll have you know this *mere* ageing mortal, who is nearly a seventh of your years and with no magical ability, has saved your ungrateful ass many a time, so show some respect before I beat it into you!"

Before this escalated any further, I turned a concerned gaze to the large hole in our kitchen wall. Two other pairs of eyes quickly followed suit and the lightened atmosphere was soon replaced with an ominous tension, only broken by Monroe's curious mutterings. "Well, well, what do we have here, I wonder?"

Vylnor

Cursing to himself, Vylnor stared at the ruined wall he was unexpectedly thrown through by a strong force of magic. He knew instinctually that his injuries were rather severe, despite his immortal heritage and had little choice but to mutter the word "*healios.*" This allowed his magic to mend the shattered sternum and punctured lung, while leaving any minor injuries untouched, in a bid to avoid depleting his magical stores.

Vylnor could already feel the ill fates of the two Skygge demons he had summoned with him and, disgusted by their swift failure, turned towards the farmhouse, now more intrigued than ever by the unexpected turn of events. Narrowing his eyes, Vylnor decided to tread carefully, but remained determined to test these new opponents and the extent of their abilities. Knowledge was power after all and if he could drag a Portalis and a mage back to Oromos with him, his Master would be somewhat appeased.

Aria

Monroe eyed the crumbling stone structure curiously for a few moments, before an impressed whistle flew from his lips and he turned to me with an arched brow. "What manner of magic did you use to throw this foe through a wall I wonder, young Aria?"

Believing he mocked me, I snorted in reply, "After witnessing you casually cast a spell of searing light that destroyed two demonic beings, I doubt whatever I did accidentally is worth questioning." Although, I did briefly ponder over the concerning thought, but decided not to add anything further.

Scratching his chin, Monroe responded thoughtfully, "They are called Skygge demons and it seems I have much to teach you, Aria. Magic requires commands from even masters before it can be performed. You, on the other hand, produced a magical force with no command whatsoever, so I believe my question is still valid."

We all jerked to a stop upon hearing movement from beyond the wall and our small group cautiously turned in that direction, while I absently grabbed a dust-coated frying pan hanging above the hearth and watched as Monroe's lips twitched.

"I think I will take this fight outside Jacoby my old friend, to try and save some of this dreary farmhouse at least." He paused and looked about the space seemingly dissatisfied, before kicking a piece of rubble with his boot, much to Grandfather's annoyance.

I had the distinct impression he would have thrown his dagger at Monroe, if the situation wasn't so precarious. Surprisingly, he did not deign to reply to Monroe's ill-timed insult and instead grumbled with a furrowed brow perched upon his face, "Put the pan down Aria, you are to fight no one."

Monroe pulled his sword from his scabbard and murmured "*lux*" until it pulsed with an unnatural glow, before offering Grandfather a knowing look and ordered, "Clear the farmhouse and retreat to a safer location. I do not recognise this foe, so it would pay to be prepared."

Grandfather grabbed my hand, sword still drawn in his right, but before we took even two steps, a deep voice from outside jeered, "Leaving so soon, pretty girl?"

To my surprise, it was Monroe who retorted, "Compliments will not help your predicament, you demonic cur!" and launched himself through the back wall with enthusiasm towards his new opponent.

Soon after, the ominous sound of clashing blades rang in my ears and I turned to Grandfather, worried for our friend. "Will he be OK?"

"He can handle himself, Aria," he said confidently before adding with urgency, "it is *us* who must move." So we ran for the hall towards the front of the farmhouse. "Prepare the horses and carts my girl, I will go find Wendy. Geoffrey and Berta should already be amongst the farmhouse grounds."

I nodded and pulled open the large oak door, its hinges squeaking in protest, before rushing outside towards the stables.

Vylnor

It had been many centuries since someone had addressed Vylnor with such audacity, however he could not help but smirk at the mage's reply. Not much entertained him these days, so to cut out his enemy's tongue would be a delight. The brown-haired mage, *Monroe*, he overheard, threw himself through the back wall and at Vylnor with impressive swiftness, no doubt using a reflex potion to enhance his otherwise inferior speed. Drawing his twin Corrono blades (*corrupted elven craft*), Vylnor prepared to inflict some pain. They were slightly curved and wickedly sharp. Any former etchings tarnished by the dark magic which now eagerly awaited the taste of fresh magical blood.

His right sword was first to connect sharply with his

opponent's glowing blade, sparks exploding outward as light magic battled dark. Swiftly blocking the advance, Vylnor faded left with his second blade when the mage called *"protego!"* and forming a shield of protection, where Vylnor's blade would have severed his arm. Despite the mage's quick thinking, he had left Vylnor with an opening and with that, the Lord of Shadows took his opportunity. Bringing his right foot forward, he planted his armoured boot into the mage's chest and kicked him to the ground twenty paces away, his head cracking on a loose piece of rubble. Disappointingly, the mage did not rise and, unsatisfied, Vylnor hissed into the air, "What a poor challenge." His ears pricked at movement from the other side of the property and aware the Portalis was now heading towards the stables, Vylnor realised he must move quickly. Uncharacteristically, the Oromos Lord decided to leave the mage unconscious on the floor without removing his head, eager to seek out a far greater trophy instead.

Aria

Arriving at the stables, I ran past the four stabled cobb horses to my right, whose nervous whinnies and shuffles against the stall doors did little to calm my own pounding heart. Grabbing the reins off the far wall, I reached up onto my toes and pulled the last one from its hook, when the sound of booted feet made me pause. I slowly lowered my shaking arm from its outstretched pose and froze like prey, caught under the piercing gaze of a predator, unsure of what to do or when it would strike. Knowing I should face my enemy and not stare at the worn, timber-clad walls like a coward, I turned warily, the three leather reins still gripped in my hands, until my eyes met the dark prisoner from before.

Not fifteen paces away, he stood firm, grasping twin swords of death, one of which he pointed at me and the other to the floor. In a low commanding voice, the words he uttered next frightened me to my core.

"I will speak plainly. Do not run. Do not fight me. Come obediently and I will let the occupants of this wretched little farm survive. If you do run from me, I will hunt you down and make you watch as the Norags peel the flesh from their bones, while they scream their agony to whatever gods you worship. Am I understood, pretty girl?"

Unaware of what a Norag was, but my imagination running wild as it did, I felt myself beginning to tremble. At this point he started towards me. Confidently sheathing both swords, he pulled a slim, silver chain from his pocket and gestured for me to hold out my hands. Feeling hopeless and empty of any magical push that came from before, I drew my arms to my chest defensively, hesitant even. The loud crack of a chain splitting one of the stable doors next to us, and the subsequent skittering of terrified horses, made up my mind for me. Unnerved, I met my enemy's unforgiving gaze and dropped the leather reins to hold out my wrists in defeat, while he deftly bound them together. Oddly, I noticed his pale hands were peculiarly warm, his black claws clipped but sharp, as he coldly carried out his task. No other words were forthcoming, when my skin began to prickle almost painfully, moments before a second newcomer flew through the stable wall like a piercing arrow. He slammed into the dark prisoner who held me captive, glistening frost leaving a path in his wake as the momentum thrust their bulky forms through the opposing stall wall and startling the horses for good measure.

Tied to the dark prisoner, I was pulled harshly to the ground, shoulder squarely hitting the barn floor first and I cried out wildly at the instant pain. My body was swiftly dragged toward the fragments of debris and sharpened wood at pace, however the pain in my wrists and shoulders was soon forgotten in the face of being sliced or impaled by the large jutting timbers. Mercifully, the chain turned quickly slack and my movements ground to an abrupt halt.

I looked up, gingerly testing my body for obvious wounds and caught sight of glinting silver armour and flowing, frost-white hair. Neither knowing if this new fighter was friend or foe, I could not look away while he stalked confidently and straight for the dark prisoner. Meanwhile my enemy now stood in a crouched position, poised, and scrutinising his new opponent with his mouth drawn down in an irritated fashion. In but a dial, the clashing of metal rung about the farm while the two fighters embarked in a deadly dance of steel and I quickly realised I would be of no use in this fight.

So standing on wavering legs, the cracking of wood beneath my feet seeming horribly loud to my own ears, I prepared my discreet exit and passed back through the entrance of the barn tentatively. Peering around the wall to ensure my audience were distracted, I stilled at the sudden and all-consuming silence. The two impressive combatants had paused their attacks, in favour of sizing each other up, and I finally caught a detailed glance of my saviour.

Not as thickly built, the man was clad in ornate armour and was as tall as his opponent, with long hair that brushed his tapered waist. However, what drew my attention further were his silver eyes, framed by thick grey lashes, that spoke of utter conviction and a determination to succeed.

A soft breeze ruffled his white hair to expose, *pointed ears*?! And I let out a small gasp in realisation. He was the man, nay *elf* from the mirror.

"Nice of you to join us elf, but do move along, for I would not wish to ruin your pretty face." The dark prisoner's tone was mocking, his twin blades grasped lazily at his sides, while his stance was battle ready and unforgiving.

The elf spat on the earth and growled, "You revolt me, you traitorous filth. What dark persuasion did it take for you to give up the Light, or did you just decide to betray us all on your own?" His teeth were clenched in anger and I knew I should try to scurry away, but my exit would be too easily noticed by the two fighters, and truth be told, the current events held me in a state of incredulous pause.

Huffing a derisive laugh, the dark prisoner sneered, "Spew your judgmental righteousness for someone who cares. All of you are nothing but livestock, followers, and will die at the end of my blades as nothing more." And with that declaration he launched forward and was met by an equally swift force.

They hacked, parried, blocked, the upper hand gained and lost on both sides more times than I could count, until they broke apart briefly and the dark prisoner growled the words, "*lanza ignatio!*"

To my horrified astonishment, a spear of flame was forged in his outstretched palm and now headed straight for his pale-haired opponent, who called "*mirorst!*" in response. A shield of thick ice as broad as his body encased the elf, the surface rattling and cracking as it deflected the blow.

The threat to my existence becoming increasingly apparent by each passing dial, I began to struggle earnestly out of my chains, but the bindings were infuriatingly tight and I found my movements becoming more frantic. The chains gradually shifted, and I looked up towards the two battling males, now more determined than ever to escape this strange nightmare, without losing my freedom or life in the process.

The sound of rushing footsteps could be heard from the front of the farmhouse and I turned in horror to see Wendy, Berta and Geoffrey approaching, accompanied by Grandfather who stuttered the word

"*Elf?!*" disbelievingly. His gaze rested on me, looking decidedly ruffled and cowering behind the barn when his demeanour soon turned coldly composed and he addressed the dark prisoner, overconfidently I might add.

"Scum! Where is Monroe?!" No retort was forthcoming, until a pained moan came from the side of the farmhouse, near the kitchen gardens.

"Why Jacoby, that sounded like you almost *cared.*" Monroe headed towards us, palm absently rubbing the centre of his chest and I noticed a horrid head wound at his temple that bled rather profusely and I could not stifle my glare of outrage towards our enemy.

In the interim, Geoffrey and Grandfather drew their weapons and pushed Berta and Wendy behind them while they faced the dark prisoner, who merely scowled in disdain. "And what do you plan on doing with those? Interfere and I will personally remove those pathetic excuses for sword arms."

Angry that he would dare threaten my family and possibly feeling more confident due to our new elven acquaintance, I stepped from my hiding spot, now devoid of chains, and fixed a glare firmly on him.

"Oh please do join us, pretty girl, I would like you to see me remove the elf's head from his shoulders, before I deal with the farmhouse pests."

I turned to him, feeling as though I'd reached my limit of threats for the day and spoke icily. "No one threatens my family." Like before, I swiped my hand in his direction and the same previous push of power radiated from my palm, but disappointingly, he seemed to expect such an assault. Calling a black shield to his front, its dark form cracked and then to my satisfaction, shattered under the force of my power. In the end, his efforts accomplished little, only dimming the attack and not stopping it entirely. He flew across the yard, twisting his airborne body to dig a clawed fist into the gravelled earth and slowing his movements, before he hit the treelined border of our land.

I felt the stunned silence and wide-eyed stares of my family at my back, including from the elf, but paid them no mind, my attention still trained elsewhere. The dark prisoner was now breathing heavily, his eyes narrowing from his crouched position on the floor and I noticed blood dripping from his mouth. For some profound reason, this upset me deeply and I was shocked by the sharp turn in my emotions. He must have understood the look on my face, for he frowned back at me in disgust, as though to say without words, *'attack with conviction you weak fool'*. The next reply, however, came from the elf.

"Well cur, it looks like you are out of options, other than to perish!" With his mighty blade in hand, that glimmered like a sheet of ice upon a lake, he charged, while our injured enemy wisely chose to retreat. With a swift call of *"arvemnico,"* his eerily dark stare remained fixed upon me and I struggled to look away, even as his imposing form unnaturally shifted before disappearing entirely in a scattered cloud of black smoke.

♦ 5 ♦

Aria

"I doubt that is the last we shall see of him, but you girl are in need of a magical tutor." The elf spoke in my direction while arching his white brow. At first glance I thought he was jesting, but the seriousness of his tone soon convinced me otherwise.

Irritated, no doubt by tonight's events, I retorted sharply, "If you must deliver criticism, I suggest you work on your timing elf, for I am not in the mood to receive it."

I stormed off towards my grandfather, where Wendy hurried around him to embrace me, soon after holding me at arm's length and assessing for any injuries. I smiled warmly at her motherly attentions, but quickly waved away her fussing as she picked pieces of wood and straw from my hair. "See to Monroe, Wendy, I am fine for the time being."

"Nonsense, he is well enough," she added dismissively, while I looked to the mage in question who appeared rather ghastly, sporting a pale and bloodied face. I turned to her, incredulous, and she muttered,

"Besides, it is his pride that has taken the worst beating tonight." And Monroe physically stumbled at the insult, while Grandfather fought the smirk from his face.

Clearing his throat, he added with authority to our group, "Let us speak inside, Aria, some explanations are needed and we must form a plan of action. And Wendy? Please take pity on Monroe, he looks like a Corkcat's chew toy."

With little argument we all followed Grandfather's instructions, the grumpy elf included, and slowly moved to the large hall inside the farmhouse.

We entered the vaulted room, Monroe following limply behind and supported by Wendy who saw him gently into a chair on my left.

"Thank you, darling Wendy," he offered before speaking, "*healios*." His skin glowed softly and the wound and bruising on his head swiftly disappeared, leaving behind dried blood.

"You wicked man!" Wendy rallied, swatting his arm before moving away. "You can drag yourself into this house next time for all I care!" She huffed irritably and stood behind Grandfather, who was sat to my right.

Monroe smiled broadly at her and explained, "Magic is useful, but it is no substitute for honest care and affection."

"There was nothing honest about that care, you scheming little man," she grumbled begrudgingly, a small smile twitching across her lips. Finally, we had all gathered around the large oak table to the far end of the space and I noticed Monroe's focus had turned on our new guest. The elf had such a commanding presence, that even the sizeable room felt inadequate. Interestingly, Monroe spoke first rather than the elf.

"Before we begin, Geoffrey, Wendy and Berta, please could you excuse us for a moment? Perhaps ensure the hole in the farmhouse wall is suitably covered for the time being and the kitchen usable? The stables also require some attention."

"And what is it that you do not wish for us to hear?" argued Wendy, her hands now on her hips.

Monroe glanced at Grandfather, who nodded in agreement and uttered, "Do as he says and I will let you feed him your most wicked concoctions afterwards, Wendy, as recompense."

She huffed at the placating smile Grandfather sent her way and then towards his two other most loyal household members. Geoffrey looked rather put out, but our main farmhand did not argue as he led the two women reluctantly from the room.

Before they left, I grabbed Wendy's hand and murmured, "I will be along shortly to help," which she gave a small squeeze in return, before closing the large oak doors behind her.

Facing the elf across from me, I was taken aback by his expression. He appeared to be studying me, which I found particularly unnerving, so I decided to arch an eyebrow in challenge. It must have done the trick, for he quickly looked elsewhere.

"So ..." Monroe sighed, "may we start with your name and how you came to be here at such a convenient time?"

"If that is your way of saying thank you, it needs work, mage. My name is Erondriel Malvious Oakwald, First General of Elavon and protector of the elves." He paused dramatically and I had the urge to roll my eyes. "As to why I am here, I think you know, don't you girl, for this is not the first time our paths have crossed?"

Narrowing my eyes, I gritted through my teeth, "This *girl* is named Aria and you would do well to remember my name, for I suppose you desire my future cooperation, isn't that right *Oakwald?*" Monroe snickered beside me, while Grandfather sighed hopelessly, no doubt expecting my short reply. Erondriel's full lips twitched upwards and he surprised me with his next words.

"I confess it has been some time since I spoke to mortals. Their small levels of respect for those who saved them from a dismal fate centuries ago still surprises me."

I retorted quickly, "Respect is earnt Oakwald, and if you expect me to grovel for your heroic deeds centuries past for the sake of your own ego, you are sadly mistaken."

Erondriel was now frowning at me, but I would give no ground.

"Aria, I would not expect a child to understand the depravity which your people were saved from and I do not expect you to *grovel*, however entertaining that would be. But your naivety betrays you. Were you not in danger a mere hour ago and have yet to even thank me for coming to your aid? Sadly, such poor manners must be a reflection of your upbringing."

A blush stole up my neck at this comment and I suddenly felt ashamed. Grandfather had taught me better and I had let my sore feelings of tonight's events affect my manners. I bowed my head to hide my guilty blush and spoke into the awkward silence that followed. "This is no reflection on my grandfather, it is a reflection of my ill-controlled temper while in distress. I apologise, Erondriel, and thank you for your assistance earlier."

I felt rather than saw his nod of acceptance and peeked up gingerly when Grandfather intervened. "I would not judge her so harshly, Erondriel. Events like this are here to test us, are they not?"

Steeping his fingers, Erondriel leant back in his chair. "Indeed they are, and you have youth on your side, Aria, with which to learn."

"Manners are wonderful and all …" Monroe added, "but how are they to aid us against the Lord of Shadows himself and his minions?"

"You think it him?" Grandfather questioned and Monroe winced. "His last spell confirmed it. No doubt their scourge of a master is now after Aria. A Portalis under our nose this entire time no less!"

The mage smiled at me as he spoke and I couldn't help but feel clueless as to what he was talking about. I echoed the word Portalis around in my mind, racking my brain, in a vain attempt to not look stupid in front of these men, when thankfully Grandfather indulged me.

"Think of a Portalis as a key through the worlds, Aria. Oromos, the Mortal Realm, which includes the Kingdom of Arckus and the Ingoreen Mountains as you know, and Elavon, home of the elves. There is no current way of amassing an army of troops and transporting them all through these worlds at once. Only a few powerful magic wielders are able to travel across the worlds individually and perhaps a handful of others at best, but it requires an extortionate amount of magic." He paused before continuing. "Now think of how a conqueror might use this key to secure his victory amongst these realms. This is why Oromos desires you so badly. You are a strategic boon to any leader, opening and closing portals at will, to use to their advantage."

Stunned and, if I was honest with myself, utterly petrified, I whispered through the lump in my throat, "I never knew such a thing existed. Nor these other realms."

"They, or rather you are very rare Aria." Erondriel turned to me, angular jaw gritted. "And knowledge of the realms is not widely acknowledged, for our gatherings are few and only in times such as these. The last known Portalis was discovered over four centuries ago, when the world descended into chaos."

"What happened to them?"

This was met by a harsh cough from Monroe, which didn't seem to deter Erondriel as he replied easily, "I will not lie to you, Aria. They were destroyed, before they became a vessel of Oromos. Usually long-lived, like immortal elves, upon their demise the realms must wait another four hundred years for another to appear. The magic within the runes hibernates, the portals closing within a short window, until the successor appears and reactivates the magic."

I didn't realise until he finished speaking that I was holding my breath, only Grandfather's grasp on my shoulder reminded me to breathe. "Aria, look at me," he implored and I turned slowly, the contents of my stomach threatening to claw its way out of my throat. "I have protected you your whole life and that protection does not stop now." His blue eyes were earnest, loving even.

"Indeed, my darling Aria!" added Monroe. "We already have the advantage, you are with us after all and even the elves are upping their game from last time it seems."

I gritted my teeth. "What is *that* supposed to mean?"

"Well," he carried on, unperturbed and unaware of my inner turmoil, "the last Portalis was captured by Oromos despite our interventions, but I was only a young man at the time. The poor fellow sent his own dagger through his chest before they could drag his body back to be tortured." He then muttered none too quietly, *"That was a mistake of gargantuan proportions."*

This knowledge did not improve my escalating fears and I could feel my hands beginning to tremble in my lap. "I think that is enough for one day," finished Erondriel, looking pointedly at Monroe, seemingly as unimpressed as Grandfather with his graphic tale. Instead the elf changed tact and saved my ravaged emotions from further abuse.

"Monroe, are you able to set some wards about the property to ensure it is secure? I would ask for your hospitality Jacoby Torvel, so I can guard the premises and arrange watches, until I can find a way to contact the elven Elders."

At this I glanced at Erondriel. "Would the mirror not service a second time?"

His eyes widened. "You have it?"

"Pah! Of course we do, Eron my majestic elf. You did not think I would let that Oromos hag keep it did you?!" the man crowed, while I just rolled my eyes at his over exuberance.

"You irritate me, mage," Eron grunted and it seemed I was not the only one annoyed by Monroe's antics.

Eron

Deciding to speak with the elven Elders in the morning was a good idea despite Eron's impatience, but he worried that the girl, Aria, seemed as if she would fall over at any given moment. No doubt, he thought, from that vast push of magic she threw at that traitorous letch.

It still surprised him, what level of magic she was able to achieve without any prior incantation at all. It was told that the original magic wielders of these realms were able to accomplish such feats at one time, but that was only a myth, even to his immortal kind and sworn to fade in the memories of history. For the first time, however, Eron suspected differently. Aria was no ordinary Portalis, of that he was certain. Of course, some form of magic usually accompanied their gift, but nothing to this magnitude.

Eron sighed as he keenly watched the night-shrouded surroundings from the tiled portion of the Torvel's uneven farmhouse roof and pondered his next move. He would need to explain to Aria that now her abilities had manifested, it meant that portals across the worlds were now activated and would need to be closed. Thankfully there were no more than a score on record across the realms, but still, this was going to be an infernal job. Just one open portal was enough to incite a war and the records were far from accurate.

Running his hands through his white hair, Eron knew that a sound strategy relied on gathering more information regarding the mortal portals' locations and something that the elves struggled to obtain last time. He would speak with the Elders to see what they knew and what areas would be most at risk of an Oromos invasion first. Over the last millennia, each world had catalogued information on the locations of their realm's portals. However, his mortal neighbours were forgetful and suspicious creatures, hiding and burying this information away from prying eyes, including the elves. Not that Eron could blame them. Since the rise of Oromos even before his time, the realms turned suspicious and untrustworthy, in their bid to survive the ever-encroaching darkness, watchful and silent as it was. Eron grimaced.

Soon his thoughts returned to the new Portalis and, if he were honest, she was not what he expected.

Fiery yet contrite, strong yet fragile. He seemed to enjoy her verbal sparring and that blush when she was reprimanded. Eron admired that she would defend her family fiercely but was humble enough to acknowledge her mistakes. Hopefully this meant she would be open to allying with the elves and to the rigorous training he had planned. Eron was determined to provide her with the basic tools she would unquestionably need to survive the coming days. Sadly, it was almost a certainty that she would need to defend herself against some foul Oromos beast at some point in the future, if her protectors were otherwise indisposed.

Arriving at that conclusion, Eron kept watch until the brisk early hours, as a soft-pink dawn broke out behind the treeline and Monroe strutted outside, his head having healed nicely when he called, "I'll take over so you may have your beauty sleep, elf!"

Aria

It was morning and for the first time I didn't wish to face the day. So much had happened and I was finding it difficult to process. Now aware that the gravity of the situation was frighteningly not something I could ignore, my mind began to rally against the truths that were thrown at me the previous day. Why was I a Portalis? Why was I chosen? I had no such ambitions and only desired to live peacefully on our farm. I wanted to hide back under my bed coverings as I had when I was a scared child and life was much simpler. Willing the tears to not fall from my eyes, I stared out at the early morning sky from my window and rose towards the beckoning blue scattered with thin ribbons of white. I decided then, that I could not go back to being ignorant as I once was. Despite the revelations from my grandfather, I understood very quickly it did not matter to me. I still loved him, as I loved Wendy, and I knew she wasn't my birth family. It seemed more special that they had chosen to love me, despite our lack of blood, but the lie still shook me, the trust between us more fragile than I ever thought possible.

I sighed aloud, my breath misting on the small windowpane while I absently ruffled the dried lavender around the frame. I needed more information and I needed to control whatever this magic was that I possessed. I discouraged my doubts, thinking of the scuffles I'd had as a child. Grandfather would always sigh despairingly at my stubbornness but however inappropriate my actions were, it would not stop me from righting any wrongs that I had witnessed. Luckily, I'd avoided any such incidences since then, *apart from that unfortunate encounter with Thomas the toad*, so it was now more glaringly obvious that I needed a tutor and my thoughts wandered to the elf. He was very beautiful, but had enough strength in his jaw and eyes not to appear too feminine. Distracting as his facade was, I could see from his mannerisms he was unyielding yet wise and probably didn't suffer fools gladly.

I moved from the window, the elf and his pleasing face soon forgotten while my ire grew instead. I was so very ignorant of our world and those around me had allowed that ignorance to fester throughout my entire life. Jaw gritted, I proceeded to dress for the day ahead. There was no going back now, so all there was left to do was to push forward and refute those doubts that seemed determined to destroy what little remained of my courage.

I walked into the kitchen wearing my sturdy woollen skirt. The cornflower blue had faded over the years, but it was the warmest one I had and I needed that thickness to act as an armour, wary as I was about what the day ahead would bring. I spotted Geoffrey still working on the back wall. He had covered the large gap with timber boards to keep the worst of the weather out, but sadly it would require a stone mason to repair the wall and I grimaced at the additional expense to the farm. Other than the occasional grumblings from Geoffrey that I could hear from the other side of the planks, Wendy was the only one in the kitchen as it was still early. I could see her kneading bread for the oven and called "good morning," before grabbing an apron and helping her with breakfast. While I weighed out the oats for porridge and chopped an array of vegetables for a morning broth, Wendy approached tentatively.

"I imagine your thoughts are as troubled as my own, Aria, but remember your grandfather and I will support you, as we always have." I stilled my knife and turned to her, my eyes pricking with unshed tears that I blinked rapidly to clear.

"Did you know?" I whispered, thinking over the relationship I had with Grandfather. At her lack of response, I looked up to see her damningly confirm what I suspected to be true. I clenched the knife harder. "What about the others?"

She shook her head vehemently, "It was not for them to know. I wish things were different Aria, but maybe you will understand, given time. You must know that it does not change his love for you, and I hope it does not dampen your love for him."

I nodded swiftly and went back to my task with some intensity, tears falling across my cheeks which I brushed furiously away. "You could always read me like a book, Wendy, and have always known the right thing to say to lift my spirits, but I am uncertain if it will work this time. I am ... frightened. Unsure of myself. A danger to you all. To this world." I frowned at the half-chopped carrot in my hand, as though it miraculously held all the answers I sought when, to my surprise, Wendy's sharp grab at my shoulder had my body spinning to face her fully, her blue eyes softening as she spoke.

"You always were a sensitive child, more concerned for others than for yourself. If protecting my family is a danger to me, then so be it. That is *our* decision, Aria, and we would never abandon you. But it is *my* decision. You cannot burden yourself with guilt for the choices of others."

With her words, she cupped my cheek and gave me a warm smile that temporarily pierced through my fog of fear. In that moment, I knew I would do whatever it took to protect my family and as if sensing a change, Wendy nodded swiftly and moved away to continue with her tasks.

The normality of our chores settled my nerves somewhat and a few dials later, another set of unfamiliar footsteps entered the kitchen. I turned to find Erondriel standing awkwardly in the doorway, misguided in his belief that the other men would already be awake at this late hour, and I smirked to myself before calling behind me, "Make yourself comfortable, Erondriel, breakfast will be ready in a moment, I just hope it is to your elvish tastes."

A huff of laughter was my only reply as he took a seat at the large kitchen table, devoid of his armour and now in a set of dark leathers. Wendy quickly approached him with a tray of fresh bread from the oven, while I placed the vegetable broth on the worn table, along with some plates and utensils.

"It may still be hot ..." Wendy warned maternally, "but please help yourself. The porridge will also be ready shortly," and she smiled warmly at the elf before walking back over to the fireplace. "Aria, do sit, I will finish this while you eat with our guest and shall rouse those lazy swines from their beds shortly."

Once placing the porridge on the table, she removed her stained apron and walked out of the room with a large metal ladle in her hand, while I could only wince in sympathy for Monroe and Grandfather, should they remain in a state of slumber when she found them.

Taking a seat opposite, I looked about the room,

unwilling to meet the elf's gaze while the silence continued to stretch, until I mustered the courage to ask honestly, "I cannot ignore this task set before me, can I Erondriel?"

He paused before taking his first bite of fresh bread, the enticing aroma floating about the room and yet I lacked the hunger to reach for a piece.

"We all have a choice, Aria." His silver eyes were piercing, like that of liquid steel and I blinked forcefully, breaking away from his enigmatic gaze when he continued. "And you may call me Eron, for I have no doubt we will be spending much time together in the near future."

Surprised by the familiarity, I still replied bitterly, "And what choice is that? To run and let the world descend into chaos, in the hopes that I am not found? Or fight to stop that chaos, in the hopes I am not killed or enslaved?"

Eyebrow raised, Eron stood firm "A choice is still a choice."

"Well you are lucky that I have already made mine, despite how terrified I am." The whispered words were followed by my hands twisting restlessly in my lap, the breakfast before me completely forgotten by my rising nausea.

"I would think you a fool if you weren't, Aria, but in times of great fear, we find even greater courage." His eyes softened towards me and I'm sure a blush stole across my cheeks. Thankfully he seemed to ignore this and saved me from further embarrassment by elaborating, "And in rare cases, we accomplish feats we would never have dreamed we could, so believe in yourself, Portalis." And with that final statement he grinned around a mouthful of bread and at that point, I forced myself to look away.

♦ 6 ♦

Vylnor

Vylnor could not recall the last time he felt such anger, such *failure*. But a moment or two more and he would have secured his Master's prize and the conquering of the worlds would have been a certainty. That elf had decided his fate when he stood against Vylnor and now he would suffer for it. Vylnor would need to move more pawns across these forsaken realms to secure the Portalis and the chase was becoming tiresome.

His thoughts wandered to the girl, Aria. Her look of concern after she had wounded him was both surprising and irritating. It did however reveal a fault. A weakness. And Vylnor would use her empathy to his advantage.

Absently stalking through the black charred rock of his mountain residence, the weight of its surrounding walls was both defensive, as well as oppressive. An impenetrable prison for all who dwelled there, its memories were drenched in the blood of its former life. The vast maze of walkways and the shadows which prowled them would lead any unsuspecting victim into the Baromorph's maws, or seek to enclose them beneath its jagged walls. Its simple wish, to savour the taste of fresh blood. It craved it and displayed it through the bright red veins that plagued the mountain range. So much death haunted the space, that it was almost alive with it.

Servants scattered at the sound of Vylnor's footsteps, their warped mortal facades a clear indicator of what they had survived, but it was nothing compared to the other horrors that lived under the mountain. Turning down a steep spiral staircase into the interrogation chambers below, Vylnor met with his second-in-command, Fellious. Vylnor himself had no qualms with violence, preferring to plot and avoid the general mess that it caused, but Fellious thrived on inflicting pain, which made him an asset to Vylnor and his Master. His current victim was, impressively, a mage and quite a rare find in the Mortal Realm, given the King kept almost all within the confines of his castle. His screams were fighting around the acidic cloth stuffed into his mouth, while he was bound with an iron chain and strapped to a worn table that gave off a foul odour. Most likely putrid blood. From the varying array of marks upon its surface, Vylnor could make out the individual instruments used to score them and was forced to shake his head to rid himself of the memories they invoked.

Fellious had taken to skinning this victim alive from the feet up. The mage had fared well not to pass out, although his face was deathly ashen. The loose skin now reached the prisoner's calves, while his torturer began perusing a more appropriate knife.

"Ah Lord Vylnor, how nice of you to join me, I do

like to show off my work." Fellious was a goliath. A head taller than Vylnor, but with limbs taken from different Oromos abominations. He could walk on two or four legs – useful when scaling a mountainside – and was now neither man nor beast, but simply a monster of Oromos.

"You would not be my second in command if I felt your work was less than adequate. Have you learnt anything from the mage?"

Smiling, he revealed rows of serrated teeth almost gleefully. "I confess, Lord Vylnor, I am yet to question him."

Tongue clicking with displeasure, Vylnor stepped forward. "You will tell us, mage, of the nearest portals to Great Barrington and will do so quickly. Your cooperation will ensure you join the ranks of Oromos, your life spared." Vylnor paused and grabbed a saw from the bench. He took his time to peruse the blood stuck to its jagged surface, most likely from its last victim, and frowned in distaste before continuing. "Or you can suffer at the hands of Fellious here and be fed to the Baromorph when we have extracted all we need from you. And we will get what we need regardless."

Tears fell from the mage's defeated and bloodshot eyes as he painfully nodded his agreement, while Fellious grumbled irritably about the torture ending too soon for his liking. But Vylnor did not have time for his Second to sate his unnatural bloodlust and instead focused on the narrow freedom he would soon obtain, once the Portalis was in the hands of his Master.

Aria

Once again we gathered about the table in the main hall, the mirror placed at my front and covered by Wendy's embroidered handkerchief. Following a brief description of the elven Elders and Generals by Eron, I began to fidget nervously, my palms turning clammy while I awaited their instructions to activate the mirror. The elven General sat to my left and Monroe to my right. Eron had assured me no shadow creatures would be shooting through the object and I wondered why my grandfather currently paced at the end of the hall. I was unsure what caused his obvious agitation, but had little doubt I would soon find out when Monroe muttered, "When you are ready, Aria."

With a glance at Eron and his tentative smile, I reached forward and removed the handkerchief before gazing once more into the mirror. Soon after the familiar flare of magic, I was addressing the intimidating expressions of five elves, their fierce beauty a welcome distraction. A female elf, Florel I assumed, smiled warmly through the mirror and made introductions.

"Greetings Portalis of the Three Realms. I am Lady Florel and one of the three elven Elders of Elavon. Accompanying us in this meeting are our Second and Third Generals."

Taking a deep breath I returned, "Please call me Aria, and greetings to you all. I fear I will say something foolish in such company so ask that you bear with me, as this is much to take in."

Florel smiled kindly at me. "I think you are no fool, Aria, but honest, and we value that highly amongst our kind. Sadly we cannot speak for long." Her verdant eyes moved away swiftly as she addressed Eron. "Erondriel, we are relieved to see you have accomplished your first task and are not the worse for wear. Our scouts have reported flares in Portali magic at three locations, the port of Framlington, the market town of Kervalis and the village of Herringlea."

Eron hissed, "They are preparing an assault to gain back the Portalis already?! Those locations will cut off any and all access to the Arckus Kingdom. We must seal the portals before they can mobilise their armies."

At the metallic taste in my mouth, I realised I had bitten my lip. They were going to cut us off from the rest of the Kingdom. From our only aide. The people I had grown up with, the people I loved would be in *danger*. Faced with an immediate surge of panic, I quickly interrupted. "What can be done? I cannot put my family and town in danger, *please*, surely I can close some of these portals before they reach all three?!"

My rant was ended abruptly when Eron grabbed the clenched fist in my lap. "Calm yourself, Aria, we will not leave your town unprotected. Have there been any reports of dark mage activity in these areas, Lady Florel?"

"How astute you are, Erondriel, no there has not, therefore we have time, Aria, so do not worry yourself so."

Another elf, Havrel, with braided deep-brown hair

and a square jaw, headed towards the mirror and I quickly noticed his imposing stature. "We will approach this strategically. You will head first to the port, for that is the closest portal to seal shut. It also provides a nautical escape route through the Ageless Sea, should the other locations be commandeered before we can reach them. From our scrolls, Petriel will advise of the nearest available portal to you from Elavon. Here we will station three hundred elves, armed and ready to be deployed, should you need us to come to your defence. Our best bet is to stay one step ahead, but there is still a risk of the town being taken before you get there."

Eager to speak, I questioned, "Can we warn the town at least, so they are not defenceless?" Those earthy eyes bored into my own, strong and unwavering, and I found it difficult not to appear overwhelmed.

"Yes, Miss Aria, we would not leave any town defenceless and have forewarned its Lords. However, if they choose not to take action, we cannot be held responsible."

Nodding, I looked at the table, ignoring Eron's next response in favour of turning over that word, *responsible*. Because of this power, did that make me responsible for protecting our world? Whether I accepted it or not, I was responsible for these people and the burden of such a responsibility suddenly threatened to crush me. I felt, *alone*. If I failed to seal the portals, they would be left to face such horrors that even I could not comprehend.

Gritting my teeth, I looked up to see all eyes now faced me. Embarrassed and assuming I had missed some crucial point, I stilled.

"Aria?" Grandfather walked over to me and I winced nervously.

"I apologise, Grandfather, was I being spoken to?"

He gingerly knelt beside me and took my hand. "No my girl, but we all felt your sadness, your isolation." I was shocked and appalled to say the least.

"But … but how is that possible? Am I *that* easy to read?!" Good grief, no wonder I couldn't get away with sneaking extra puddings from Wendy when I was a child!

Monroe responded with a smile, "No Aria, it was magic. Your feelings must have been very powerful, for they needed an outlet to maintain balance."

"Miss Aria." It was Florel's voice that relievedly drew our combined attention. "I will only say this once and hope that you take these words into your heart." My shoulders straightened at her direct tone. "You are not alone in this fight and this fight is not yours alone. We will face this evil together and honour that allegiance by protecting you as if you are one of our own kin. Should fear or doubt creep into your heart, look to your family and companions, for they will not easily fail you."

And with that declaration, the ethereal image in the mirror faded before disappearing entirely. Eron was the first to look at me, those beautiful silver eyes filled with compassion and strength.

"We shall succeed or fail together, Aria." The finality in those words resonated within me and, despite my fears, a spark of hope ignited within my chest before we all rose in preparation for the journey ahead.

After our meeting with the Elders, packing for our journey was swift. Grandfather decided it was not safe to remain at the farmhouse, or in Great Barrington for that matter, so Wendy, Geoffrey and Berta would take up residence at Monroe's spice shop and keep us abreast of any changes. As it turned out, the spice shop was merely a facade for collecting rare herbs and tinctures used in the magical arts. But I rather believed it was to keep an eye on his old friend, as much as Monroe was unwilling to admit it.

In my room I began packing two spare sets of clothes for my journey, along with soaps and my one other pair of boots, when Wendy walked in.

"Miss Aria?" I turned to see her rounded frame perched in the doorway and noticed a set of clothes in her arms.

"It's alright Wendy, I have already packed a thick woollen skirt, my working trousers and two shirts. Do you think that will be sufficient?"

Wendy shook her head and held her own pile aloft, as if in offering. "These are what you will wear to begin your journey."

"Oh?" Intrigued, I watched as she walked into the room and set the clothes out on the bed. Curious, I moved closer and arched a brow at the new garments while she grinned enthusiastically. "Let's get you dressed, shall we?"

Eron

Erondriel finished his preparations quickly and was ready to leave before the rest of the party, so found himself patrolling around the front of the farmhouse impatiently. Many centuries of battle and travelling had taught him to be ready at a moment's notice, so he had to rein in his instincts to bark orders when Monroe walked leisurely out the front door, as if they had all the time in the world at their disposal.

"Lady Florel, is she mated?" Eron rolled his eyes and decided to ignore the idiotic mage.

"Oh come now elf, it is a harmless question."

"It is a pointless question Monroe, for matings are of equals." Eron spoke the next sentence as if addressing a youngling. "*You* are the equivalent of a mouse and the Lady a tiger."

Smirking, Monroe replied wistfully, "Oh and what a tigress she would be."

Eron tried and failed to hide his huff of disgust and left the fool to his musings before eyeing the front door to watch Aria step through and was left rather stunned by her appearance. What she wore was not particularly special, for she was dressed in brown studded leathers and solid boots, but it was the way they hugged her slim figure perfectly. She looked *alluring* to him and that was a feeling he had not experienced for some time. It surprised him. Left him feeling uneasy and undoubtedly with a frown marring his face.

Monroe decided that was the moment to clear his

throat and let out a small whistle. "Well you certainly look the part, Aria, ready to go?" Aria blushed slightly at this, then nodded, steely resolve in those deep-blue eyes and was shortly followed by her grandfather, as well as the other members of the household who gathered at the front of the property. The housekeeper, Wendy, had a handkerchief pressed to her face and tears in her eyes, until Aria moved and embraced her fiercely, muttering that she would see them all soon and to stay safe. Eron admired her concern, even when it was herself that was the target, but he would have to set boundaries. It was commendable and endearing, but also dangerous. Sympathetic souls were easily manipulated by those that would otherwise do them harm and her compassion would be a risk to them all, if she failed to control it.

Aria

I embraced Wendy, for what could have been the last time. We had already talked while she helped me don the travelling leathers she had brought with her and hinted that it was in fact Monroe who had helped procure them before our departure. Despite Monroe's forethought, Wendy was not so impressed with their snugness. They were not uncomfortable and allowed me to move fluidly, but I also knew they accentuated areas that had not been highlighted with my previous attire.

I failed to miss the look of surprise on Eron's face when I exited the farmhouse and just hoped his frown was not one of disapproval. I was embarrassed enough as it was and remained rather tempted to cover myself in a cloak, had it not been such a warm autumn day. Leaving Wendy's embrace and sending a smile to Berta, I mounted one of our sturdy brown mares called Mavel, my favourite, which Geoffrey walked from the stables along with three other horses, who all nickered and swished their tails at our approach. The two taller stallions, one a dark brown and the other black and white, were to be ridden by Eron and Grandfather, while the third, another mare called Floxy, was taken by Monroe, who declared he was far more bearing of the title *ladies' man* and so should have the other mare, which drew further eye rolls from all parties.

Patting Mavel's flank, the smell of hay bursting from her fine chestnut hairs, Geoffrey deftly attached my belongings to her saddle before I waved once more to the friends and family I was leaving behind. Before I knew it, my thoughts drifted back to my earlier conversation with Wendy.

"I know it is far too dangerous for you to write to me whilst on your journey, but you must promise me, Aria, no matter the challenge, you will not give up. I must know my wonderful girl, that you will fight, not just for others, but for yourself should the need arise? Let your old cook have some peace knowing that."

It broke my heart to hear such fear in her voice and I could not help the tremble of my lips, or the tears that threatened to fall in that moment. My last words to her echoed through my mind as we left the farm, *"You are no simple cook to me Wendy, you are family and I will fight for us all."*

Following the treelined road, their leaves swiftly falling in a rain of oranges and reds, I steeled myself for a long journey ahead. Upon setting out on our expedition, Eron had scoffed at the term when I described it as such. The ride to Framlington port would take three days, the longest journey I had ever taken on a horse, but Eron's response made me feel even more inadequate, so I remained quiet for the remainder of the morning. It was Grandfather who broke me out of my reverie some three hours later, when we stopped to stretch our legs and have a quick luncheon of bread, cured meat and cheese.

"I know I have said this already, but please forgive me Aria for not being honest with you about how you came into my care those years ago."

Even though the reminder still stung, I had already decided that it didn't change how I felt about him. "I'll admit after the shock I was deeply hurt, but you are and always will be my grandfather, despite my true heritage. The thought that my original family did not want me, only saddens me further." I tried and failed to stop the huge sigh as I spoke. "Can I ask who they were?"

Looking at me sympathetically, Grandfather replied, "I was not privy to such information, my girl. All I know is that you were given into my care by the King's court who oversee such matters and that it was my sworn duty to protect you."

"The Jaguar's court are not very forthcoming with information, pompous toads they are, but compared to the former Mage Council, they are practically gentlemen," Monroe added.

"Former?" I asked him, not having heard of this council before, or mages for that matter.

"They were disbanded shortly after you were placed into our care. The newly appointed King Lenard did not like their sway and power over his court, smartest thing that fool did, *ever* in fact, now that I think about it."

Changing tact, Grandfather interrupted. "Nevertheless, how are you holding up my girl? Days of riding are not for the faint-hearted after all?"

I huffed at that statement, my reply bitter and loud enough for Eron to hear. "The definition of a long journey clearly belongs to the experience of the rider and therefore my feelings on the subject are not valid, for to some it has been no time at all."

I sent a glare at Eron, who seemed unimpressed with my little outburst, before turning to Monroe, who was now chuckling heartily and trying not to choke on his water. "Hear, hear Aria!" he crowed, while Grandfather looked pointedly at the laughing mage.

"Monroe, you blathering oaf, do not add fuel to the fire before we have even finished our first day of riding!"

"It is OK, Grandfather, I have made my point. Besides, if anything, this has taught me that no matter how many centuries old you may be, it is still no guarantee of proper manners or even empathy."

A low rumble came from Eron's direction. "Aria, you misunderstood my intent. It was not a criticism, but a way for you to gain perspective *through* my experience. You are clearly sensitive and I will mind my words in future, so that they appeal more to your delicate young ears."

The elvish snowflake was mocking me and before I could answer he walked away to mount his horse. I was about to charge after him, when Grandfather grabbed my arm and stilled my advance. "This is not the time, Aria, we must reach the port, *that* is our priority. And please try not to fling him off his horse in a temper on our way there," he added with an exaggerated sigh before releasing me and heading for his horse. Thankfully I found my frown dwindling at Monroe's next words.

"Now *that* I would love to see, the elvish General flung off his horse by a mortal. It would be a thing of legend!" Clearly amused by the thought, given his smirk, and despite his irritating tendencies, the mage knew how to make me smile and that's just what I did for the rest of the day.

♦ 7 ♦

Aria

Perched on the border of Harkwood forest, we reached an inn just after twilight called the Bluffing Boar. Monroe had recommended it, no doubt being a regular patron. He also suggested that Eron cover his elvish charms, citing that no one would loosen their tongues in the presence of an elf and we needed to know if any of the locals had noticed strange activity in the area.

"We don't need rumours of a large noisy elf floating around the Kingdom. The King's spies would have a field day," Monroe muttered casually and Eron's grunt was his only reply as we walked inside the building. It took mere seconds before my hand covered my mouth and nose and I had to stop myself from gagging. The smells of ale, tobacco and body odour so strong, they attacked my senses like a physical blow. Some were perfumed and pleasant, but the most pungent stench was that of unwashed bodies. Monroe inhaled deeply. "The smell of a fine establishment," and I thought Grandfather was going to throttle him, as the colour of his face was turning decisively redder by each passing moment. Before things could escalate, Monroe called the innkeeper over.

A short, stocky fellow with no hair atop his head, but interestingly sporting a long, dirty, blond beard, trudged over. "What can I do for you fine travellers?" he asked in a gruff voice, so Monroe quickly requested four rooms and disappointingly, only two were available. It was decided I would have my own and the three men would share the larger room next door, so paying the fee, we hesitantly entered the main bar area behind an excited Monroe.

It was dark. The space lit dimly by a few sporadic lanterns and a large fireplace towards the back of the room, which made it uncomfortably warm. The ceiling was low, its beams a hazard to the men's tall statures and was unpleasantly covered in a thick layer of tobacco smog. A large number of long tables were crammed together in the tight space and occupied by rowdy men of all ages and a few women.

A barmaid sauntered over and gestured for us to follow to what I hoped was a free table. She would have been pretty, if not for the layers of rouge on her lips and cheeks and what I assumed was a fake beauty spot just above her top lip. Sadly the table was half occupied and I was ushered into a chair next to a strongly built gentleman, with a short beard and dark hair, who unabashedly ogled at the barmaid's low-cut dress. I began to panic when his eyes turned to leer at me until Eron grabbed my waist, hoisting me into the air and placed me between himself and Grandfather. The gentleman however, decided to protest.

"Oi! The lady and I wanted to get better acquainted," and I cringed.

Slowly turning, Eron's silver eyes and strong jaw were the only thing visible under his hood as he muttered in a low tone, "You would do well to keep your interests in your card game and not on the lady."

It was then I noticed the glimmer of a blade pressed to the man's lower abdomen and I glanced nervously at Monroe across the table. Clearing his throat, he called heartily, "Drinks for the table on us!" Which was greeted with a round of cheers and had successfully stopped an all-out brawl before it could start. Eron retracted the blade and faced forward once more, while I admired Monroe's quick thinking and hoped he hadn't just spent our entire travel purse.

After nearly two hours, the residents of not just our table were looking decidedly rosy-cheeked, Monroe included. Even Grandfather seemed to be enjoying a few tipples, although, unlike the other patrons, he knew when to slow down. The only other sober member of our party, apart from myself, was Eron. He hadn't moved and refrained from joining in. At first I thought him just standoffish, but after a while I noticed the exchanged looks between himself and Monroe and realised swiftly after, that they were gleaning information from the rowdy patrons. Impressed, I decided to remain as invisible as I could, although how invisible was a woman to a table of drunken men? Not very. I lost count of the number of lewd comments or innuendos that were thrown my way, but instead of being offended, I found it rather amusing. Although things may have been decidedly different if I were not sandwiched between Eron and Grandfather, as a few men seemed to be getting handsy with the barmaids, some of whom did not seem to mind.

The hour was growing late when Grandfather spoke to me. "Aria, I think it's time for us to retire, we will be rising early and unfortunately Monroe will be entertaining for some hours yet."

Pleased to be leaving, I did not argue as we stood from the table, and Monroe's jeering began. "Going to bed so early, my friend your age betrays you again!"

Laughing heartily, Monroe was taken by surprise when Grandfather threw an empty tankard of ale at his head, which he luckily dodged before it made contact. This was met with a round of cheers as Monroe stood and took an exaggerated bow and I failed to stop my chuckle.

"Come on now Aria, lest you be taken in by this rabble as well!" Grandfather growled, so I threw a sympathetic smile towards Eron and Monroe, before mumbling placatingly, "Yes Grandfather," as he stormed off towards the crooked timber stairs at the far end of the bar. I followed quickly but was stopped halfway by a drunkard who smelt particularly foul. My words to him were short. "Move Sir, I will not ask again."

"Oh lovely lady, my companions and I would wish to spend more time with you," he crooned and the sound was like the scraping of metal against a plate. Smiling broadly, his yellowing teeth on show, he took a step towards me, eyes roaming my body while he muttered, "We could learn a lot about each other." He moved closer and I could now smell his rancid breath, which left me shaking with disgust. My eyes darted about the room as I wondered briefly if Eron or Monroe would assist, but unable to see them, I understood quite quickly that I would have to deal with this wretch myself.

Eron

Eron remained seated uncomfortably at the table when Aria smiled and left to retire for the evening, all the while considering at what point he too could leave this table full of prigs in favour of his cot. Knowing these drunken mortals were less than honourable, he decided to keep an eye on Aria as she walked away. Monroe was currently on his sixth ale and doing well to keep his focus on the task they had planned. Simple really, ply the mortals with ale and loosen their tongues. Unfortunately, there was nothing to note. One man had confided that his brother, who was an armed guard for the port Lord in Framlington, had begun to prepare arms, but that was of little consequence. Havrel had said he would warn the towns at risk.

Glancing back to Aria, Eron's eyes narrowed at the inebriated fool that had stepped in front of her and his two lackies who were slowly circling behind. Swearing to himself, he calmly slid away from the table and headed towards the group, the man now less than an arm's length away from her. Eron soon reached the bar preparing to intervene, when he was quickly stopped in his tracks by the right hook Aria threw at the man's face. Knocking him out completely, his overweight body fell uselessly to the floor and Eron's eyebrows rose in response, impressed. The whole bar went silent for a moment or two, before cheers and laughter rang out from some of the patrons.

"Watch yourself lads, there's a she-wolf on the prowl hah!" came a cry from some lunatic across the room and Eron watched the two accomplices slink back into the crowd, while a slightly flustered Aria headed up the stairs. Wandering back to the table, Eron struggled to supress the smirk on his lips and was pleased that this Portalis had a lot more tenacity in her than he first suspected.

Aria

Reaching my small room and grimacing despairingly over the behaviour I had just witnessed in the main bar, I bolted the door shut and settled my bag on a small stool that sat next to a worn chest. The hinge however refused to open, despite my persistence, so I chose not to unpack. Instead I turned to a large basin filled with fresh water that sat atop a simple table and, even though the water was now cooled, I was grateful to be able to wash before bed.

Changing and settling into the small single cot, I thought over the day's events. My hand still throbbed from where I hit that drunken boar across the face, but I felt my decision was easily justified. I had to make an example of him, or the other patrons would also have taken liberties. Thankfully the man remained unconscious and I avoided an even bigger scene. Not that I couldn't handle myself, but I'm sure Grandfather wouldn't have approved of drawing such attention to our travelling party.

My thoughts strayed to Eron and how he had reacted when I first sat down. I doubted his actions were the result of any kind of affection when he moved me from that man's reach, but I couldn't help feeling warmed by the gesture nonetheless. It took me an hour or so to fall asleep, what with the noise downstairs and my mind racing frantically, but eventually I must have drifted off. The words *"pretty girl, where will I find you?"* echoed unpleasantly in my mind, until I awoke with a start and covered in a thin layer of sweat. Frustratingly I couldn't remember my dream, despite my efforts, but those soft, sinister words remained in my mind for the remainder of the morning, while I dressed and then met with my companions downstairs for breakfast.

I soon spotted Grandfather, his hand raised and waving me over cheerfully. "Good morning my dear, I trust you slept well?"

The remainder of our party appeared surprisingly well, in spite of last evening's revelry and the usually bustling room was now mostly quiet, which I assumed was due to the early hour. Not willing to disclose my disturbed sleep, I uttered, "As well as can be expected," while grabbing a boiled egg and some bread and taking a seat next to him. He frowned a little at this, but did not question me further, for which I was grateful and instead scowled at Monroe across the table.

"We unfortunately had to share with that animal and was subject to all manner of noises."

Monroe said nothing, his defence muted while he chewed on a piece of ham hock, with part of the meat hanging out of his mouth. Amusement flashed in Eron's usually stoic eyes and I couldn't help but snicker; perhaps today's journey wouldn't be so demanding.

Unfortunately I was wrong and Eron set a punishing pace over the next two days. The ride was harsh and my legs were straining against the stirrups as we cantered through the tall grass, while I tried determinedly to keep up with our party. Breezily riding ahead were Eron and Monroe, whose horses had begun to kick up dust when the hard ground quickly turned to sand and I was forced to squint and move abreast of their path. I knew then we must be close to the port, for I could also smell the salted seawater in the air.

I had been happy to vacate the inn and its unfortunate inhabitants, however it had not been an easy journey. Despite my pained legs and back, I had managed to avoid a verbal sparring match with Eron, so considered the trip successful thus far, until high-pitched screams of terror and black smoke rising into the crisp autumn skies jarred me from my naively optimistic thoughts.

We stopped abruptly, Mavel whinnying at my harsh pull on her reins when Eron raised his right arm and called for a halt to assess the situation before us.

Past the sea of blackened smog, atop what I assumed was Lord Framlington's pearlescent tower, poured all manner of gruesome creatures that tore savagely through the property and spread like a disease into the ill-prepared city below. The areas which had yet to be destroyed, were like nothing I had ever seen.

Whitewashed buildings dressed with what looked to be scalloped metal roof tiles, that I imagined gleaming like iridescent scales on a warm summer's day, were now being marred by the growing shadow moving across the sky and blocking the sunlight. The atmosphere was growing eerier by the second and Eron cursed into the wind.

"Havrel should have sent forces by now, what is the delay?! The entire port will be slaughtered within a few hours at this rate!" Turning his steed to face us, he added grimly, "We must provide what aid we can, but I am reluctant to send you anywhere near the forces of Oromos, Aria."

Gritting his teeth and closing his eyes, Eron looked to be seeking patience and perhaps, an alternative answer. I however knew there wasn't one, so I decided to make the decision for them all.

"I must close that portal. It will at least give the residents a chance and we do not know what manner or number of creatures will pass through, should it remain open."

Eron's distressed eyes met mine, when Grandfather retorted shortly, "I cannot put you in such danger, Aria, the risk is too great. Not just for me, but for the success of our task."

Clicking his tongue Monroe nodded, but surprised me with his reply. "We cannot keep her sheltered forever, Jacoby. If we do not close this portal, there will be many innocent lives lost." Grandfather tried to interrupt, but Monroe continued regardless of his opposition. "It is a gamble, Torvel, I concede this point, but if you and Eron can create such a diversion as to draw the eyes of the enemy, I will sneak us in and out before they realise we are there … at least that is my plan." He muttered this last part and winked in my direction, while the screams and roars of dark creatures only continued to worsen and I knew I had to force my grandfather's hand.

"We ride Monroe. Grandfather, Eron, please be safe."

Grandfather looked incredulous, while in contrast, Eron's tone was supportive and stern.

"Get in and get out, rendezvous here. If you should fail, unleash your magic and I will reach you."

"I won't allow it Aria!" Grandfather exclaimed and attempted to grab my reins, but I ushered Mavel into a gallop along the sand-dusted path and was followed swiftly behind by Monroe.

When we were out of earshot and closing in on the port, my magical friend sported a wicked grin and hailed, "Let's show that old miser what we can do, Aria!" before we rode beneath the main gate. Its white stone was decorated with carvings of cresting waves and cawing sea birds beckoning us to enter, before my friend raised his hands to the sky and cried, "*invisor reflectay*!" A slight shimmer surrounding our forms like an invisible cloak.

"They cannot see us, Aria, but can hear and smell us. Should my concentration break, the barrier will fall, so let us try to avoid any flying daggers before we reach the northwest tower."

I nodded, too nervous for words, but remained determined to see this task through for the sake of the people in this town. I would prove to myself that I could do this and be what these realms needed in times of uncertainty, and of fear.

We followed the white cobbled streets that meandered down the cliffs, the horses reluctant to press forward at speed due to the steepness, but eventually we reached the large bay filled with merchant ships at the bottom. People were fleeing chaotically as we passed, some carrying their possessions, others clutching their small children who were wailing with fear.

How it angered me, the cruelty of the evil that we were heading towards, and I used that anger to feed my resolve, my courage. Eventually Floxy and Mavel were too large to press through the throngs of people, so we were forced to dismount. After releasing the horses, Monroe grabbed my hand and led the way as we snuck through a narrow but steep passage, dwarfed by white buildings either side. Hidden amongst the towering shadows of the structures and nearing ever closer, the bloodshed became inescapable. Bodies started to appear along the streets, some human, others malformed creatures of nightmares. I thought their mangled bodies, displaying rows of teeth and blood-tipped claws were frightening, but nothing compared to the horror of seeing them alive and hunting the guards, who courageously tried to hold them back from defenceless citizens.

Their tarnished armour gleamed in few places, each swipe of their swords deft and determined, despite the monumental task before them. Such bravery would struggle not to inspire any who witnessed it and I found myself bolstered by their courage.

A creature with midnight fur and an elongated muzzle caught my attention as it started stalking towards a woman carrying a young child of no more than six seasons in her arms. Her husband stepped in its path and brandished a small knife while ushering her to run, yet still the creature prowled ever closer.

"Go my loves, do not falter! I will meet you at Humbridge, go now!"

Their eyes met for less than a breath, before his wife let out a sob of utter anguish as she sprinted away, clutching their child and leaving her husband to face his death.

Monroe gripped my arm hard and pulled me in the opposite direction. "We must get to the portal, Aria! Only then can we help these people."

But his words did not register as I watched on in horror while the creature lunged towards the man, who, despite his thin frame, held his ground. The dagger was poised shakily in front of him, his expression torn between sheer terror and resolve, as he likely knew that his approaching death would ensure the life of his family.

My inner voice screamed; such injustice could not be tolerated in our world. Such sacrifice for love deserved so much more than a death by that monster's jaws. I flung my hands out, thinking of an arrow, sharp and true. My magic melded into physical form and I knew it struck its target when the crunch of bone and splitting of flesh reached my ears. It screeched and writhed, demonic eyes seeking out a new enemy it could not see, while a golden arrow lay imbedded in its hide and slowly leached away its life.

My relief was almost violent as I staggered into Monroe. The townsman, although briefly baffled, shrewdly did not wait for the creature's life to end and instead sprinted away after his family. I could only hope that I had given him a chance to reach them before more beasts could stalk their steps.

Monroe hauled me away from the scene and grabbed both my arms, frustration clear in his expression. "Aria, you can not interfere further, there is too much at stake. Time is of the essence! Eron and your grandfather will be fighting through these monsters to create a diversion; the more time that passes, the more at risk they are!"

He was inches from my face at this point and I could not blame him for his reaction, so answered placatingly, "I understand."

Nodding, he spun quickly and ran, holding my hand in a vice-like grip as we weaved through the chaos and desperately tried to avoid the weapons and jaws that threatened to cut us down in the process.

Eron

The booming roars from creatures not of this world sounded from the parapets of the manor perched upon the cliffs, as Eron carved his way through the city with a tiring Jacoby in tow.

"We can't just peck off a few of these blighters one at a time, Eron, we must create a distraction large enough for Aria and Monroe to reach the manor!"

Eron huffed while facing off with a mangey-looking canine with the head of a reptile and retorted, "I cannot utilise a vast amount of magic too early, we need to reach the south-easterly quarter of the manor to inflict the most damage and scatter the Oromos forces."

He sliced through the creature's neck easily and its black lifeblood spilled satisfyingly onto the cobblestones. It had been some time since his elvish Frostblade had met Oromos flesh he mused, as Jacoby nodded towards a side street away from the fighting. Here they paused for breath and eyed the surrounding city guards currently keeping the monsters at bay.

Panting harshly, hands on his knees, Jacoby acknowledged, "I cannot follow, as I will only slow you down Eron. I will remain here to help contain these creatures and rescue as many folk as I can."

Seizing Jacoby's shoulder before turning away, Eron declared, "Stay alive until I return" and sprinted towards the darkness at immortal speeds. It was becoming harder to dodge the growing hordes as Eron traversed the steep steps towards the eastern side of the manor. Its lowest courtyard exposed to the ocean and edged with a small stone balcony, the only barrier between him and a watery grave at the bottom of the cliff. It was here that Elavon's General bellowed his order "Retreat or die!" to the few remaining soldiers still able to fight. The bodies of their brothers littering the once beautiful space, some now reduced to nothing more than a meal for its new horrific inhabitants.

The enemy numbers were overwhelming, so Eron did not wait long to see if the soldiers heeded his warning and drew his Frostblade high. Forged millennia ago for the forbears of his house, from the glaciers born of the Elavon Sea, he pointed it towards the darkening sky and cried *"archtore!"* and slashed the blade down with all his might at the enclosing enemy ranks. An impenetrable arc of wicked sharp ice cut through the swathes of darkness heading his way and, having caught their attention, Eron waited while rows upon rows of the enemy turned upon him. They jumped from the higher balconies and scaled up the cliffside and, only when their forces thinned from the western side of the manor, did he decide to unleash the full force of his magic.

♦ 8 ♦

Aria

I sensed the surge of magic before I could see it. It was vast, powerful and what followed baffled my mind and senses, as a wall of water surrounding the eastern tip of the manor rose from the sea to crash against a massing horde of dark creatures.

"Keep moving Aria! This is our chance!" Monroe urged and pulled me more forcefully through the western gate, but my gaze remained captivated by the water as it cascaded from the balconies and stairwells. It flowed in great cleansing waves and dragged the enemy with it, wiping their tainted existence from this world while I remained stunned by Eron's power and its ferocity.

Our invisibility remained an advantage for the time being, as we evaded countless enemies and skirted our allies while they traded deadly blows within the courtyard. The water's wrath thankfully subsided by the time we reached the space, but the liquid now posed a challenge, as it gradually settled into deep puddles about the manor. Those innocent pools soon became a threat to our presence, should our tread be too obvious. So moving carefully forward, the sounds of carved flesh and shattered bones followed us as we headed ever closer to the portal, my eyes immediately spying the magical doorway and I frowned, for it was not what I expected.

The runes glowed around what looked to be a stone column. A pillar to be exact and one of four currently holding up a small, delicate bridge, to what I assumed was the Lord's quarters. Suddenly a sound, that I could only describe as a thousand mirrors shattering, pulled my attention to the east. The remaining wells of water rose to the skies and dispelled into razor shards of ice that rained upon its enemies lurking below, impaling their forms as well as any steel spear. Howls and cries of pain that I did not recognise reverberated across the port and were broken only by Monroe's next words.

"Corkcat's balls! I can neither sense nor see any immortals or mages guarding the portal, which means, Aria, that they are hiding as we are."

Having ignored the great display of magic I had just witnessed, or unbothered by it, Monroe stood grimacing, before sharply pulling me into an alcove to the left-hand side of the open-aired space. We crouched under its arched structure, Monroe leaning towards me conspiratorially, eyes occasionally darting in the enemy's direction as he whispered, "We must be tactful, Aria. The longer we lie in wait, the more beasts we unleash on the city."

I worried my bottom lip between my teeth and toyed with the handle of the blade Grandfather had given me. Taking a deep, calming breath, I considered our options, of which I soon realised there were very few. Stealth or haste. The cries of the fleeing residents resurfaced in my ears and quickly decided for us.

"This situation is very precarious, I will do what I can to clear a path for you Aria, but they will soon realise our location as the spell will falter."

I nodded, understanding the danger he was trying to convey.

"Remember Aria, close the portal and flee to safety. No matter what happens, do *not* engage the enemy, we cannot risk your capture."

We stood and, with a dramatic bow, Monroe murmured, "Ladies first."

Cracking a smile I replied, "Your manners are impeccable as always, Monroe" as we stormed forth in unison, my heart in my throat, and surged towards the bridge.

Monroe cried *"propellore!"* and blasted through the wall of creatures that awaited us at the base of the bridge. Despite his prior manners, the mage had charged ahead of me as we approached the gathered monsters, that were either crawling through or guarding the portal. His spell had thrust them back at least ten paces in different directions, with the mage remaining at its epicentre. Immediately I ran through the lull and onto the stone bridge before they could regroup and block our advance. I dared not look back, even as I heard rather than saw Monroe aggravating our enemies.

"Let us dance, filth of Oromos. Come and meet your end!"

But at his words I instinctually twisted and spied a number of demonic eyes now fixed upon him, the mage's invisibility and mine, I realised uneasily, were now completely gone. The slight shimmer of his incantation had faded as I peered nervously down at my leathers, but I still pressed on. My hopes for success glimmered when my hand collided with the portal runes, the magic greeting me as if in welcome and just as the incantation was perched upon my lips, all thought stilled when a pale, black-tipped hand clasped around my wrist from the other side. I screeched *"sigillum!"* desperately, but no longer in contact with the pillar, the portal remained open. So abandoning that course of action, I began to tug my hand free, a frenzied panic overtaking rational thought as I struggled helplessly against my new enemy, only pausing my movements upon hearing a short and malicious laugh which turned my blood to ice.

"Hello again, pretty girl."

And I began to scream.

Eron

Feeling depleted with heavy limbs and covered in all manner of gore, Eron sensed Monroe's magic which led him to the western gate. Having destroyed the south-easterly tip of the manor with his magical assault, Eron remained satisfied with the distraction, despite it costing him much of his magical reserves. But the expenditure was worth it he reasoned, for it kept him alive at least.

Havrel had sound reasoning for sending him here

first, water being Eron's mastered element and that of his house. The rhythm of water hummed within his very being, and what better way to secure the best offence than to place him in a port surrounded by water, in the unfortunate event the elvish reinforcements did not arrive on time.

Dodging the battle around him, Eron was intent on reaching Aria and Monroe post-haste and it wasn't long before he entered the inner courtyard. At first glance, he saw Monroe hacking his way through a swarm of Oromos creatures, casting spells at whim and with a sinister smile plastered on his face. Eron's keen gaze next roamed the area in search of Aria and was immediately drawn to the ornate, white-stoned bridge, following a cry of utter terror.

Eron's eyes widened, fear seeping into his very bones when he met Aria's blue gaze filled with panic and despair. The traitorous letch from before was currently dragging her smaller frame through the portal and all Eron could do was uselessly roar his dismay and his challenge towards the enemy, for it to be drowned out by the cries of battle that surrounded them all.

Moving on instinct, he charged forward, hacking and destroying any creature that dared to enter his path as he tried desperately to reach Aria, her arm now extended towards him pleadingly. It nearly broke his heart. He moved with grace and deadly skill, honed by centuries of training, and flowed unchallenged through the swathes of enemies, leaving a river of inky blood in his wake. Eron only paused his assault as a threatening echo danced along the sea breeze and reached his keen ears. The words of his enemy. His cowardly form hidden behind the shimmering veil which purred, "Follow us into the bowels of Oromos if you dare, General," before Aria was hauled through the portal and into the cesspit of nightmares, all the while screaming his name.

Aria

The cold. It pierced my lungs, halting my screams while my mind raged wildly and begged for Eron to rescue me.

My back was held firm to a strong chest and I willed my eyes to open, but fear held them tightly shut, until my irrational mind conjured images so frightening that I had little choice but to tear them apart. Gaze now darting in every direction, I firmly expected any manner of creature to slice at me with their claws or worse, swallow me whole, but instead I was greeted by a suffocating bleakness, enhanced by the growls and shrieks of the monsters residing within the mountain. The derisive words from my captor only seemed to enhance my despair, "Look around little Portalis, no one is coming for you in this place."

The onyx and red-veined rock that enclosed the cavernous room looked as though it *bled* and my eyes travelled about the space via the unnatural and twisted rivulets, until I caught sight of my only salvation. The portal. Thankfully it remained unsealed and offered a seductive glimmer of hope, when the hands that held me pulled harshly at my hair and drew my face back, to look deep into a set of eyes filled with loathing.

"You will seal this portal and you will do it now."

Without thinking, I grabbed the handle of my blade and aimed for his throat, my brief assault stopped almost instantly by his hand, as though expected.

"Stupid girl," he sneered and squeezed my wrist harshly, until the bruising pain forced my hand to release the blade with a clatter. He leaned closer, fangs bared and hissed threateningly, "Close it, *now*."

Knowing this next response would seal my fate as a prisoner, I steeled my resolve and stared back defiantly, not daring to utter a single word. He smirked knowingly, playfully, not dissimilar to the expressions of Monroe, but this was sinister and full of an age-old malice that made his green eyes glow with spiteful challenge. Suddenly he turned and I was thrown to the nearest soldier. At first I thought him human, but his black eyes determined that there was nothing human left in this shell. My arms were quickly secured behind my back and a blade pressed dangerously to my throat and I knew it was now my turn to wait expectantly for the threats to begin.

Surprisingly, the dark prisoner, as I still did not know his name, merely his unfortunate title, ignored me for the moment and addressed the vast number of creatures in the room. "Guard the portal until it is sealed. Kill any who enter. Fellious, with me."

The guard holding my arms hissed, "You will wish you had complied, Portalis," and dragged my trembling form behind them as we exited the cavern.

I decided that walking rather than being dragged was my best course of action as I was led out into a hallway, softly lit by iron torches perched on the walls. Even they hissed while we walked the unpleasant halls and pressed on down a jagged stone staircase.

The prisoner and this new arrival, Fellious, who I immediately noticed was a proverbial giant and dressed in a long black cloak and hood, strode ahead with purpose. The only sounds were our footsteps crunching against the uneven rocky floor until we reached the bottom of the stairs, where I heard the muffled groans and sharp screams from behind the various iron doors we passed. My panic started to grow frantic when we reached the end of the hall and I was ushered into a door on the left. My sharp intake of breath felt like it echoed around the room, for in its centre sat a long wooden table. The top must have been five inches thick and was marred by an assortment of carvings and blood stains upon its surface. A set of chains looped along the top and bottom, but it was the bench and wall of instruments scattered across it that had my whole body trembling with fear.

"Now then," the dark prisoner turned to me, "you have two choices, Portalis," he sneered, before circling me like a hunter.

I wished I weren't so intimidated, but my current situation being what it was, I had little options left but to cower.

"Become a servant of Oromos and aide in the conquer of the Three Realms, or Fellious here will gladly spend the remainder of your life persuading you to."

At this declaration, Fellious took down his hood and removed his cloak and I had never seen or imagined the like. He was a mismatch of bestial limbs with a human head, devoid of any hair and smiled with unnaturally sharpened teeth in excitement, waiting for my reply.

Chuckling, the dark prisoner uttered, "Not really much of a choice I suppose, so save us all some time and agree to the terms."

Remembering Wendy's words, I knew they were all counting on me to be brave. Regardless of my fear, I could not give in, not yet. I made my decision then, as completely terrified as I was. I would buy my friends and family as much time as I could withstand, before this wretched place broke me. The horrors of Oromos would pay witness to my courage, no matter how short-lived, because even in this hell I had a choice and I would not give it up so easily.

Breathing in deeply, my mind settled, I steeled myself for what was to come before I met my enemy's gaze and uttered, "You will have to break me first."

His expression shifted to one I could not recognise, before his dooming nod to Fellious settled my fate and, despite my earlier words, my legs began to quake.

Vylnor

Vylnor could not quite believe his ears. The girl was obstinate, he would admit that much, but foolishly so. After seeing the room and hearing the screams of those tortured around her, he assumed she would easily concede to his demands. It was rare that someone surprised him. He'd seen grown warriors piss themselves just walking up the hallway, however, her naivety would be her undoing. Unfortunately for him it now meant the process would take a little longer. It was a shame to see Fellious break her, but once she became a servant of Oromos, the dark magic would simply render her body and mind a shell to be controlled at his Masters' whim. He knew first-hand of that dark magic and what it could do to someone's mind. Perhaps it was best she not know of it.

Shaking his head to stop the direction of his thoughts, Vylnor replied smoothly, unperturbed, "Very well, let us see what you are made of, pretty girl," as the guard holding her drew a cloth over her mouth. Vylnor watched on as her eyes widened in terror and she struggled pointlessly for a few dials before she was rendered unconscious. Turning to Fellious, Vylnor reiterated, "Break her mind, but be careful of her body. The consequences should you get carried away will be *far* severer than anything you can imagine, Second."

Fellious said nothing, merely tilted his head eagerly in silent acknowledgment before it was time for him to begin his work and for a spark of a moment, Vylnor was tempted to pity this Portalis.

Aria

I awoke strapped to the table in my underclothes, arms and legs bound in chains and utterly petrified. A chuckle came from my right and my eyes immediately followed the sound to where Fellious currently perused a table of knives and other instruments in front of him. Without picking one up, he wandered over to me leisurely and placed a leather strap across my forehead. His cold, scaled claws brushed at my temple, forcing a wretch from my throat before he moved away and purred in mock sympathy, "T'would be a shame if you knocked yourself out and missed all the fun now, wouldn't it?"

My panic was becoming tangible, frantic even, as he moved to another table and I noticed a woman standing next to the dark prisoner. She seemed elven, but something about her beauty and frame appeared warped and unnatural. Her eyes were replaced by two pits of darkness, darkness which held such an endless and desolate depth, that one's soul would be lost, should they gaze upon them for too long.

I tried to disperse such wayward thoughts but felt as if this place encouraged and festered my fears wherever I looked. Regrettably my eyes were drawn back to Fellious, who now held a large club hammer in his right claw.

"A healer," he explained and nodded to the woman. "You are too useful to kill after all." The mountainous creature strode over casually and stood at my feet, while all I could do in my vulnerable state was hold my breath at his violent smile. "This will hurt," he chuckled and raised the hammer carelessly, tears pricking my eyes moments before he brought the weapon down upon my right ankle with an audible crack and my lungs exploded with my anguished screams.

Eron

Eron's roar of dismay fell on deaf ears as he and Monroe cut through the tide of foes to try and reach Aria before the portal was sealed shut. Monroe's actions became hectic when he called spell after spell to try and disperse the number of enemies in haste.

"*Propellore!*" Slash. "*Illumenti!*" Parry. And Eron's own fear rose in tandem with the mage's desperate actions. He had seen what that place could do to even the strongest warriors and began to growl in frustration, spearing yet another enemy, which was rapidly replaced by two more. The situation seemed futile, until his ears fell upon the sound of their salvation.

Looking to the west, atop the cliff they had descended only hours ago, the Horn of Havrel was singing the tune of battle. A line of elvish warriors on horseback, three hundred strong, peaked over the cliff edge towards the port, led by Havrel and Talos, his Second and Third Generals. His kin had made it, but were they too late? Knowing there was no time to lose and releasing the last of his magic, Eron cried "*lanciaglas!*" and shot a spear of ice towards the sky. It erupted into a shower of frost that glittered like the ocean on a summer's day and Eron followed his signal with a resounding boom. "FOR LIGHT AND PEACE!" With a pride born from the love of his homeland, Eron watched as hundreds of lethally trained elven warriors charged, the beat of hooves echoing like thunder towards the port of Framlington and finally, to their aide.

Aria

Pain. It was unbearable, unimaginable, and it was now my closest companion. Fellious brought that hammer down thrice more, my ankles and kneecaps now shattered. I bit my lip so hard upon anticipating the last hammer blow, that blood was now running down my chin. Even oblivion was no longer a salvation, for they would use amandine salts to rouse my weary mind each excruciating time.

Inhaling sharply, expecting my wrists or elbows next, I was relieved when Fellious called the healer over. The relief was short-lived however, when he uttered his next words. "Fix her for stage two."

The woman pressed her hands to my shattered ankles first, none too gently, and chanted as she did so. Delicious warmth suffused my skin and the pain soon dissipated. It was only when she was finished tending my knees, did I notice the two posts and subsequent chains Fellious was attaching across the room.

Cold terror gripped me and I began to struggle against my restraints. Fellious laughed as he crossed the room to throw a scaled claw across my cheek and, stunned, I could do naught when he breathed into my hair, "Struggling will only make me enjoy this more."

After roughly undoing my restraints and despite my newly healed state, I had little energy left in my limbs with which to walk and so was hauled towards the dreaded posts. Swiftly tethered and now standing weakly with one hand tied to each post, Fellious stood back and grasped hold of my breast band, ripping it off completely. My head throbbed painfully and my situation was too dire to be mortified at my state of undress, as I realised rather quickly what my next 'stage' was. *Whipping.* Breath now coming in sharp pants, I felt lightheaded, as the air around me grew increasingly thinner by each passing moment. I repeated Wendy's words over and over like a mantra, the only thing that kept my mind tethered to my body as the first blow struck. Razor sharp, it prised open my skin and forever tarnished my mind to the horrors of this world. I wailed and strained uselessly against my restraints, my back arching to absorb the pain before her words resurfaced once more. *"You will not give up."*

Vylnor

Vylnor felt … uncomfortable. It was a long-forgotten feeling and not a pleasant one. The girl, Aria, let out a scream of agonising pain as Fellious used a barbed whip, one of his favourites, to carve into her previously perfect back. For each scream Vylnor witnessed, the more enraged he became and the reaction was … *unusual.*

Normally Fellious and his talents for torture were barely of interest. He had seen hundreds of beings face this torment across the centuries and not battered an eyelash. Being on the receiving end, he'd endured more than most, but as his soul darkened over time, he found his empathy and feeling had disappeared with it. On the fifth lash, Aria uttered not one sound, but a despairing cry echoed in his mind and shocked him to his very core. '*Someone help me.*' And Vylnor instinctually boomed, "Fellious cease!" But before he could make any sense of his reaction, shouts sounded from beyond the chamber and one of his subordinates rushed in, the iron door shuddering as it hit the wall of rock.

"Lord Vylnor! The elves are attacking the portal. Your orders, Sir?!"

Aria

Slumped against my chains, I replayed the guard's startling news again in my mind. '*The elves are attacking the portal.*' My friends and my allies had not abandoned me, despite the odds.

Tears streaked my face while I listened dazedly to the words that followed, in spite of my agony.

"Heal her enough so we can relocate her to the Master's wing and do it quickly. If the elves are foolish enough to attack us on our own soil, they will pay for their insolence with their lives. Second, you will accompany the Portalis and I will deal with the cretins."

I heard Vylnor's retreating footsteps as warmth again radiated across my wounds and I quickly realised this would be my only opportunity to escape. This chamber was not far from the portal, so I just had to reach the cavern and hope my friends would find me. My magic had failed me so far and no matter what I tried it did not surface. I simply prayed it would not fail me again.

The worst of my wounds were healed, but the sites of the injuries were sore and itchy. An old tunic was thrust over my head and ropes were tied about my wrists, before I was hauled out of the chamber by Fellious, now equipped with a vicious-looking war hammer strapped to his back. His touch was callous, his claws puncturing the skin on my shoulders while we ascended the stone staircase away from the dungeon, I at his front. Arriving in the hall, we were greeted by the cries of battle and the clash of blades to my right. Fellious paused and leant down, his voice exuding smug delight.

"This way, Portalis, the Master is keen to meet you."

His insipid breath invaded my nostrils when I decided that now was my only chance. I threw my head back and, with a satisfying snap, it hit Fellious's nose. Slightly stunned, he released me on instinct and I sprinted up the hall with my hands still tied behind my back. Fear gripped me like a vice, while sweat streamed down my spine and I could hear his sadistic laugh and heavy footsteps giving chase through the mountain. They grew closer and closer still. The jagged rock began to cut into my bare feet, but fear pushed me further as though a phantom wind at my back, and I gritted out as I ran, "Faster, I must go *faster*!" As if hearing my desperation, my magic roused and I flew across the uneven black rock at speed, until, in no time at all, I recognised the hallway and the door housing the portal behind. Without thinking, and desperate to escape this place, I collided through the heavy doors and staggered, my uneven footsteps quickly halting at the scene of utter carnage that played out before me.

◆ 9 ◆

Aria

I scanned my surroundings desperately, unwilling to allow that monster behind to reach me. My arrival had to remain inconspicuous, so picking up my momentum, despite being surrounded by creatures of varying size and deformed shapes, I weaved through the fray with a light tread and kept to the shadows. Thankfully my enemy's eyes were trained on their opponents. There was a line of rapidly thinning elven forces being pushed back through the portal by a wall of Skygge demons and I knew my only chance of survival was to reach them.

Hearing *"illuminenti!"* my eyes turned to locate the mage and found Monroe across the cavern. I let out a brief sob, my relief almost palpable at simply beholding his familiar face in such a horrifying scenario. His spell did not have the blinding power as it once had in the farmhouse, no doubt Monroe's magic was weakening, but it did blast two Skygge demons back, before a beast of black fur and large canines took their place.

I ran towards the mage, desperate to reach him. I heard him call "switch!" and my hope was nearly derailed completely by the retreating forms of Monroe and the elven forces through the portal, until I saw Eron stride through, replacing Monroe and the previous elves with a new line of warriors.

They charged at their enemies with a renewed vigour and before I could stop myself I sobbed *"Eron!"*

He span immediately in my direction, shock and relief clear in his eyes. He looked so exhausted. Parts of his leather armour were shredded, dried and fresh blood splattered over his face and clothes, but I'd never seen a more welcoming sight. Eron arced his blade and slashed through an attacking beast's hide before spinning away, just as its fangs attempted to clamp down on his calf.

"Aria, to me!" he boomed and I recognised his alarm, moments before the tread of thundering feet reached my ears.

Fellious was still giving chase. I sprinted as fast as my legs would carry me towards Eron, his blade now protruding through the back of the beast, before he withdrew it in a spray of black blood and charged towards me, arm outstretched, while mine remained bound behind my back. I barrelled into him and was immediately thrust out of the way as Eron brought his blade up to collide with Fellious and his war hammer. The strain of the blow was severe, the rock beneath our feet trembling in answer and brought Eron to his knees, where he now grappled to keep the heavy weapon from meeting his skull. Through his gritted teeth Eron barked an order.

"Rendon! Get Aria to safety now! Warriors, defensive positions!"

The elf I assumed was Rendon ran from the line, while I shuffled uncertainly away from Eron and Fellious. The warrior's golden braid whipped in his wake as he ran to us at immortal speeds. Carefully he lifted me into his arms and offered an encouraging smile before we dashed through the bloodshed and towards the portal. Elves quickly rallied around us and formed an arrowhead blockade while I looked to my new ally, incredulous when I saw Eron and Fellious fade into the background.

My concern for my friend rising, I argued, "We cannot leave Eron to face that monster?!"

But Rendon merely smirked, "He is the First General of Elavon, it is the monster that should be frightened."

I blew out a huff at his arrogant response which was of little comfort, when an unexpected blast of fire exploded through the elvish line to our left and forced Rendon and I to the ground. The elven warrior swiftly countered and thrust out his arm crying, "*jordmur!*" A wall of rock and stone was pushed from the ground and caused the entire cavern to rumble ominously, when a second barrage of magical fire was unleashed upon our party. Its flames whipped and scorched the already blackened rock and I gripped my new ally tighter, my dread rising upon recognising who now sought to hinder our escape.

Vylnor

Vylnor was both incredulous and enraged by what he witnessed. Hidden behind a wall of earth was the Portalis and in the hands of his Master's enemy no less. Turning, he saw Fellious now battling that pathetic elf and he rather hoped for his Second's demise. Not only had he lost the Portalis, but was also failing to execute that elven whelp in good time.

Focusing back to the task at hand, Vylnor raised his arm and spoke "*frioterra*," which caused the earthen barrier to splinter and crumble, until a cry of "*astio!*" sounded from behind the wall. Disappointingly, the trembling earth ceased its movements and strained, unmoving against the two opposing spells. Two elves stalked boldly to the front of the barrier. The larger of the two, with dark-brown hair, carried a battleaxe and called arrogantly, "You meet the Second and Third Generals of Elavon Lord of Shadows! And also your end!"

Vylnor tsked, deeming the threat as little more than a bluff of bravado, when the other elven General sprinted towards him at deadly speed, his glaive aimed directly at Vylnor, thirsting for blood. But they would have none of it.

Drawing his twin Corrono blades, the shafts decorated with blackened steel, Vylnor charged with equal fervour and deflected the tip of the glaive before it could impale him through the stomach and swiped back, eyeing the General's white strip of hair and assumed he must be Talos of air and lightning. Blunt force would be needed against this foe, he quickly deduced, for the current battle was within a mountain, lightning could not be summoned and air was limited in such an environment. Ducking the elf's next attempt at removing his head, Vylnor looked for an opening and was distracted by the rantings of an old fool.

"Can't he just suck the air out of that filth's lungs, Monroe?!"

"Jacoby, my senile friend, not without sucking the air out of half the cavern also!"

Aria's protectors had located her. Gritting his teeth, Vylnor knew it was only a matter of time before Havrel entered the fray and should his magic waiver, the Portalis would be lost. He was now forced to do something drastic, so grabbing his Eldua chain, Vylnor hissed *"entwinor"* and watched as it discreetly slithered to his next target.

Eron

Eron held his ground, despite the mountainous weight of the war hammer pressing him towards the bedrock. The elven steel of his Frostblade held strong and after assessing this monster's unhurried movements, he decided speed was his best option. Pivoting on his feet, Eron twisted away from his opponent moments before the war hammer hit the granite with an audible thud, leaving a deep crack in the earth below. Advancing with elven speed, Eron rushed his enemy while the war hammer lay stationary and landed a vicious slash to his scaled abdomen. A fierce roar erupted from his foe, but it was more the sound of hurt pride rather than a killing blow, as he assessed the shallow wound he had inflicted. At least it would slow the monster down, Eron thought, but the more pressing issue was the environment. He needed to finish this bout and quickly. Aria was vulnerable, even with Rendon's protection, but as he rushed forward to land a second attack, his enemy retreated and drank a small black vial from its person. Eron recognised it immediately for what it was. A *potion*, which gave him reason to pause. Potions were deadly in battle, if one had the opportunity to consume it. Not only used for healing, they could also improve speed, strength, stamina and even knowledge, if brewed by the right hand. His foe now smirked, wiping the residue from its horrifically scarred maw and set down the war hammer. The slice to its abdomen was bleeding steadily and his opponent's breath still remained quick and sharp, so it was not a healing potion Eron acknowledged, but something offensive. Grimacing, Eron knew his enemy's battle prowess would be much improved with this potion and was reminded swiftly that true warriors succeeded with the tools they had at their disposal, not only their skills.

Bracing his stance, sword placed before him, Eron tried to analyse the giant's next move, when suddenly he charged with wicked speed. Claws replaced the war hammer and naturally his foe was faster as he struck, *hard*. Ducking and slashing, Eron danced with this demon of speed and power, before it drew its clawed arm back into a fist and aimed for his chest. With little time to react, Eron twisted his Frostblade to its flat edge and locked both ends with his hands. The clawed fist clashed with elven steel and flung Eron back twenty paces with incredible force, his body rolling roughly across the jagged rock and winding him in the process. His training instincts surged and Eron used the momentum to jump to his feet and face his enemy once more. It seemed this fight would not be as simple as the General first anticipated, so spitting blood to the floor, he quickly readied for his next assault.

Aria

I began to panic as the wall of rock and earth in front of us started to crumble, when the word "*astio!*" boomed from General Havrel and it ceased its movements. Slightly relieved, I quickly took stock of my surroundings and stilled at hearing Vylnor behind the wall, Talos and Havrel having now met the Oromos Lord in battle. But what disturbed me the most was the state of the five elves around us. They all suffered from varying degrees of burns and struggled to rise and reform the blockade. Their beautifully intricate elven armour was tarnished with soot and some warped by the heat of the blaze and my heart ached at the sight.

"We must leave, Miss Aria, are you able to stand?" Rendon stood at my back, cradling his left arm, before pulling a dagger from his belt to cut my bindings and I gestured worriedly to the elves around us.

"Will they be OK? They cannot fight in this state!"

Rendon's wintery blue eyes softened, his face marred by small cuts and dirt. "The line will switch as soon as we reach the portal, Miss Aria, so we must move."

I turned towards the portal and gasped as my eyes beheld a face I cherished most of all. *Grandfather*. But warmth was soon replaced by cold fear as I realised he should not be here. He and Monroe rushed towards me, their faces filled with relief when Rendon and I hurried in their direction, our elven convoy in tow.

"Grandfather!" I called, my voice struggling against the sounds of battle around us.

"Faster my girl!" he shouted desperately back and reached for my hand, now mere steps away, when my eyes widened at the sight of a moving chain that slithered with malicious intent across the black rock and towards him.

"MOVE!" I cried out shrilly, but it was too late, the chain had wrapped around his calf and dragged Grandfather down, surrounding his entire body in less than a dial. Monroe dropped to his knees and chanted urgently beside him, while Grandfather howled in agony. My panicked, tear-filled eyes began to blur as I looked at Monroe and Rendon pleadingly, willing anyone to fix this. To save him.

"An Eldua chain, Aria."

Monroe held my gaze, fear and defeat reflecting in his own eyes, while Rendon's were achingly sympathetic. With naught else to do, the elven warrior began directing the remaining elves into a protective circle, fending off any beasts and magical spells that tried to reach us.

"What is it?!" I snapped, ire rising at their jaded reactions.

"A corrupt magical chain, said to be forged with the scale of an Eldua serpent. It is used to seal and constrict its enemies to death."

I reached for it frantically, unwilling to believe such tales while Grandfather's cries continued to lash at my heart.

"NO ARIA!" Monroe barked, holding back my shoulders and I shrugged him off irritably. "It is unbreakable and will harm any but its master. You must heed my words!"

His grip was tightening, but Grandfather's screams were almost deafening and would surely haunt my nightmares for decades to come, while the chains continued to wind tighter and tighter still. *"Pretty girl, I can end his torment, just give yourself over and you will spare his life."*

The unexpected voice in my head caused me to start, momentarily halting my struggles and the tears that streamed down my face. I reached towards my grandfather, the air between us empty and cold.

"Miss Aria, there is nothing we can do," Rendon urged placatingly, but his voice soon grew faint, as did the cries of battle while I stared at the man who was my world, as he slowly faded before my eyes. His gasps of soundless breath were my last view before I launched both hands at the chains and, with gritted teeth, endured the searing pain that ravaged my body. Like scorching coals, it burned me from the inside, but I refused to give in. They said I would be the one to break, but whether it killed me or not, I would shatter these chains or die trying. Cries of alarm from my allies sounded around me, while fearful hands tried to pull me away and, in my rage, I released a cry of agony and a surge of vengeful power.

Vylnor

Vylnor looked on towards the beacon of energy emitting from the Portalis. He did not know if her screams were from grasping the Eldua chain, or her own powerful rush of magic trying to tear her body to shreds. All he could do was wince at the piercing rays of light that lit up the cavern and caused all manner of carnage to cease, lest the occupants go blind trying to look through such light. The only creatures that remained active were the Norags, blind as they were, however, in but a few moments, Vylnor found himself blinking rapidly as the brightness dimmed. Impressively, the Portalis had destroyed at least fifty Skygge demons, while the other beasts continued to shy warily away from the source of such power.

Before long, he felt her eyes of retribution cast on him and met them with equal fervour across the cavern. Twin scorching globes of gold tried to pierce into his very dark soul and in her hands, she held the broken remains of the Eldua chain. Shocked, his eyes widened and Vylnor hissed disbelievingly, "That is not possible."

Laying prone but breathing by her feet was the old man, Vylnor's leverage and still useful alive. As if understanding his thoughts, she spat across the vast space with a humbling and ancient baritone, "You would *dare*?!"

Her hand slowly rose and Vylnor chanted his strongest shielding spell, when a powerful force struck across his body. Vylnor, along with a line of demons, were thrust back violently at least forty paces and crumpled harshly against the Oromos rock face. Unsteadily rising to his feet, Vylnor spat out the blood that gathered in his mouth, lungs and ribs surely damaged by the force of her attack, but still he remained vigilant and braced for another. He needn't have bothered. The runes around the portal swirled and glowed and, to his astonishment, began to pull her allies to safety.

In a desperate effort to halt her, Vylnor was forced to bellow "*feranox!*" and threw his remaining shadow magic at the Portalis. It burst forth from him in the shape of giant dark wings, intending to encircle her form and stop her advance into the portal, but it did not reach its target. His power shattered against the Portali magic that surrounded her, preparing to pull her through also, when she turned to him and with that same ethereal voice uttered, "*valore.*" The lone word resonated deep within his soul, scattering all sane thought to the winds and left Vylnor nothing but an empty, useless, vessel, as he watched unmoving, while his prize disappeared entirely from view.

Eron

Eron relived those moments in the Oromos mountains over and over in his mind, but he still could not make sense of what happened. That magic, Aria's magic, was nothing he could have ever predicted. Crouched on the ground, he saw her blazing power before the runes pulled his body through the portal and he was once again at the western gate in Port Framlington, surrounded by his kin and allies. All of them. Alive or perished, she did not leave a single one behind.

Eron quickly shook himself and barked, "See to the wounded. Those who are able reform the lines, we must ensure the Portalis is safe," but before his orders could be met, Aria walked languidly through the portal and called "*sigillum*," sealing it closed behind her.

All activity paused as elves and allies alike took in her changed appearance. Hair ablaze around her form, eyes glowing golden, like that of a rising sun, Eron held his breath when she met his gaze. This was not the Aria he had come to know and Eron's hackles rose when he realised that staring back at him, was a being of far greater knowledge and power. Her attention soon turned to her grandfather, currently being tended by Monroe's healing chants, but the man still remained unconscious, with harsh bruises covering most, if not all of his body.

Striding over with the poise of a lady, despite her ragged clothing, she knelt next to him and placed her hands either side of his face whispering, "Wake." Magic streamed in scroll-like patterns around Jacoby's form, surrounding him in a warm glow and, before long, he opened his eyes and whispered gruffly, "There's my girl."

Aria's smile was achingly soft, Jacoby's bruises having disappeared and a single tear fell over her cheek.

"Do not frighten me like that again."

Her words were gentle and yet berating and Eron found himself rushing to her side as her slight form crumpled exhaustedly to the limestone floor of the courtyard.

Aria

I did not want to wake. Wrapped in a cocoon of warmth as I was, only encouraged me to fall back into a deeper slumber and yet, a soft voice was determined to pull me awake. The accent was melodious, feminine and sung softly *"orlandro aliva Aria niso rello* ... awaken Aria, follow my song." The words kept echoing in my mind and, after some time, I felt I could no longer ignore them. Forcing my eyes open, I squinted at the brightness of the room, framed by two tall silver-rimmed windows and blue curtains, which gently rustled against the limestone walls. The soft breeze bringing with it a welcoming smell of the ocean, before I bolted upright.

"Grandfather?!"

"I am here Aria," came an indulgent rumble to my right. I turned to look at his welcoming face and was immediately taken aback. Still the face I knew, although slightly exhausted, appeared decidedly younger by at least a decade or so. His bushy moustache was more brown than silver now and I noticed fewer lines around his tear glossed eyes.

"Yyou …?! *Your face*! Are you well, Grandfather? What happened?!" I looked around frantically and saw Monroe perched in the corner of the room in an armchair of navy-blue velvet.

"Well Aria, it seems old Jacoby wanted to keep up with the young sprites, he may even be in fair shape to enjoy a bit of female company again." And he waggled his eyebrows.

"Watch your tongue Monroe, or by the Light I will cut it out and shove it up your arse!"

A huff of laughter came from the doorway as Eron entered, looking refreshed since our last encounter. "Glad to see you are awake Aria, you had our healers worried." And that was when I noticed a female elf, dressed in tarnished armour but looking no less regal, standing to the right of the room by the bathing chamber.

"My name is Oriella, Miss Aria and I will leave you to speak with your friends, but you are to stay in bed for the remainder of the day." Her tone was stern as she made her way towards the door and I made a grab for her hand. Surprised, she looked at me, with short blonde hair and delicate features pulled down in confusion, while I spoke with as much sincerity as I could muster.

"Words cannot thank you enough, not only for myself but for my grandfather as well."

Smiling now, she squeezed my hand. "I will gladly accept *your* thanks, but it was not me, Miss Aria, who healed your grandfather." Pulling away, she turned to address the others. "I will let you talk," she said, before bowing her head subtly and exiting the room. Confused, I looked around at the three male faces for clarification. It was Grandfather who spoke first.

"My girl, it was *you* who healed me." Offering a gentle smile, Grandfather took my hand in his own. "You saved us Aria, the elves included."

"And did not leave any behind, alive nor passed, which their families and I am eternally grateful for." This came from Eron, arms crossed over his chest but gratitude shining in his eyes. However, my confusion only grew.

"But I do not remember any of this?"

Monroe chimed in, "What was the last thing you *do* remember Aria?" He leaned forward, hands steepled and seriousness in his tone. Frowning, I thought back, reliving the moment I saw Grandfather in so much pain and closed my eyes as if to shut the horrors out, before whispering "Grandfather, you … you were in so much pain, I couldn't bear it. My last thoughts were to shatter that chain … to protect you." Eyes still closed, familiar arms pulled me into a reassuring hug.

"And you did just that my girl and so much more. I have never felt such pride, well compared to that time when you were nine and delivered a right hook to that bully Finley," he added, I assumed to lighten the mood.

"In all seriousness Aria, your magic is much more complex than I or Eron first thought," added Monroe pensively. "I've never read or heard of a Portalis drawing those who are away from the portal through."

Eron confirmed with a shake of his head, white hair shuffling in tandem with the movement when Monroe continued, "You need to control this power, Aria, and with Jacoby's support, I would ask if Eron would take you to Elavon and begin your training."

Shocked, I blurted, "*Training*?!" and looked to Eron.

"This is not conventional, Aria. The few historical records we have garnered on previous Portali relay that they are to be protected and hidden. Magic is present but not significant enough to defend themselves, or others. You, on the other hand, possess a power even I am unsure of. Petriel will know more and perhaps it will aid us in our future battles."

"It would take years for me to be able to master any type of combat," I challenged and, feeling rather defeated, sighed, "I am no warrior."

Eron smiled and it almost melted my resolve then and there. "But you have strength, Aria. I know of very few warriors who have entered the bowels of Oromos a captive and fought their way out."

I grimaced to myself. "It was nothing like that, Eron. All I experienced was polarising fear and pain. It was Wendy's words that helped me survive those dials, strapped to that table ..." I cut myself off, not wanting to talk about what had happened in that place and could feel Grandfather's frown.

"What was that, my girl, about a table?"

I hid my face and turned away, uttering, "Do not make me relive that horror, Grandfather."

I could hear his teeth grinding as the silence in the room stretched and became almost painful. Thankfully it was Eron who broke the awkward moment.

"I hope in time, Aria, you will tell us your story, but until then, do not let certain experiences consume you. Lest it hinder your spirit that we so admire and lessen your resolve to continue on this path."

Sending him a small smile, I nodded my assent and waved them all away so I could rest. Sadly I did little but fall prey to the swirl of anxiety my thoughts conjured. Knowing that our paths would cross with the realm of Oromos once more, all it did was inspire thoughts of the foul place, which leaked like poison into my dreams.

◆ 10 ◆

Aria

I'm again strapped to those whipping posts, my shakes
are uncontrollable and wrists raw as I try desperately to
wrench myself free. I can feel each lash shredding into
my flesh, as Fellious laughs delightedly behind me. I
wanted to scream, but silence reigned despite my efforts
while I begged in my mind for someone, *anyone* to help
me. Eyes of the deepest green pierced my vision, before
strong arms grasped my shoulders and shook me awake,
mercifully freeing me from my memories. The smell of
crisp air and snow hit my nose when I realised Eron was
cradling me tightly in his arms, his voice soothing as he
murmured, "I am here Aria, you are safe."

After a moment or two, my trembles subsided
somewhat and he pulled away, a frown set about his
beautiful face, filled with concern, before he wiped the
tears from my cheeks. It surprised me, his gentleness, for
I had only ever known his character to be the righteous
and stern General of Elavon. My confusion must have
shown on my face when he huffed, "Do not look so
surprised Aria, you are not just the Portalis to me,"
before offering a warm smile, while I openly gaped in a

very unladylike manner.

The thunder of leather boots turned our attention to the door and Grandfather stormed in, including half a dozen elven soldiers and rushed to my left.

"Who was here?! Were you attacked my girl?! I could hear your screams from the Lord's study!" He clutched my hand fiercely, but it was Eron who replied evenly, "A nightmare, Jacoby, warriors stand down. Meet me in the Lord's hall when you are ready, Aria, Elavon awaits our arrival." And with that order, Eron and the warriors left, while I stared at Eron's retreating back thoughtfully, questioning his reaction and words.

"My girl, please tell me what frightens you so?"

I turned to Grandfather, his eyes concerned and the line between his eyebrows deepening. Not willing to hold his stare, I looked down at my hands in my lap, their paleness stark against the blue bedspread and I whispered almost dazedly, "I'm not ready to talk about it, Grandfather."

Instead he pressed, "But you cannot continue as you are. I can see you are frightened and this hurts me, my girl. I am and have been your protector your whole life and if you feel threatened, by the Light I will not have it!"

His impassioned speech built to a crescendo as he finished and I could not help but smile, my eyes drawn upwards as he stood outraged. Always in my corner, I knew he would do anything to protect me, but I answered in truth, "You cannot shield me from my past experiences, Grandfather, or the nightmares that follow."

He sighed sadly. "Then I will be here to support you and dry those tears whenever I can."

Once again my eyes misted, but from a feeling of love rather than fear. I would cling to this feeling, use it to rage against my terror and deter my nightmares, before they were allowed to fester and haunt my waking days as well.

Vylnor

Resonating from the shadows, the disgusted hiss of Vylnor's Master crawled about the cavern walls and pierced his ears painfully.

"You failed me ssservant."

Head pressed into the rock, Vylnor chose his short reply with care. The promise of death and torment hung thickly in the air and from experience, he would rather the former than the latter.

"My Second was not up to the task, he will be dealt with."

Vylnor felt magic forcing his head further into the jagged rock, the pressure building, until a searing pain exploded from his skull and cruelly, this remained his Master's only response for some time. But Vylnor knew better than to react and reined in his instincts to fight back.

Eventually his Master rasped, "I will deal with the failed crafted one," and the surrounding temperature dropped sharply, a sure sign of his dissatisfaction.

The pressure built along his torso, Vylnor's lungs

now straining for breath before becoming short and difficult, while the freezing air burned through his chest like shards of ice.

"The Portalisss was mine. You have taken those realmsss from me ssservant, ssso it ssstands to reassson you will be responsssible for getting them back."

"Yes Master," he gritted, while blood began to pool around his eyes, the slice deepening in his forehead and the force threatening to break his nose next. But still Vylnor offered no voice of protest.

"You will have until the Winter Solssstice," and after a pause, the pressure began to lift. "Newsss of your demotion will reach the bowelsss of Oromosss sssoon, replacementsss will be aplenty. Ssshould you fail, the Maliskasss will eat your flesssh and bring back your sssoul ssstone as payment."

With that ominous threat, Vylnor stood silently, shoulders hunched in a cowardly fashion, although he felt anything but cowardly in that moment. Instead his veins thrummed with challenge at the thought of the witch cannibals that would soon hunt him. Grinelda would no doubt enjoy the chase, but likely send one of her leaders to fulfil the task in her stead. A few witches he could deal with, but they liked to attack in packs and that would be a nuisance. Not one he couldn't handle though.

"Yes Master," Vylnor replied as he strode from the chamber with purpose, anger and contempt seeping from his pores, along with the blood that covered his face. He would be strategic and while competition for his standing as Lord was always fierce and previously a nuisance, it was now an obstacle to his success and to his survival. The threats to his existence growing rapidly, Vylnor began to plan and intended on vacating the Oromos range immediately, before its other inhabitants attempted to maim him first.

Deliberations moving to the journey ahead, he listed the items he would require while he walked towards his personal chambers, lower-ranking creatures recoiling and scrambling from his path in earnest. Reaching his rooms, a bare cot within a pile of windowless black rock, he skirted the pathetic place in favour of his study. His main place of sanctuary within this filth of a mountain. Adjacent to his room, via a small archway littered with wards to keep out prying eyes, he stored a collection of weapons and magical tomes mounted to the unforgiving walls. Efficiently he gathered the necessary objects he would need, including a handful of potions, maps of the Elven and Mortal Realms, as well as weapons. Picking up his favoured Corrono blades, Vylnor's thoughts returned to the Portalis and that word '*valore*'. It whispered around in his mind, unfamiliar and unwelcome, but he felt its significance as if it were a part of himself. Unworried, but his curiosity peaked, Vylnor settled himself quickly. The time to question the Portalis would arrive soon enough and Vylnor would have his answers one way or another.

Aria

It was half a day's ride from Port Framlington to reach the portal that the elven Generals had used, along with their army. As it turned out, the resident Lord Framlington fled the city with an escort of twenty guards when it was first attacked, so an assignment of elves had been instructed to remain and assist in rebuilding what they could. It didn't bode well for any future alliance however, if the King's Lords fled at the first sign of danger and I couldn't help but feel enraged for those people who had been left to face such peril alone.

Monroe and Grandfather were stationed either side of me while I sat astride Mavel, beyond relieved she had survived the battled unscathed. The elven Generals had dismounted their horses and now surrounded an unremarkable stone boulder, bordered by tall evergreen trees and thick shrubbery that had turned autumn hues of orange and yellow. I paused for a moment intrigued, for I could not see any visible runes, yet I could *feel* the magic humming in the air.

The earth had been disturbed, or rather trampled by the elven soldiers and their steeds and I arched a curious eyebrow at Eron, who stood a couple of paces away. He grinned, his handsome face lighting up knowingly before he gestured I step forward. As I did, the shimmering veil of the portal came into view and the dark wet earth which would have marred the runes, had begun to glow with power at my approach.

"Aria." Eron was by my side now and paused my

advance with Mavel, hand now resting on the horse's neck. "We cannot take her to Elavon."

Surprised and a bit put out, I huffed, "Well I can't just leave her out here, Harkwood forest is vast."

He sighed and pinched the bridge of his nose with his free hand and I got the distinct impression he thought me a petulant child. "Laurel!" he barked, startling myself and Mavel who whinnied, until an elven soldier arrived. His plaited brown hair and grey eyes were all I could see beneath his helm. "Yes General?"

"Can you please ensure the horse …"

"*Mavel*" I quipped.

"Yes, *Mavel* …" he added with emphasis and no doubt irritated by my interruption, "… is taken back to the city and cared for until Aria's return."

I climbed down from Mavel's back and itched behind her chestnut ears while the soldier replied, "I will see to it now, General."

Laurel grabbed her reins from me and I blurted nervously, "Her favourite treats are apples!" And then more quietly, "Please take good care of her."

Laurel smiled gently and confirmed, "Of course Miss Aria, lots of apples" with a playful wink and headed eastwards towards the port.

My attention then turned to Monroe who dismounted his horse with an elegant jump and requested jovially, "So Eron, as we head into Elavon, I expect you will introduce me to the lovely Lady Florel as was previously agreed."

"I wouldn't introduce you to a hog, even that would

be disrespectful," he tsked and I had to stifle a laugh. Waggling his eyebrows at Eron, Monroe began to belt out a song as he strode casually through the portal.

"Oh Lady Florel, your beauty is legend, to be in your presence, is a gift from heaven!"

I winced as we followed him through, Monroe repeating his basic tune over and over while garnering many frowns from the surrounding elven party.

"Bloody fool," Grandfather muttered and scowled at Monroe, when suddenly all sound ceased, barring Monroe's embarrassing tune. We passed into the Elven Realm and I stopped short at seeing Lady Florel, standing opposite us and flanked by the remaining Elders on the other side. Several highly decorated warriors surrounded them and glared openly at Monroe.

"Monroe's going to get us killed before we even begin training!" Grandfather hissed at me, exasperated, and probably a little worried, when the mage baffled us all by addressing the Elders first.

"Ah my Lady!" Monroe greeted Florel with an exaggerated bow, ignoring the disapproval which hung thickly in the air. "What an honour it is to be in your presence, perhaps a kiss would be appropriate?" And with that, Grandfather clipped him across the back of his head.

"Ow! I mean really Jacoby my old friend, I was only trying to be polite!"

Grandfather's fists were now clenched, his teeth grinding together to the point I feared they would crack and a small chuckle erupted from Lady Florel, immediately disbanding the thick tension.

"Greetings to you all and welcome to Elavon."

It took me a moment to realise that our surroundings had changed, for we still stood in the middle of a forest clearing, but this one was nothing short of magical, not just in essence but in design. The forest was decorated in a blanket of colourful wildflowers, set amongst a scattering of tall grasses bathed in verdant greens that peaked out above the dark-green needles littering the floor. The eye was drawn to the imposing trees, their height so vast and dizzying, as though they intended to inhabit the skies. I could not view the treetops and it would take at least ten villagers to circle around the wide and reddened trunks.

"Cedaris trees," Florel explained while gesturing to the giant tree I was currently admiring. "A source of life to Elavon, providing much of what our people need to survive." She smiled proudly as she spoke and I could practically hear Monroe sigh in appreciation of her beauty. Unlike the mage, it was more than just her beauty that I noticed, although she looked dazzling in a deep-green robe, edges embroidered with gold which complemented her eyes perfectly. The Lady had a warmth that was undeniable and she spoke with such love of her home, that it was hard to be anything but endeared. General Havrel stepped forward and addressed all the Elders present.

"I will have the soldiers retire to the barracks, my Lady, and issue a report."

"Glad to see you are home safe, Havrel, although I am told your numbers are fewer." A sadness filled her tone and she looked to me again, eyes now glittering. "But I must thank you, Aria, for bringing all our warriors home." And with that humility, I felt nothing but a heavy wave of guilt.

"Do not thank me, Lady Florel. If I had not been captured, there would have been no need for them to charge into that massacre." My lip trembled as I looked to the forest floor, not wanting to hold her gaze and the judgement I might find there. The guilt had weighed heavily on my heart and mind since I saw those scorched elven soldiers in the mountain. Their dedication to protect me, to put their immortal lives on the line in that terrible place, even if it was for the benefit of the greater good, inspired me to do better, to be braver and to not take any of them for granted.

The sound of rustling leaves moved closer and Florel's delicate slippers came into view.

"Do not burden yourself so, Aria." She touched my chin and drew my face up to hers. "You care for our warriors and that is a comfort, however, we each decide our fates, as you will decide yours in the battles to come." With that she smiled, but there was a strength and belief in her eyes and words which had me breathing a little easier, at least for the time being. "Now then," she began and clasped my shoulder familiarly while my eyes widened in surprise, "to the barracks, Portalis Aria, we do not have much time. Dusk will soon be welcoming the stars in Elavon, so your training will begin on the morrow."

The barracks were maybe a three-hour walk from the clearing on foot. Grandfather remained with Monroe, most likely to try and keep his behaviour in check, while Eron travelled beside me, enthusiastically describing the plants and animals we passed and, truth be told, it all fascinated me. The fact I knew nothing of this world mere days ago was astounding and I peered curiously when my eyes caught sight of an unfamiliar animal. About two feet long, with a shimmering golden coat, it sported a pointed nose that highlighted a set of pale canine eyes. Eron explained it was a *"Mukasa"* which fed on the cedaris roots that were a source of magic for this land and caused the animal's fur to glow almost luminescent. Not only smart but mischievous, he warned that Mukasas were rare and to be admired from afar, but sadly did not elaborate further.

I noticed quickly that Eron seemed happier and more content in his surroundings, which was a joy to see. Maybe he would stop being such an old crank and we would get along for more than a day without squabbling. Soon enough we reached what I assumed was the barracks, nestled easily amongst the woodland landscape and hidden behind a magnificent golden gate. Strong wooden doors held together by what looked like gilded hinges, the gold swirled through the wood in waves, and converged around a medallion in the centre. It depicted a majestic bird, but unlike any I had ever seen, that hovered above a star. Its sharp talons and determined eyes gave it a fierce quality, however the rest of its body was elongated and graceful, with a tail and wings etched in flames. In a way, it reminded me of the dragons of old in our history books, which disappointingly remained just a tale of legend and now extinct, but it remained unclear when or why.

Just as I began to ponder this point, Eron startled me with the word, "Locksnight," and gestured proudly to the medallion.

"Excuse me?" I looked at him, baffled, until he explained, "They are one of our oldest and most powerful elven houses. The Locksnight bird is said to have been one of the first creatures born when Anala's star fell from the sky and created Elavon."

"I am not familiar with that story Eron, although it sounds magical," I sighed wistfully and looked up at the rustling canopy.

He chuckled, "I'm sure Petriel will provide more details, but know that the Locksnight house produced the most feared and loyal warriors in Elavon." Even Eron's voice was bathed in awe, as he stared at the medallion proudly.

Beyond curious I asked, "Are any of the Elders or Generals from that house? Wait! Are *YOU*?!"

Eron blushed profusely and replied quickly, "I am honoured you would think so, but sadly no."

I looked to his armour and for the first time noticed a small insignia of an oak tree, pressed into the thick leather, but instead of conventional roots, it looked to be floating on waves of water.

He observed my stare and tapped the symbol knowingly, "*Oakwald*, it means river through the forest," before continuing his explanation. "The Locksnight line was wiped out some millennia ago. However the teachings they instilled live on in our future warriors, the bird a symbol of our warrior spirit and our song is the fire, which breathes it into life." He paused for a breath before beginning to sing. "*I will be the force and searing fire, to eliminate evil, its wants and desires. Shine bright the elven, raise your shields, we will defeat the darkness, across all battlefields.*"

The other warriors in our party joined with Eron's fluid baritone and once the song ended, the only sound was the rhythmic rumble of weaponry thudding against their shields. It was beautiful and inspiring and I felt my magic stir in response to their tune.

◆ 11 ◆

Aria

A fortnight had passed since we arrived at the elven barracks, its yellow stone facade and four observation towers feeling more like a prison than a place of training and wisdom. I had wanted to explore more of Elavon and its famed Citadel, but Eron outright refused. We were currently in the courtyard training grounds, it was early and my morning drills of deflect, lunge, swipe, retreat were only fuelling my irritation. However, that was nothing compared to my hatred of running.

You need to be fitter, faster they told me, so running it was, consistently, every evening to *"close the day and settle my mind"* Oriella would say. Not only a healer but a fierce warrior in her own right, she had become a friend in such a short space of time. Perhaps it was because she reminded me of Wendy, with her wise words and humble manner, despite looking no older than five and twenty years, but the similarities led me to think of my home.

The farm, with its smell of fresh bread, Berta's short mannerisms and Geoffrey's stoicism, until Eron brashly interrupted my thoughts.

"We do not have time for sightseeing, Aria. Oromos

could mount an attack at any moment, most likely on your home world." He sounded exasperated, but after asking for the fifth time, I wasn't surprised. In fact, I rather enjoyed irritating him. I know it seemed juvenile to keep asking, but my pessimism was overwhelming. I reasoned that if there was a possibility I would be either captured or killed, I wanted to see as much of these worlds as possible beforehand. Also, the fact he appeared unruffled by these drills and I was sweating profusely and covered in a layer of dust from the training grounds, did nothing to improve my cooperation.

"It may not seem important to you, but after recent life events my priorities have shifted." Exasperated, he rolled his eyes, "And seeing the elven city is more important than your training and the probable death and destruction that this delay could cause?"

My anger grew rapidly at his patronising tone and I blurted, "Will you desist with your lecturing and for once see things from my perspective!" I swiped the blade more vehemently in my maddened state and was surprised to feel my magic surge.

Eron swiftly blocked the swipe, the blunted steel clashing, but was forced back several paces and raised his eyebrows, no doubt mirroring my own surprise. Instead of cursing my recklessness, he smirked almost proudly, "Well, well, that's more like it. Your swings are usually so mundane … AGAIN!"

Conversation forgotten, Eron charged back at me, grinning wildly as he did so and with a renewed enthusiasm that was so infectious, I jovially goaded back,

"I'll show you *mundane*" and attacked once more.

The next two days passed quickly. Encouragingly, I was now able to manipulate my magic to provide extra strength to my attacks, which although significant in battle, was not particularly impressive by elven standards. Eron was now satisfied with my basic drills, so the next stage to test my control were the block holds. Here Eron would swing down his blade repeatedly and I would have to stop its trajectory with my smaller double blades. Lightweight but strong, the weapons were engraved with decorative scrollwork and symbols which related to the master craftsmen that forged the steel. In some early cases, the blade markings also represented the bearer's house, but this was very rare. The elves later choosing to display their house emblems on their armour instead, for the risk of losing such an item was much lower. In any case, these lighter weapons allowed for faster, more fluid movements and so suited my form and fighting style better, or so Oriella had explained.

Each time Eron added more and more pressure to his blade and by the tenth manoeuvre, my arms shook violently.

"This is not even half my power!" he growled disappointingly and continued his tirade. "Your magic is a part of you, of each breath. You instinctually know how to apply power to your swings, now use it to reinforce your arms. Allow it to give you strength, not just expel it from your body."

Blade after blade I blocked until my arms gave out

and I was thrown to the floor. Panting, dust pluming around my body, I stared at the sky, feeling exasperated and wholly out of my own depth. A feminine chuckle came from across the yard and I knew it was Oriella.

"You cannot pummel her magic out of her, General." His unblemished face came into view above me, blocking the otherwise cloudless sky and looking exasperatingly beautiful with his silver eyes. I felt myself blush and was relieved that my skin was already flushed from the training, or he may have noticed the reaction.

"Perhaps not Oriella ..." he groused amusedly, "it seems the only way I *can* get any magical response is to irritate her."

He was smirking now, so I groaned in dismay at my initial reaction to his handsome face and rolled to my feet, with the intention of verbally insulting him. Sadly I could not do much physically in my current state as I scowled openly at the General, but I planned for my next curses to be colourful, when they were halted by Oriella's tactful words.

"I would like to take Aria to the healing rooms, mayhap her talents lie in this area, to challenge her mind and not just her body?" Eron tapped his chin in thought and nodded his agreement.

"A change of environment may be beneficial, after all you did heal your grandfather. I will speak with the Elders in the meantime and establish if there has been any progress from the Mortal Realm."

Without another word, Eron turned and strode off the training yard, sheathing his Frostblade, while I shook my fist aggrievedly at his retreating back.

Oriella looked at me shrewdly and winked. "You can thank me later."

Eron

Eron approached the rooms reserved only for the Elders when they were in residence at the barracks. Usually the warrior rooms were simple in design, but these were decorated with arched windows and metallic hues, as fit for their station. Eron entered the vaulted room where silk ribbons of the fallen decorated the beams and remained a stark reminder to all dwellers in the room who it was they served and what it cost, should their decisions fail.

Kalor did not halt his speech at Eron's approach. "... her time here is limited and unless she shows signs of improvement soon, we will have to amend our course of action."

"And what would that entail, Kalor?" Eron asked as he bowed and greeted the room, before taking a seat at the kuldera stone table.

Florel tapped her nails against the golden polished surface and replied, "Greetings Erondriel. We are discussing the time restrictions on Aria's training. It will not be long before Oromos launches an attack on the Mortal Realm and thus far, our requests to have an audience with King Lenard have not heeded any results."

Kalor's fists hit the table. "He is a fool and from his

foolishness many lives will perish and not just his own subjects!"

"Now, now," Petriel's calming voice halted Kalor and his rantings, "we have knowledge of several rune sites in the Mortal Realm and can assume Oromos also has similar information. This is not the first skirmish of its kind after all. We will plan our offensive strategies based on these locations and Anala willing, we will be prepared if King Lenard calls for aid."

A roar erupted from Kalor. "You think we will run to the aid of those who would so happily snub us?! I will not risk elven lives for such corrupt selfishness!"

Eron was not surprised by the outburst, Kalor had a fierce temper to match his mastered element of fire, but Eron did not agree with his sentiments and replied evenly, "The King may be a selfish boar, but his subjects are innocents. Allow the Mortal Realm to fall and Oromos will just enslave a larger force with which to attack us."

Kalor sneered, "With the Portalis, our portals will be sealed and render an assault by Oromos useless."

Shocked, Eron retorted, "You would leave the Mortal Realm to rot under the hand of Oromos because of your wounded pride?!"

"Hold your tongue, First!" Kalor bellowed at Eron, before they were cut off with a curt command from Lady Florel. "ENOUGH! Centuries of experience and wisdom and *this* is how you act?"

Kalor had settled back in his chair reluctantly and Eron steepled his fingers, waiting for her to continue. "I agree with Petriel."

Kalor was about to speak and she raised her hand for the Elder's silence. His mouth closed quickly, which only amused Eron further and it took him a moment to mask his smirk. "Request Havrel and Talos to meet us here on the morrow, so we can begin preparations."

It was Petriel who replied, "And what of the Portalis? The Winter Solstice is drawing closer, the days are darkening and Oromos will be stronger for it."

"They will likely amount an attack on this day," mused Kalor. "We should assess her progress over the next sennight and no more. The portals must be sealed in the Mortal Realm as they are the greatest risk, but also our greatest chance for success."

With a satisfied nod of agreement, Eron was dismissed. Leaving the warrior halls, he remained more determined than ever to see Aria's training offer more fruitful results and refused to leave her defenceless against the scourge of Oromos again.

Aria

After changing my sweat- and dirt-covered attire, Oriella took me to a large hall along the west wing of the barracks. Despite having resided within the structure for some time, many of its spaces were still unknown to me. Thankfully the square design, centring around the large training courtyard was simple, otherwise I feared becoming lost amongst its halls. My arms still ached from training with Eron and I rubbed them absently as my friend spoke.

"The healing rooms are on the ground floor," she explained, "you do not want to be lifting male elves up four flights of stairs. They may look trim, but trust me they are *heavy*," she added with a grin and I chuckled.

"Welcome Oriella," a slight female elf with midnight hair and dark eyes greeted us. Shorter than myself and Oriella, she was dressed in white robes, decorated in silver filigree and resembled an enchanted spirit.

"Aria this is Lady Yelena, she is our Second Healer and has graciously travelled from the Citadel to oversee your healing abilities."

"That is correct," Yelena continued, "after word reached the First Healer and I of the events involving your grandfather, I had to see you for myself. Although gifted, our healers cannot alter the ageing process of mortals." My cheeks reddened in embarrassment.

"That was an accident I can assure you."

Pursing her lips, Yelena grabbed my hand. "And that is all the more curious, young Aria, now this way please, we have many patients to tend to."

Moving further into the hall, I noticed the swooping forest-green curtains first, which gathered atop the high beams and provided privacy for the cots and patients they surrounded below. Yelena soon gestured for us to stop at the end of a male elf's cot. Cropped blond hair highlighted his pointed ears and angular jaw, and I idly wondered if there were any elves who were average in appearance. So much beauty threatened to hurt my eyes and warp my vision, until I returned to the Mortal Realm deeming everyone positively hideous.

"Greetings Lady Yelena," he murmured, his voice strained and sweat beading on his forehead. I saw that his left leg was currently splintered and bound in strips of white linen.

"Greetings Darnel" Yelena responded and frowned. "Your potion has been waning for some time if you are in this much pain, you should have called myself or one of the other healers to administer more."

"Forgive me my Lady but I am a warrior, pain is part of our journey."

Yelena tsked. "*My* duty, young warrior, is to relieve you of your pain and you dishonour me if you do not accept my help graciously." Darnel balked, his eyes widening as he quickly spluttered, "Forgive me my Lady," and Yelena nodded before gesturing to me.

"This is Aria, my understudy for the day. Will you allow her to assist me in your recovery, Darnel?"

I waved and thought how ridiculous I must have looked, but Darnel only smiled.

"I remember you Miss Aria and thank you for bringing my comrades, as well as myself home that day. For a moment I thought we would be lost in the darkness, until we saw your light."

My face must have deepened several shades, mouth bobbing open and closed like that of a wordless fish and it was only Yelena's next words that saved me from further embarrassment.

"Let us continue." The Second Healer began to remove the linens and splints carefully from around Darnel's leg. From the look of the slight protrusion under his skin along his shin bone, it was most likely a break. "Now Aria, I would like you to place your hands on Darnel's leg and use your magic to ascertain how bad the break is. You will only assess the damage, do not attempt to heal it, understood?"

I worried my bottom lip through my teeth and confirmed nervously, "Yes, Lady Yelena. Assess the break. But can I ask how exactly do I do this?"

Folding her arms, she replied, "Let us see how your magic reacts naturally, before we move any further."

Putting my concerns to the back of my mind, I smiled encouragingly at Darnel who sat patiently, not displaying an ounce of fear, before placing my hand on his shin and was immediately met with a rush of agonising pain.

"ARGH!" I cried, my magic bursting forth to protect me from the assault on my senses and I could see little but light flashing behind my eyelids.

"Remove her!" Yelena ordered and still my agony continued. I could hear my screams rising, my voice turning hoarse when I was pulled sharply away from the source. Once the pain dulled somewhat and my breath returned to normal, I opened my eyes to see Oriella, her face pinched in concern.

"Are you well Aria?"

I brushed myself off and shakily moved out of her grip, afraid to meet Yelena's eyes and instead looked at Darnel. "Yes, I think so. Darnel?"

Darnel's eyes were slightly aglow, the protrusion in his leg now gone and his gaze remained intent on my face.

"I, I feel ..." He looked down at his body as if it were new and I finally met Yelena's gaze, worried I had hurt him in some way, when suddenly he exclaimed, "I feel incredible! As if not only my body is healed but my magical essence somehow ..."

"Somehow *what?*" Yelena pushed, eyeing the warrior intently.

"Replenished?" His reply was uncertain and Oriella turned sharply to Yelena and whispered, "How is that possible?" Meanwhile, the Second Healer of Elavon stared at me warily, no explanation forthcoming before sharply dismissing us for the day.

That evening at dinner, I stared at the watery wild hare stew that normally would have sung along my taste buds, but instead I found myself reflecting on the afternoon's events. Following my little stunt in the healing chamber, Yelena requested a consultation with the Elders and summoned the First Healer from the Citadel.

I could feel Grandfather's wary gaze watching me as he sat across the table. The benches could seat twenty warriors comfortably, but many were still on the training yard or carrying out various duties, so we ate alone. Eron told me the large tables were carved from the cedaris wood that surrounded the barracks. Cut in their raw form, the grain was beautiful, polished veins in shades of bronze and warm reds, which he said reminded him of my hair. *That* conversation had set my face aflame, but my musings were quickly interrupted by Grandfather's concerned voice.

"I heard you caused quite a stir today, my girl," and raising my face, I looked to his newly altered one, another reminder of my power.

"I thought that by training here Grandfather, I could grasp more control." I paused, trying to find the words, "But my magic surges around me like a vast hurricane and I fear I am being swept away." I dropped my face into my hands. "How can I survive the chaos around me, when I cannot even master the chaos within me?"

My words were muffled, but they did not stop Grandfather from pulling my reluctant hands away from my face. Taking a deep breath, he held them gently on the table. "This is not a criticism, my Aria, but you are foolish to think that anyone has the power to master their magic within a few weeks. You think that in my youth, after a few seasons as a soldier, I became the warrior I am today? Or was in yesteryear?" He added the last words sadly and any attempts to interrupt failed as he pressed on. "We can only control how we react to the chaos and so far, my girl, you have shown nothing but your determination to do what is right and that is all anyone can ask ... and it is also all you can ask of yourself." Silent, I mused over his words until he added, "I hope one day you see what I see. A beautiful, strong and compassionate young woman, who no matter what the outcome should be proud of how far she has come."

My bottom lip trembled and I replied honestly, "I will *try*," and he squeezed my hands encouragingly before letting them go.

"Well, well, well am I interrupting a fatherly

moment, Jacoby?" Monroe sauntered over and patted Grandfather on the back patronisingly before winking in my direction.

"And where have you been, you lazy toad?" Grandfather retorted, while Monroe acted as though he had been stabbed in the chest.

"You wound me, Sir Torvel!"

Almost immediately, the gravity of our conversation had lifted and I struggled to keep the grin from my face.

"In all truth, we have been summoned to the Elder's chambers, something about Aria accomplishing impossible feats yet again." The mage spoke with a yawn and I complained good-naturedly, "You exaggerate, Monroe you swine!"

Shortly after, we all stepped away from the table.

Deciding to put my fears to rest for the time being, we followed at Monroe's back towards the Elder's chambers, when my thoughts turned to another predicament. Would the Elder's grant us sanctuary for a few more days and the relative peace it provided? Or would I be forced back into my home world otherwise filled with uncertainty and turmoil? Sighing aloud and garnering a concerned look from my grandfather, I squared my shoulders and stepped with purpose, for there was only one way to find out.

We arrived at the Elder's noticeably decorated chambers and each took a seat around the large stone table. Eron and Grandfather were perched either side of me, while Monroe interestingly stood behind. Grandfather described him as "prancing around like a peacock in search of Lady Florel's attention" which forced a laugh from all of us before the Elders entered, including Elavon's Generals, and I struggled to feel anything but intimidated while waiting amongst such high-stationed company.

"Welcome all," Lady Florel greeted the group. "We have called you here, Aria, to discuss your feelings on returning to the Mortal Realm within the next sennight."

A little disappointed I replied, "So soon?"

"We have spoken in length and Petriel has garnered as much information as possible relating to the portals in the Mortal Realm. Sadly our information is limited and we have not received word from your King in response to our war council summons. Thus you will be instructed to close the portals known to us, before returning here and sealing the elven ones."

Confused I asked, "But I am already in the Elven Realm, why not close the portals here first?"

It was the golden-haired Petriel who replied, "Because, Miss Aria, it is unlikely Oromos will attack the Elven Realm first. We are the stronger opponent and they would expend much energy and lives assaulting us in our home world."

Kalor, with his blood-red hair, added in his usual uncompromising manner, "Over the next seven days your training will intensify. You are the only limit to your progress, so I hope you make this a priority. From the information we have received so far, your magical control is erratic, fuelled by your emotions or on your survival instinct."

Eron spoke sternly. "That is unfair of you, Kalor," but his words still struck a chord and I felt myself physically recoil.

"How dare you." All eyes turned to my grandfather, his posture tense and anger dripping from each word. "Elder or no, you do not insult Aria's integrity by suggesting she has not made this a priority since she arrived here. I have seen how hard she works, the mental and physical toll it is taking. Do not forget, Elder, that it is by *her* grace that she aids you also in this war."

Kalor sneered, "Is that a threat, mortal?" And my guard immediately rose, the hairs on the back of my neck standing in unison, while my magic rallied in response to his words.

"However entertaining it would be to see you continue your little tete-a-tete, can I ask if anyone has considered what Aria's magic *is*?"

Monroe's words halted the rising tension in the room, when Petriel replied, "I have yet to study today's events, although my initial thoughts are that Aria here could be a source, given your renewed condition Sir Torvel and the warrior who she tended earlier."

Curiosity growing at the direction of conversation, I found my anger had dissipated somewhat and instead I asked, "What is a source?"

"A source is a well of pure magic, able to expel, absorb and replenish another's if necessary," the Elder explained evenly before continuing. "There hasn't been a recognised source for millennia, as they went into hiding or were killed. Corrupt mages, elves and mortals alike, hunted them for their power."

A "hmmmm" came from Monroe. "I have never heard of a source directing their magic for combat?"

"Our earliest records suggests that they can push and pull their magic in defensive and offensive manoeuvres," but clearly unconvinced, Monroe cut Petriel short. "What about forming an arrow or healing wounds?"

"No, err no, there is not. But it does not disprove the theory either." Petriel looked a little harassed at Monroe's persistent questions, until the mage addressed the whole room.

"Does anyone else have another theory?"

Silence.

"Oh this is intriguing," he murmured, before offering a dramatic pause, to which Grandfather snorted impatiently, "Well get on with it, you imbecile."

Pouting, Monroe finally continued his explanation. "Always spoiling my fun, Jacoby. As we all know, magical ability grows overtime, it learns with the bearer if you will and their magical capacity is exposed. The more practised it is, the more adept it is at reacting to your will."

"We know this mage, so get to your point," sniped Kalor and Monroe's gaze turned to me. "*Your* magic, Aria, seems to have skipped these stages. It instinctively reacts on its own accord, to keep you alive and those around you. It does not require commands at all. This speaks to me of a sentient magic, an aged magic and possibly an *ancient* magic. Whether it is innately yours is another question entirely."

I stilled, blood rushing to my face while the whole room remained pensively silent and eyed me with fascination, for what seemed like an age.

♦ 12 ♦

Aria

My healing lessons had sadly halted with Yelena. The Elders felt that until they distinguished what magic I possessed, that it would be safer for the patients if I did not practise administering care. Yelena was displeased with this turn of events and assured me this was not the end of my schooling, merely an unfortunate delay. In the meantime, special attention was paid to my physical training with Eron and Oriella during the little time we had left in the Elven Realm and I wasn't wholly ready for the new challenges they began to throw my way.

I lunged over giant logs, climbed trees and scaled boulders within the surrounding landscape of the barracks. Training was intense and gruelling on my body, but my mentors stressed that I must be able to keep up with my comrades as we travelled. On the other hand, something I *did* wish to master was the blade-throwing exercises.

"Focus Aria!" Eron shouted, which drew me from my musings and only added to my general feelings of inadequacy.

I currently held three curved daggers, each sporting

a set of growing vines down the steel. Eron explained that they had been forged by a famed elven blacksmith known as Liefka, while I stood nervously twenty paces from my target, that consisted of a wooden shield with a red star painted in its centre. Each tip was to be my target, although thus far I had struggled to hit the shield itself. Oriella had suggested that I should avoid close range combat in the first instance, so long range attacks were our next focus. The small weapons reminded me of the blade Grandfather had gifted me, which vexingly had been stolen by that wretch Vylnor, and my hands instinctively clenched tighter around the hilt at the thought of the Oromos Lord.

"Your attempts thus far have been inept at best! With your magic, you should be able to hit targets from a hundred paces away with ease!" the First General of Elavon barked across the large space, his stern tone drawing the intrigued eyes of other soldiers as we trained.

Gritting my teeth, I imagined his face as the next target and yet, even with this incentive, I barely managed to hit the wood.

"ARGH! This isn't working!" I groused at no one in particular and Oriella chimed unhelpfully, "Your mind is elsewhere," as she gathered the blades and brought them back to me. "These skills require not just accuracy, but the ability to calm your thoughts in the midst of battle."

"Exactly," Eron persisted. "If you cannot focus now, how will you manage with the distractions of war and possible injuries?"

I sighed despairingly and stared at the cloud-dusted skies; there was much at stake and I couldn't afford to be unprepared.

After our initial meeting with the Elders, I requested that Monroe work with me on my magical training. Eron seemed most put out by the request, but Monroe's words resonated within me and as his methods were usually unconventional, I felt that if anyone could understand my magic better it would be him. Despite his talent for being the jester, he was most astute at noticing the small details and asked me to meet with him outside of the barracks, by one of the many cedaris trees that littered the forests.

Grandfather walked beside me, my surprise escort for this lesson and I asked, "Why have you decided to oversee my training with Monroe, Grandfather?"

Eyebrow arched, he replied, "He may be a great mage, but he is an even greater nitwit and I mean to keep an eye on him, as I have done throughout these passing decades."

I chuckled. "So it is not necessarily for my benefit, Grandfather, but more to ensure Monroe does not hurt himself?"

And he laughed, "Exactly my girl! You I trust implicitly."

I found his response amusing and unsurprising, despite being the one who had little control over my magic.

"There is my favourite student," Monroe called and

greeted me with a wide smile, which dropped slightly at spotting Grandfather, "and you have brought a test subject, very smart indeed."

I smothered my chuckle while Grandfather huffed, "I shall observe over there," and pointed to the far side of the clearing, before warning Monroe, "Do not do anything foolish." With a pointed stare that lasted longer than necessary, he reluctantly stalked off in that direction.

"You know," Monroe began and leaned closer to me conspiratorially, "I feel privileged the old miser would trust me with this task. I hope these lessons will be beneficial, Aria, but results will not surface easily."

I nodded solemnly, "I understand," and he clapped his hands smartly, startling me and added with enthusiasm, "Very well, let us begin!" He gestured we move to the nearest cedaris tree and inspected it closely, as though he were a famous botanist. "Do you know the origin of these trees, Aria?"

"Very little," I admitted, "but I do know they were here at the creation of Elavon."

Placing his hand on the tree, Monroe confirmed, "That is correct. They are also a source of magic to this realm, the roots themselves writhing with magical essence." This made me think of the weasel-like creatures that Eron described when we arrived here. "My suspicions are that they act in a similar manner to a source, Aria, and I wonder how your magic will react upon touching one?"

Confused I asked, "But why? I have climbed these trees many times during my training here, Monroe, and have felt nothing other than a slight hum of magic."

Monroe looked pointedly at me. "One cannot hear if they are not listening, Aria. Place your hands upon the bark and listen to their song."

I walked over and hesitated slightly. Placing my hands on objects or people previously had not heeded the best of outcomes in my recent experience, but Monroe gave me another encouraging smile, so I moved and laid my hands tentatively against the thick bark.

At first I heard nothing. The slight hum of magic yet again present, but little else. No *song* as Monroe described, so I pulled away, shaking my head as I did so. Monroe looked momentarily disappointed, while I pondered over the Mukasas and asked, "What of the roots?"

Eyes roaming to the base of the tree, Monroe spoke "*cavoterra*" and the surrounding earth began to crumble and move aside. "Why can't I do that?" I huffed bitterly, gaze fixed on the glowing roots which were now exposed.

"We all have our talents, Aria. I am a mage of tricks if you will, but no master of water and ice as Eron is. I could call an ice shard, but could not pull the ocean to do my bidding as he can, the lucky sprite."

I looked into Monroe's hazel eyes. Despite his light-hearted attitude, there was such depth behind the facade that I couldn't help but admire his candour at times like these.

"Try again, Aria," he pressed, so I reached for the roots and as soon as I made contact, my mind and body were lost to its power.

I felt my essence, my very soul splinter painfully upon contact with the cedaris roots and yet I could not scream my agony or my panic. My body remained numb and unmoving while I was dragged through the interconnecting web of roots across Elavon. Its magic was like a sonnet and its tune the only entity holding my spirit together.

Finally the roots coalesced into an epicentre under the Citadel and I could feel the elves walking languidly above me, their magic humming into the ground. In front of me sat a glowing boulder the size of a carriage, which pulsed eerily with a wild and volatile magic, but also *life*. Unable to escape, it pulled me in, closer and closer, absorbing my essence to feed its insatiable hunger, when suddenly a vision filled my mind.

A black armoured hand crushing an elven sword, while a giant maw spewed breaths of unstoppable flame. The vision was chaotic, all-consuming and I could make little sense of the events unfolding, so instead I tried to focus on those which I could recognise.

Familiar runes glowed across the face of a shield, while a stone tower sat scorched and covered with ash and soot. The mighty structure crumbled under the pressure of magic, when suddenly I was soaring amongst the peaks of an unfamiliar mountain, the biting chill of a phantom wind piercing my eyes and distorting the view.

I could not grasp the details in these visions, they passed by too rapidly like a fast-flowing river and unperturbed by the boulders in its path. My mind wavered, the power of this place too much to bear, when a small stone of deep evergreen halted all sense of time and settled the erratic pace. I gazed upon nothing but the rock, everything else dimming behind its presence while I remained uncertain and cautious of its purpose. Reaching out to grasp it, it was flung unexpectedly at my chest. The impact was painful but manageable, until it refused to move and began to melt away at my flesh and bone. I screeched and writhed in anguish, my mind and magic abused and now threatening to shatter, when I was abruptly brought back to my body and felt my legs give way.

Ears ringing and now detached from the roots, I tasted the fresh forest air and felt my magic scrambling to refuel my drained body. It took a few moments to realise Monroe was slowly walking towards me, hands raised placatingly as if to calm a runaway horse. His mouth was moving, but I was unable to hear the words, when gratingly, they began to pierce through. "Hold Jacoby!" Monroe's arm was now pointing at my grandfather, who also stood about ten paces away, his face flushed and eyes panicked, so I rasped quickly, "I am well Grandfather, Monroe, I am sorry to have worried you." They both simultaneously sighed in relief and rushed over to my side.

"What happened, Aria?" Monroe questioned, currently bearing a worried expression, while I patted my chest, expecting to find a burning hole in its centre where an echoed pain still rang freely.

"I have never seen the like, one minute I felt your magic, the next ... it was as if it disappeared?" Monroe spoke almost nervously, so I cleared my throat and uttered, "I ... I am not sure what to make of what I saw, but I would like to only repeat this once, should I forget any details."

Grandfather frowned. "We should send you to the healers, my girl!" While Monroe in contrast, nodded swiftly, "I will gather the council," and offered me his outstretched hand.

"How dare you, mage!" yelled an offended Kalor, the council meeting having taken a turn towards the unexpected. "We had word that someone had been snooping around our ancient scrolls, have you no respect?!"

An unflustered Monroe simply sneered, "As one of Aria's guardians, it is my duty to ensure she is as prepared as possible for the task ahead. Any advantage I can give her, the better, and do not take me to task Elder, for you have been withholding vital information."

All light-heartedness had disappeared in the wake of the mage's annoyance, but it was Florel who replied, "We had already discussed this possibility, Monroe, but Anala's star is not to be trifled with. Only the wisest and strongest of elves can witness and make sense of those visions. There are few who could even survive an absorption of magic on that scale."

"Ah, so that was the disappearance of magic I felt, the roots absorbed it?"

"No, the star requires a price for its visions, not just anyone can look through Anala's eyes. Those who do not have the reserves of power would die, for she would deem them unworthy."

"Hah!" mocked Monroe, "wouldn't you think that an important fact to *note* in your historical scrolls? That explains the cedaris cages I stumbled upon in the council building," he finished on a murmur and Kalor's cheeks flamed in indignation.

"*That* information is of concern to the Elders, *NOT* a mage who acts beyond his rank!" Kalor was gripping the table at this point, trying in vain to rein in his temper.

With Havrel's assistance, Eron was currently arranging a troop of elven warriors to escort us on the next leg of our journey and was now missing the current arguments between the Elders and Monroe.

"Had I approached you on this matter you would have declined and thwarted any of my attempts to pursue it."

Florel sighed and admitted, "That is true, but only to protect Aria, we could not risk her safety."

Monroe scratched his head and looked at me apologetically. "Neither would I, had I known the full risks … forgive me Aria."

With understanding I replied, "Even with the risks, I would have done it Monroe and with all due respect, the decision should have been my own to make."

"Pah!" snorted Kalor, "your age betrays you. Your decisions are spontaneous, possibly reckless and we could not have you killing yourself and leaving the Three Realms to wage war through unclosed portals for the next luna cycle until they eventually closed. Consider the consequences of your actions girl, or leave the thinking to those wiser than you."

Before Grandfather could reply, I threw back my own words. "Through all your patronising speech, Kalor – that I have taken so far with grace I might add – I would remind you that I am no pawn and reckless decisions or not, I will forge my own path in these days to come with or without your council."

It was Monroe who added, "We either treat each other as equal allies in this battle, with all information shared, or I fear the mistrust will rot away our alliance and doom us all to fail."

With that, the three Elders looked to one another before nodding their assent, so I took the opportunity to ask Petriel, "Is the information I gathered of any use?"

"Hmmm ..." he murmured, "the visions are rarely exact predictions of future events, merely possibilities. The weapons could represent sides of the battle to come. The stone tower seemed very vague, although at least it points to a battle within the Mortal Realm. But my main qualm is with the stone you described," and he looked to Florel. "At first I thought it a shadow stone, but they do not hold that colour?"

"Forgive my ignorance, but what is a shadow stone?"

Petriel leant forward, his pale eyes piercing, "It is a magical artefact forged from the bowels of Oromos. Though the colours are usually black and red, a reflection of the mountain it was created from. They are used to forge a soul link between the Overlord Ramos and his servants, creating living puppets if you will, a very cruel thing indeed." Petriel's frown deepened and I could imagine his mind ticking over as he spoke. "However, I will investigate our records to see if I can find anything befitting your descriptions, it may prove beneficial in the days that follow."

Vylnor

Vylnor weighed the risks of his current predicament irritably, but his newest plan offered the best chance of securing the Portalis before any of his subordinates could interfere. Although his decision to travel and infiltrate the Elavon Citadel remained one of his more ambitious ideas, sadly he could not travel through the available portals, for they would likely be protected by elvish curs and thus too hazardous to chance. So instead, he had to expend much of his power in travelling there via his *arvemnico* spell, which was no mean feat and had he been a lesser being it would have killed him. After his arrival, he spent the better part of five days hiding amongst the cedaris forests, the vibrant shades almost irritating to his eyes while he gathered the required ingredients, but at least it afforded him time for his magic to revitalise. Very few could concoct a believable disguise, but that alone would not be enough to fool the elves. He needed to infuse his elixir with a *flectil*, otherwise known as a mirror potion. This would give his aura the appearance and essence of pure and uncorrupted elvish magic. It was difficult to accomplish and had he not been afforded some unknown elven heritage, it would have been impossible. Mayhap that is why he despised them so. The elves and their self-righteousness. Too concerned with the existence of their own world, they had not dared enter the realm of Oromos even to save their own kin, preferring to leave them to rot for eternity. And Vylnor had witnessed the few husks that were left. But the Portalis was different and it spoke of their thirst for power and control, but soon, even the elves would cower. Those airs and graces good for naught in the face of torture and corruption, once his Master had conquered their lands. Then and only then would they understand what true suffering meant.

His mind had wandered to a useless place and Vylnor was careful not to touch the cedaris root he had unearthed and deftly gathered, before placing the fragment with his other ingredients. He eyed his Corrono blades, unwilling to be parted from them, especially in Elavon, and had temporarily bewitched the scabbards to hide their physical and magical presence, should the elven whelp somehow catch on to his schemes. Seeing his blades were close at hand, Vylnor paused to gather his magic and after inhaling a deep, settling breath, he began the incantation. *"Higulf flectil ur'ov concil, follier elva havitch degrise … hidden mirror let us disguise, fool the elven and bewitch their eyes, to see what was past and what now is true, imbue the power within this brew."* The spell was spoken in the language of Oromos, founded by his Master and after pronouncing each word, the metallic taste of blood grew stronger and stronger in Vylnor's mouth. To warp something as pure as elvish magic required something as equally foul and he did not relish its use. Did not relish the reminder of his connection to his Master, which afforded him its use either.

Thankfully the ingredients began to fester and glow, the smell growing potent and foul and within the hour, Vylnor knew it was ready. He swallowed the potion reluctantly and retched several times against the acrid taste, before his body collapsed into a fitful state on the floor. Back arched and feeling as if his very skin was aflame, it was only the centuries of torture in Oromos that prevented his roars of anguish from spewing forth and out of his blood-coated lips. But sadly, Vylnor had to avoid discovery at all costs, so he endured the harrowing pain for what felt like a lifetime, until his body lay limp above the trampled foliage.

Evening out his breath, Vylnor soon gathered his strength and stood on weakened limbs, before stumbling to the nearest brook to look upon his reflection. His fangs and claws were now replaced by a smooth elven complexion and long golden hair that would be the envy of many. Eyes that remained green were instead paler, like twin jade stones that sat beneath the clear and unhurried water. Pleased at the results, Vylnor sneered, "Now to gather information from those loose elvish tongues. Even the Elven Realm cannot hide you from me, Portalis."

Aria

It was the last evening before we left for the Mortal Realm and excitingly, I was finally able to witness the Citadel.

We were to meet the Generals, Elders, Monroe and Grandfather at the feast and I fidgeted in my cushioned seat, slightly nervous for the elvish dress style was rather more fitting than back home. To my relief, my midnight-blue dress was adorned with long sleeves, the panels artfully stitched together with thin silver lace. At first glance, the entire outfit appeared to just glitter subtly in the light, but if you looked closely, it was actually adorned with an array of small stars and I marvelled at the intricacy.

My friend, who sat regally opposite, was dressed in emerald-green, with golden lace-capped sleeves and a matching belt. The solid gold band, set in an array of scattered leaves in her short hair, finished her ensemble and she looked every inch the elven lady.

"Stop playing with your hair, you look lovely Aria," she chided and I released the tip of auburn hair I had been absently twisting, the remainder of which was pinned back in a mixture of curls and intricate plaits running down my spine.

I struggled to retain my grimace. "I do not wish to give my grandfather a heart attack, or worse, Monroe a chance to jest at my expense!"

She barked a laugh. "They will do neither. In all likelihood, you will need to run from the many suitors asking for a dance."

I clamped my hand over my eyes, embarrassment growing, and muttered, "Give me strength," when the carriage jostled slightly and Oriella threw her unimpressed gaze to the driver in front. The small but beautifully crafted midnight carriage had arrived a few dials prior to take us to the council building that was hosting tonight's feast. Its open top allowed me to observe the vast array of stars woven across the cloudless Elavon night and as I did, a light warm breeze, milder than back home, flowed across my flushed cheeks. At least the sensation served to soothe my frayed nerves somewhat, but tonight was not only held in our honour. It also highlighted that we would soon be leaving this incredible world and the prospect only seemed to fuel my more anxious thoughts.

We entered the golden-stoned city at a leisurely pace and truth be told, I expected it to be larger, but Eron had cited previously that throughout centuries of war, the population had remained stagnant. Elven mate pairs were becoming a rarer occurrence, so the expansion of the city followed suit. Despite this, everything seemed to have its place beautifully and I could see no evidence of the destitution, rumoured to have plagued some of our own overflowing towns and cities in the Mortal Realm.

Although it wasn't bathed in sunshine, the soft glow of the lamplights flickering against the kuldura stone buildings was magical. Oriella explained that each property was etched in intrinsic designs based on the families in which they housed. A prancing stag adorned one handsome building in particular. Its antlers extended into tree branches and leaves that gathered around the windows, while shadows danced across the etchings, almost bringing them to life. I marvelled at such a simple trick and yet it was so wonderous to witness. Despite each design's individuality, as we moved further down the paved street, it became clear that they were intended to work in harmony with one another. All contained the arched elven windows that I had come to associate with their architecture and, clearly noticing my gawping, Oriella explained, "They are arched that way so your eye is drawn skyward and to the stars. A reminder of our history and whose legacy has been left for us to covet and protect."

I considered her words as we approached the council building and wondered at the deity who was behind such a legacy. A deity who harboured the imagination and the power to forge the entire Elven Realm. The thought was not simply inspiring, but also a chilling reminder of the powers that plagued these worlds, powers who now fought to conquer them, and I their key.

Hidden behind a narrow curtain wall, the council building's ornate silver gates yawned open in greeting, exposing a large veranda, tiled in subtle silvers and golds to depict scenes of the forest and sea. Nine magnificent archways stood tall and proud at the front of the structure, the stone masterfully shaped to look like the cedaris trees while the branches entwined as if holding the property together. A foundation, that's what they were and how the elves saw the cedaris forests, as well as their Elders. In its centre courtyard stood a five-pointed stone tower, that climbed higher than the trees surrounding the Citadel. Branching from it were three smaller circular blocks, each designated to an Elder so they could carry out their various duties. Oriella gestured to the tower and my eyes remained riveted on it as she spoke. "The Numei tower. An elvish word that conveys the spirit of souls. When it is viewed from above, it depicts the shape of a star. The tiles are made of silver ore from our northern mountains and gently glow in the face of a full moon."

"Tis a shame you cannot witness it from the ground," I whispered regretfully and she smiled.

"Here we have a yearly Luna festival. Legend has it that the timeless moon protected Anala's soul as she fell from the sky and released her power into our world. The three chambers are not simply for the Elders, but a depiction of the moon protecting her soul. They each play a defensive roll should the council building ever be sieged. There are few weak points, you see."

I was hanging on Oriella's every word, so intrigued to know more about the elvish history and did not interrupt as she continued. "During the festival, those without the talent of air are able to rise above the Numei tower on winged ships, to pay their respects and admire its beauty, so perhaps when this is over, you could return and celebrate with us?"

Warmed by her invitation and excited by the prospect, my answer was easy. "I would love to."

◆ 13 ◆

Aria

We entered the courtyard to see it filled with unusual, sweet-smelling flowers and soft candlelight. To my delight, there was what appeared to be a brook running from the east and feeding a deep pond at the base of the tower, where a group of musicians were currently playing a cheerful tune on a floating platform.

Oriella nudged me. "A water source for the building. Try not to fall in." She chuckled at her own jest, while I simply gaped at the general splendour, until I heard the clearing of a throat. "You look beautiful Aria, and Oriella of course." Oriella chuckled once more, her eyes turning mischievous. "I will see you two later, there is someone I would like to ask to dance while they are unaccompanied."

Without another word, she strode off confidently into a crowd of unfamiliar elves and I turned to see Eron smiling warmly at me. Again my treacherous face was set ablaze as I took in his appearance. He was handsomely dressed in a silver tunic and navy-blue trousers, reminding me of the element which he so gracefully commanded, when a whistle to our right drew my attention and saved me from further embarrassment.

"Not the attire we are used to, young Aria, but if I do say so, we wear it well." Monroe spun in a circle, parading his forest-green tunic, matching trousers and brown boots.

I pouted. "Yes Monroe, but at least you can dance. I shall more than likely fall on my face."

"I would not let you fall."

I glanced immediately to Eron. His surprising mumble earned him an inquisitive glance from Monroe also, before the elvish General looked away sharply and called, "Good evening, Jacoby."

Grandfather strode over in his all-black ensemble and appeared irritated. "Aria, I would ask that you stay with me this evening. They may be elves, but I have seen far too many send admiring glances in your direction."

My faced turned as red as a radish in spring and I could not stop my spluttered reply. "You exaggerate as usual, Grandfather!"

"Yes Jacoby," chimed Monroe, before adding unexpectedly, "you are right and here comes one now." The mage was now grinning wildly as Darnel walked towards our company, no signs that his leg was broken a mere sennight ago, when he addressed our group confidently and with a small bow.

"Good evening all. If I may be so bold, Miss Aria, would you do me the honour and dance with me?"

He held out his hand to me and Grandfather visibly stiffened, hand raised as if to bat the poor elf away, so I quickly grabbed him and replied, "Of course," before rushing us towards the dance floor.

Eron

Eron ground his teeth, irritated by Darnel's audacity and forwardness, but in reality, he could not blame the warrior for acting before him. In the art of war, his speed and strategy were incomparable, but when it came to matters of the fairer sex, he was decisively slower and overly cautious.

"Better luck next time old fella," Monroe whispered and patted Eron's back in mock sympathy, but before he could spit his scathing reply, Jacoby spoke.

"Don't be absurd, Monroe. Eron's intentions would be to protect Aria from roaming hands, isn't that right?"

A second thud on his back signalled Jacoby now looking for support and Eron drew his tunic collar away from his neck anxiously before offering the courteous answer, "Of course, Jacoby."

Monroe surreptitiously mouthed "coward" in his direction and, having had enough of this conversation and the nosey mage, Eron prepared to stalk away, when he noticed a new partner now danced with Aria. He did not recognise this elf and grew especially vexed at how closely they danced. His aura, although nothing out of the ordinary, felt unusually *fresh*, like that of a newly birthed elven child and threw Eron's instincts immediately on guard. Intent on removing Aria from the elf's embrace, Eron stilled as the blond male moved even closer and whispered almost secretively in her ear. Conflicted and unwilling to act rashly, Eron hoped Aria would shove the elf away, or bestow one of her right hooks across his face for his audacity. Disappointingly neither occurred and what left him the most maddened was that she stayed close in his arms and looked uninclined to move away.

Aria

Darnel was a fine dancer and led me around the floor with the grace and strength you'd expect from an elven partner and thankfully the steps were not too taxing for my amateur abilities.

"How do you like it here in the Elven Realm, Miss Aria? I trust your intense training has not left a poor taste in your mouth, with regards to our usual hospitality?"

Smiling I replied honestly, "It has been a challenge I will admit, but I believe I have made some life-long friends from the experience, which I am very grateful for."

"You have a very positive view and I hope you keep it through your future trials. I also hope you may count myself among those newfound friends?"

Warmed by his words, my answer was easy. "I would be honoured," I said, then frustratingly, another elf interrupted the sweet moment and requested a dance. I frowned slightly at his forwardness, having not spoken with Darnel for long, but my new friend took it in his stride and bowed graciously, asking that I save him another dance later this evening, before walking away.

I turned to the newcomer and absurdly was instantly

drawn to him. He was beautiful as usual, even by elven standards, with golden-blond hair and pale-green eyes, but there was something about those eyes that had my body leaning closer. I even began to breathe in his scent and promptly stopped myself, thinking I had lost my mind.

"Miss Aria?" His confusion apparent, I sent the stranger a tentative smile before I was immediately swept off my feet. He pulled our bodies closer as we danced, the experience growing oddly intimate, when the elf began to speak, "You seem uncomfortable?"

Blushing, I replied shortly, "I don't know what you mean."

A subtle smirk crossed his full lips, "Your blush is adorable and very endearing."

My face turned even rosier under his scrutiny, words vacating my mind at an alarming rate, but thankfully he saved me from further embarrassment with his next words.

"May I tell you a secret?"

His gaze was intense and curiosity piqued, I moved my head closer. His warmth and scent wrapped around my senses almost aggressively and I welcomed it, keen to draw out the moment when he whispered, "I have missed you, pretty girl."

And that small sense of sanctuary his proximity created instantly collapsed. My shocked eyes widened from their haze as the cold realisation of who I embraced pierced my heart and with his next damning breath he called, "*arvemnico!*"

I struggled in earnest, power rising to my defence while the picturesque courtyard surrounding us began to disappear before my eyes. My head whipped about the space, eyes desperately seeking help, when the lonely weight of this fight settled gravely within my heart and I was dragged away by this monster once more.

Eron

Eron beheld Aria's expression of terror moments before he felt an expansion of magic surround both their forms. He raced towards her, bellowing for the available warriors to take their defensive positions and put on a blast of speed. But it was not enough, and Eron found himself tackling nothing but thin air while Aria's form disappeared between the worlds.

Deftly rolling to his feet, he quickly took stock of the situation, eyeing the surrounding area for any other immediate threats, which now stood in a state of pause. There was nothing but deafening silence in the courtyard. The band had ceased its playing, warriors had taken position at the perimeters of the structure and Eron felt crushing panic enter his bones when he felt the eyes of Jacoby Torvel burning into his back.

Fists opening and closing, Eron's magic was primed to attack and yet there was no enemy with which to strike. His foe had somehow reached this realm undetected and outsmarted them all. The elves relied on their auras to detect any unfamiliar energies in their world, thus easily routing out enemies and spies. Eron now realised that he had been too complacent. He felt the aura was off and did *nothing*, too distracted by their closeness. Now that mistake had just cost them the Portalis. Had cost him *Aria*.

Jacoby broke the silence with a pained voice. "Where is she, Eron?"

Monroe placed a hand on the mortal's shoulder placatingly. "My friend, please" and Jacoby shook him off quickly before roaring, "WHERE IS MY GRANDAUGHTER?!"

Eron could only respond solemnly, the weight of his guilt pressing soundly into his shoulders, "I cannot tell you, Jacoby."

The man charged and Eron allowed the first punch to hit his face, but grabbed Jacoby's fists soon after to stop the remaining blows.

"What *do* you know Erondriel?! Are you not the First General of Elavon?! Are you not her trainer, her *protector*?! Instead you allowed her to be taken from me not once, but *twice*! She could now be stuck in the bowels of that place, tortured and alone. MY ARIA!" Jacoby was now screaming irately and Eron had neither the fight nor the inclination to argue against his obvious failure.

Monroe once again halted Jacoby's tirade, brown eyes filled with concern. "That is enough Jacoby."

The mortal spun, now face to face with Monroe, his words eerily calm but cutting. "And why is that?"

Monroe took a deep breath, eyeing his friend with resolve before he spoke. "I know you well Jacoby and berating Eron for *our* failure, will neither absolve you of your guilt or help Aria."

Crack! Jacoby hit Monroe squarely in the jaw, causing him to stumble back a step.

"Do not lecture me, you fool, you have no idea what I have lost." Jacoby's voice trembled, when he raised his hands to cover his eyes, the picture of a defeated man, but Eron was not so ready to give up.

Aria was resilient and her magic would instinctually protect her, so his next response was honest and brought them all a slither of hope.

"She is not lost, Jacoby. Aria is your granddaughter and if that tells us anything, she will not go down without a fight."

Aria

"Release me!" I screamed and struggled viciously against Vylnor, whose foul magic now wrapped around our forms, the spell seizing my body and I knew it wouldn't be long before I was dragged away. Away from my home, from safety and from the people I loved. But I would rally against such a fate with all that I was and threw out a burst of desperate power, all the while thinking, flee just *flee*. Our surroundings twisted and pulled unnaturally, distorting my vision as both our magics battled for dominance, when we were thrown to the ground. Panting, my left cheek pressed to the dirt, I gripped the mossy floor of the forest and rose up, gaze darting about wildly, when I spotted Vylnor across the clearing. He remained crouched on the ground and raised his head warily, chest heaving with exertion while anger spewed from a gaze which had now returned to the Oromos torturer that I had come to know.

I scrambled to my feet and bolted as fast as my legs could carry me, ripping my skirt in the process when I heard the worrying sounds of his pursuit. Closer and closer he drew and I could hear his steps and hissing breaths stretch across the narrowing space between us. Drawing from my training with Oriella, I directed my magic into my legs and flew across the forest floor. I could hear Vylnor's curses growing fainter as I broke away, but then a distinctive clink followed and he was again in hot pursuit. Bounding over rocks and fallen tree trunks and uncaring what laid ahead, I pushed through a thicket of ferns when suddenly I tumbled. The embankment was steep and all I could do was curl in on myself, arms raised to protect my head while I attempted to slow my chaotic fall. I hit several protruding tree trunks and rocks, winding myself in the process, when the harsh ground was replaced by nothing but air and I came to a sudden halt.

"Foolish girl," Vylnor spat, his arm now banded about my waist, halting my decent over a dangerous ledge and despite my precarious position, I began to struggle anew.

"Release me!" I growled, when a smarting pain punctured one side of my ribcage and I cried out in pain.

"Enough of this stupidity, you will merely hurt

yourself more and be useless to me!" He grunted the words impatiently and I stopped moving to scowl intently at him. He looked as exhausted as I felt. Dark circles hung beneath his eyes, amid a complexion that was paler than usual and a twinge of sadness passed through me. Surprised, I swatted the strange feeling away quickly in favour of anger and remarked bitterly, "What now?"

Vylnor

This woman would be the death of him, Vylnor decided. The fool charged headfirst through the forest at magical speeds, that even a Norag would struggle to keep pace with and when he saw her tumble down that ravine he panicked. Not for his own sake, or even that of his Master's success, but because he was afraid. Afraid for *her*. The realisation startled Vylnor and he praised his forethought in arming himself with potions beforehand. Knowing his energy would be drained and unaware of the depths of her power, he did not leave anything to chance. Having caught her with his enhanced speed, they remained precariously balanced atop an unnerving drop in the forest floor, the smallest misplacement in his footing could be disastrous, given his exhausted magical reserves. But he would not admit that to her. The situation not ideal, Vylnor tightened his grip against her struggles and grunted impatiently, "Now, thanks to your dismal control, we will find out our location and survive, until I can decide what to do with you."

"If you think I shall willingly go anywhere with you,

you are lying to yourself," she said pointedly, but after a few more moments of useless protest, the stubborn Portalis reluctantly conceded, "Well get us off this cliff *oh powerful Vylnor*, as I cannot suffer being in your arms a moment longer."

Her enraged yet witty comments gave Vylnor cause to smirk. "Such a smart mouth, Portalis, but petty words will not help you."

Her only response was a disgusted snort before he swiftly navigated his way back up the steep embankment with her in his arms. He remained oddly aware of each hiss and curse which forced its way past her lips and the reaction unnerved him. The Portalis was a conundrum indeed, but all these oddities stood for naught after his Master was through with her, and soon Vylnor would return to the indifferent Lord of Shadows, as he was accustomed to.

On even ground once more, Vylnor placed her bruised body at the base of an oak tree and knew from the foliage, they were somehow within the Mortal Realm.

"Stay put, I refuse to catch you if you throw yourself over a ravine again."

"Keep talking and I might just do that," she sneered up at him, small nose wrinkled in disgust, but he ignored her little snipe and began to climb the tree. Reaching the top with ease, he took note of their location and saw a small village nestled by a river to the north, about a day's travel away. Destination in mind, Vylnor dropped gracefully back to the floor where surprisingly, the only sounds ricocheting about the forest were the crunch of leaves beneath his booted feet, so he quipped, "How novel of you to follow instructions without argument, Portalis." However, when no reply was forthcoming, he glanced at the girl more carefully. Her breaths had shortened through lips that were now pale instead of rosy. Her hunched frame hid her naïve, sapphire eyes until she began to cough violently, so much so that those pale lips were soon coated with scarlet blood, which began to trail slowly down her chin. The crimson was stark against her whitened skin and Vylnor rushed to her, catching her body before she collapsed to one side. Uneasy, he laid her atop the autumn leaves and pulled vials from his person. Picking one of his basic healing potions, he lifted her chin and none too gently, forced the liquid down her throat. Again she coughed, this time spluttering and gagging until her exhaustion consumed her and she passed out weakly in his arms. Staring at her limp form and thinking of what a nuisance this girl was becoming, Vylnor hoisted her into his arms and strode towards their next destination.

Aria

Water. That was all I craved when I opened my gritty eyes, removed the tongue stuck to the roof of my mouth and took in my surroundings. The room was constructed of wooden slats, light leaking in through the holes with a distinctive smell of damp in the air. Despite this, the linen bedsheets on the narrow cot smelt of a fresh breeze and although they were frayed at the edges, I got the distinct impression they had been well cared for.

Turning my head, I noticed a small jug of water perched on the bedside table and without hesitation, reached straight for it, immediately wincing as a dull pain stabbed at my side. I ran my fingers across the aching area gingerly and felt the coarse material of a long shirt and *only* a long shirt. It appeared clean, but for the smells of ash and woodsy earth. I frowned, concerned about who had changed me out of my clothes before reaching for the jug once more and drinking greedily. Thirst momentarily quenched, I replayed my last memories over and over in my mind, in some vain attempt to piece together how I came to be here. *Vylnor.*

A door opposite my bed began to creak open and his intense stare met mine in what appeared to be … *relief?* My brow furrowed, but before I could make any sense of his expression, my body instinctively reacted in panic and the scenes from the whipping post hit my consciousness like a battering ram. Volatile, my magic flew towards him, intent on removing the cause of my alarm, but Vylnor must have suspected as much, for his eyes widened and he called, "*absoare!*" A flash of dark energy pulsed in front of his form and harmlessly absorbed my attack. His eyes however spat fire before he barked, "You have a funny way of saying thank you, Portalis." Crossing his arms defensively before his broad chest, he simply scowled at me from across the room for some time, while my indignation swirled and I offered a scathing reply. "And what *should* I thank you for?

Memories of my shattered ankles? The whipping scars across my back perhaps? Or even better, the nightmares that continue to haunt my sleep, pray tell?"

Vylnor ground his teeth and I preened in satisfaction that my words had bothered him. Or that maybe, by recalling his previous actions, he was now upset with himself. I doubted it was the latter for someone like him, who would forever more be incapable of empathy, however, I did not anticipate his cutting words.

"Poor little Portalis having to deal with a few hours in Oromos. Go cry to someone else about your woes, for I could not give a rat's arse about them." He turned and left, slamming the rickety door behind him and rattling a few of the loose slats on the walls.

I meanwhile scowled at his retreating back and the offending door for a few additional dials, intent on devising a plan and running as far away from the letch as my legs could carry me.

It was some time before Vylnor returned. I had made several attempts to rise from the cot but was hindered by bouts of light-headedness and trembling legs. On my ninth attempt, the door opened once again and he stalked into the room, moody aura in tow. Mortifyingly, I currently stood clutching a side table that housed a wash bowl, jug and cloth and wore nothing but the ridiculous shirt.

"Well, well, well, aren't you all legs, flailing about like a new spring doe?"

The bastard was laughing at me and I imagined

head butting him in his smarmy face. Suddenly, his head snapped back and he stumbled into the wall. I would have been shocked, had his face not depicted such utter stupor that a laugh burst from my lips involuntarily. Scowl now firmly in place and a bruise slowly forming around his nose and eyes, Vylnor marched towards me, picking me up by the collar and slammed my back into the wall, jostling the slats. He then proceeded to grab me roughly by the hair, before pushing my face to the side and hissing viciously, "You forget who I am, Portalis. I have faced centuries of battle and torture, the skills I've acquired can be put to good use, should you continue to aggravate me."

His fangs were dangerously close to my neck, my scalp now aching from his tight grip on my hair and my treacherous heart only raced faster, betraying my fear. How did I forget the monster that he was, even momentarily? But I would not make the same mistake again. His callousness had my own ire rising and I decided I wouldn't allow him to make me feel vulnerable again. Vylnor of Shadows would *not* get to decide my fate, only I would.

Sluggishly, I dragged my face to look at him squarely, strands of hair snapping against his hold and spat, "You think that will stop me, you Oromos prig?!"

I threw myself sharply off the wall, my magic fuelling my limbs and offering strength, when we were thrown violently to the floor. Miraculously, I managed to land on top of the brute and begin to throw punches at his arrogant face. My first shot landed and to my delight

I heard the resounding crack of knuckle meeting bone. The second, however, he dodged at the last minute and the floorboards splintered brittlely under my knuckles. So focused on hurting him, I realised too late that he had wedged his right knee between our bodies and threw me off. Remembering my training, I attempted to roll out of range and regain a defensive position, but my opponent was fast. *Too* fast. Vylnor grabbed my left ankle and pulled me towards him, my nails struggling to find purchase and a few ripped painfully as I scrambled to grab hold of the old floorboards. In my desperation, I sent out a wild kick, hoping to dislodge his grip and let out a crazed hiss of frustration when instead, he easily grasped my second ankle, only to pull me across the uneven floor and out of the room.

♦ 14 ♦

Aria

"Release me!" I growled at the Oromos Lord, before adding a series of curses which failed to have the desired effect as he continued, unbothered, on his path out of my temporary chambers. Changing tact, I eyed my new environment desperately, looking for anything I could use as a weapon and chose to ignore my shirt as it began to gather against the timbers and ride up my torso, exposing not only my legs but my undergarments as well.

To my relief, we stopped short at a large door and I could hear a rowdy crowd in the throngs of general merriment on the other side. After throwing my legs aside, I was swiftly gripped by the front of my shirt once more and shoved through the door. Our movements stopped abruptly when Vylnor pulled my wrists behind my back and the patrons, upon seeing our little display, turned worryingly silent.

"Perhaps I should leave you to the mercy of these fine people for a day or two, while I make my travel preparations?"

It wasn't his question that frightened me, but the vast number of leers I received from almost all the men and a few of the women about the room. There were varying degrees of what looked to be dubious characters, some with scarred faces and others missing limbs. But it was the attractive ones that seemed the most calculating and sinister to me and I winced nervously at their eager perusal of my poorly clothed body. I trembled, from either weakness or fear, and stared at the stained timber floors, as though they were the most intriguing items I had ever seen, in some vain attempt to control my reaction to this new predicament.

"Alternatively," Vylnor added, drawing my attention to his pitiless tone as it hissed in my ear, "you can stay with me, do as you are told and reap the benefits of my protection."

As wearied as I was, I struggled to contain my sarcastic remark, "Do not fool yourself, Vylnor. You are no protector, just a pathetic taint on this world," and following that assessment, the front door to the building unexpectedly exploded inward.

"*Maliskas!*" cried several patrons and the building's inhabitants either fled or drew arms in response to the new threat. Vylnor, meanwhile, uttered a colourful curse before seizing me about the waist and ran us back through the corridor he had previously dragged me through. We reached our room at impossible speeds, when I was thrown haphazardly from his grip and left to stumble across the chamber.

Stunned for a moment, I watched as he diligently grabbed what little belongings he had, before my senses took hold.

"I need trousers or a skirt!"

I began to frantically look about the room despite his protests.

"*That* is your first thought?!" he asked incredulous, before hauling me over his shoulder, *still* trouser-less. I expected him to exit through the corridor, but instead he called "*argom!*" and the wall that housed a small window exploded outwards. Vylnor did not wait, even for the shards of wayward timber to settle, before launching us through the space and into the encroaching twilight.

"What ... are ... Maliskas?" My sentence was fragmented, as my diaphragm hit his shoulder repeatedly while he ran through the forest.

"Witches," he huffed derisively and I couldn't help but think his response rather anticlimactic and jeered, "The ... unbeatable ... Vylnor, afraid ... of some ... witches?"

Tsking, Vylnor sped through the undergrowth before stopping at the base of a great elm tree that still possessed most of its foliage, his only word to me, "Climb."

"But?!" And even as I stuttered and tried to muster a retort, he had already hoisted me up to the first branch, so I grabbed it wordlessly before attempting to jump over the other side in escape. The back of my shirt was gripped harshly, his vicious breath at my neck.

"Do not test me, girl. There are fouler things out there, so *climb*."

Unnerved, I clambered up and through the gnarled,

age-old branches as fast as I could, glad for my previous lessons with Eron and Oriella.

We settled as close to the top as possible before the branches began to thin and I worried briefly that they would not hold our combined weight, when alarmingly, Vylnor drew close to my side. His voice clearly irritated when he explained in a hushed voice, "These are no ordinary witches, they are cannibals and hunt in packs ... no doubt after you."

"*Cannibals?!*" I squeaked and he silenced me with a clawed hand over my mouth. Looking below, I could see some of the patrons from the property as they ran chaotically beneath us and my breath stilled when I caught sight of seven slight shadows moving closer from between the trees. The seven silent hunters converged quickly on their target and in less than a dial, a thickly built man was brought to the ground with a resounding thud. His flailing body was impressively dragged by a slender female into a clearing, the thick grass quickly trampled as he vigorously struggled, leaving a deathly path in their wake. It spoke soundly of the witch's strength and only then did I heed Vylnor's words and receive my first glance of these Maliskas.

Hair in varying shades of colour, the most unusual being a fuchsia pink, the Maliskas all looked stunning and otherworldly within the clearing, until they opened their jaws unnaturally wide and you were greeted with row upon row of sharp, boned, *teeth*. I then began to understand the weight of those patron's fears regarding these witches and could do nothing but watch on in a terror-induced fascination as the scene played out before me.

"This one is plump," a Maliska with cropped black hair purred unfazed, while the victim pleaded and screamed for mercy. Promptly hog tied, the man's mortal strength was no match for the witches and soon he was encircled by the entire pack of hunters.

I opened my mouth to appeal, wanting to help the man, but Vylnor tightened his hold across my lips and shook his head harshly in a firm no, before pulling us further into the trees' leafy shadow. One of the Maliskas stepped forward while the others held their positions and I assumed this was their leader.

The female was striking. A wild and feral beauty, her sharp facial features were accentuated by her long, blood-red hair. To add to her fearsome visage, she was dressed in dark warrior leathers and a vast array of wicked blades were strapped across her entire body. Without a word, she grasped her victim's dark hair, pulled his head back and clamped her jaws around his exposed throat. I would never forget the sound of her teeth as they crunched through cartilage and bone, nor his last gargled gasps, before she ripped his neck in two and began to chew delightedly at the human flesh.

My eyes squeezed shut at hearing the others converge and tear into the rest of the man's body, all the while trying not to retch. Absently, I clung onto Vylnor of all people for comfort in this disastrous scenario. The Oromos Lord said nothing. His body remained astute and poised, arms held firm around my trembling shoulders and face, despite what he was witnessing. It took the better part of an hour until the ordeal was over. The Maliskas had tasted their fill, their sighs and moans of satisfaction utterly horrifying before they vacated the space soon after, and we were left to bask in the empty silence. Vylnor's proximity thankfully warmed my rapidly cooling skin and upon hearing the sound of rustling elm leaves, I finally opened my eyes, only for them to linger on the mutilated limbs, shredded clothing and blood, that now tarnished the previously green forest floor.

We maintained our perch in the tree for some time. Vylnor had released his hold, no doubt deeming me too traumatised to speak, when eventually, I could no longer stand the silence.

"Must we stay here all night, I'm freezing and they have surely vacated the area by now?"

"Keep your voice to a minimum or I will gag you." His tone was short and I did not appreciate it.

Instead I spat back, "Well perhaps if you used your dark powers of communication, I wouldn't have so many questions."

"You seem to regard me as one of your companions, may I remind you that you are a prisoner and I owe you no explanations." His words carried their usual derisive bite, but given the threat that still loomed in the woods I decided to sit and wait, rather than risk escaping his clutches.

It was now dusk and the cooling temperatures did

little to help the trembles that wracked my poorly clothed body. Eventually Vylnor grunted, "Let's move" before he began to climb down the tree. I decided to follow, averting my eyes as I did so and unwilling to face the Maliskas' carnage on my own. Reaching the last branch, I hopped down onto the crisp autumn leaves and cautiously avoided the human remains on the floor, especially while I remained shoeless. Vylnor was now removing items from his pack and shortly after rummaging, produced a pair of dark trousers and my look of surprise soon turned into a glare.

Teeth chattering I barked, "You had those the *entire* time?! You sadistic boar, I'm freezing!"

Face devoid of emotion he replied, "There wasn't exactly time for a change of outfit, Portalis, and if you continue your verbal insults, I'll keep them."

My eyes narrowed, tired of his overbearing attitude, but I needed those trousers so muttered to myself, "I think you are deserving of more than a *few* verbal insults."

He paused and looked at me suspiciously before tossing the clothing at me, along with an ill-fitting pair of boots. Donning them quickly, I thought over my next move and how I could locate Grandfather, when his question startled me. "I would ask you something, Portalis."

Curious, I remained silent and simply stared at Vylnor, his deep-green eyes serious. "Does the word *valore* mean anything to you?"

As soon as the word left his lips, I couldn't help but shudder. For some reason, it resonated deep within me, making me feel warm and uncomfortable in his presence, but I had no idea why. So I replied honestly and ignored the butterflies in my stomach, "It does not."

He immediately scowled and argued, "You lie."

Startled and for some reason blushing, I was at a loss for words when his voice lowered and he stood to slowly stalk towards me, purring, "Your scent has changed."

I stepped back abruptly and hit the base of the elm tree, my fingers digging into the thick bark before I blurted, "Well if I smell, it is rude to point it out!" Feeling affronted, as well as confused, I struggled to understand his knowing smirk.

"That is not what I meant." He was now crowding my body, his face but inches from my own. "There is something you are not telling me, Portalis," he pressed, lips but a hairsbreadth away and crooned almost seductively, "and I will enjoy finding out what it is."

The moment was abruptly broken by a melodious voice that tapered into a harsh cackle and left me wincing at the painful pitch.

"My, my, Lord Vylnor, how the mighty have fallen."

My eyes widened as the red-headed Maliska leader exited the treeline and into the clearing, dried blood marring her upturned lips and jaw, before she snapped them threateningly in our direction.

Vylnor

Vylnor scowled at the Maliska, peeved at the interruption and knew the others were not far behind. Inwardly cursing that they had not left the area sooner, he snapped, "Watch your mouth, Kalida. Your teeth may be formidable, but they will not stop me from cutting out your tongue."

She chuckled, unbothered by his threat and bolstered by her newfound advantage.

"I do not take orders from the now banished Vylnor of Shadows," and she paused to add gleefully, "I intend to take your place." With that declaration, the Maliskas launched themselves at him from all directions.

Pushing away from the Portalis, Vylnor drew his twin Corrono blades. The weapons were so comfortable, so natural in his palms that they had become an extension of himself as he spun them dangerously around his form and offered a stark warning to any who dared approach. Without taking his eyes from his enemy, Vylnor barked at the naïve mortal at his back, "Run, little Portalis. *Run*," before calling, "*syndmur infernous!*"

A wall of fire encircled himself and the Maliskas, forming a barrier between his prisoner and his enemies while the battle commenced. Even at full power, Vylnor knew this would be a challenging fight. Although possessing no magical powers of their own, the witches still benefited from advantages like other immortal beings, including being armed with potion-infused strength and speed, further bolstered by his Master's own dark magic tied to their Agnicar. If surviving the mortal witch trials hadn't already turned their hearts bitter, then feasting on unnatural flesh amongst the Oromos wastes surely stole what remained of their sanity. His odds were certainly reduced by his own lack of magical reserves and the close fighting quarters, so Vylnor's plan was to stun, hopefully slay a few in the process and retreat. The Maliskas however were fast and accurate, their training brutal and their vengeful spirits only spurred their hatred for the other realms, especially this one.

Unsurprisingly, Kalida attacked first. Her curved machete sliced down towards his chest which he immediately blocked and countered swiftly with a slash from his right blade. No sooner had Kalida retreated before another Maliska, this one with short silver hair, attempted to cut through his neck with her steel fan. Vylnor deflected the assault and removed the offending weapon from her grasp, before withdrawing sharply in order to utilise what was left of his magic. Pivoting away, he stared Kalida down, their weapons still poised and neither of them willing to give ground, but Vylnor was older and much stronger. She charged impatiently, so using his strength, Vylnor met the attacked with equal fervour and thrust the witch leader back. Irritably, a third Maliska sporting braided black hair approached and swiped at him with her short sword, forcing him to retreat several steps. Only then did Vylnor recognise his error. Now standing in a small opening, the splitting of air whistled in his ears as four throwing knives were launched at his exposed back. Growling *"flecviar!"* he deflected three of the four throwing knives and grunted in pain at the impact of the fourth, which now laid imbedded in his left shoulder blade. Left arm now weakened by the assault, Vylnor begrudgingly knew he could not maintain this pace for much longer and willed that his actions had bought the Portalis enough time to put some distance between herself and the fight.

Aria

He had actually trapped himself with those monsters and I couldn't understand why as I scrambled away from my enemies and the cyclone of flames that reached high above the treetops. The emanating heat flushed my cheeks and incredibly the blaze remained contained and did not spread throughout the forest.

How I envied such magical control but having little disposable time, I thought over my next move and continued to edge myself away from the battle. Walking backwards and eyes trained on the blaze, I fully expected one of those witches to tear through and rush towards me like a demon incarnate. Knowing this possibility to be sound, I should have run as far away as possible, but something was holding me back. What, I could not articulate, while I listened to the female cries of outrage and the ringing of steel. No doubt the Maliskas were attempting to slay Vylnor and the thought left me uncomfortable. Yet why would I care? The despicable lout let me be tortured and tried to imprison me, not once but *thrice*. At that moment, three throwing knives spun out of the flames in front of me, only to imbed themselves harmlessly in the forest floor and a dull pain bloomed unwelcome across my back. Confused, I briskly rubbed the awkward area and cursed simultaneously while running over to the discarded weapons before grabbing them.

The darkened steel was light, jagged and etched with unfamiliar patterns, sporting hilts that were worn with use. Simply touching them, I could feel that these weapons yearned for murder and death, rather than defence on the battlefield, but still I stashed the blades on my person. Suddenly an unnatural and piercing howl cut through the air in the distance and I winced. The sound so shrill, I was forced to cover my ears before it clawed its way through the underside of my skull.

Even if Vylnor managed to evade the Maliskas, he would need help with this new threat. His flames were now a shining beacon for this enemy to follow and, looking to the trees, I ran towards an old elm and began to climb its knotted branches, all the while hoping I wasn't making a terrible mistake.

Vylnor

Vylnor's ire rose as the pain from the knife imbedded in his back began to throb incessantly, but the distance it placed between himself and his enemy was invaluable and allowed him to cast his magic. "*Lanza ignatio!*" he called and hurled a fire spear across the space, directly at the bitch that released the blade and watched on in satisfaction as the spear impaled her chest and dissolved, while she thrashed and wailed in aguish. Its flames entered the wound and slowly burnt her alive, which caused quite a stir amongst the remaining Maliskas for they began to attack him in earnest, even while shrieking in agony over their demised sister.

Vylnor received a barrage of superficial wounds, but also felled another two of the foul witches in the process. He even used the knife from his own back to end one of their bitter lives and felt a sense of poetic justice following the kill. Shortly after their rage-fuelled assault, Kalida called an order to regroup and Vylnor recognised that this was his opportunity to retreat. So, dispersing a section of the thrashing flames, Vylnor bolted through his makeshift doorway before swiftly closing it behind him and exited the area on a sprint. Had he the time, Vylnor would have burnt them alive within that hellfire prison, but his magic was drained and every drop was costly in his pursuit for the Portalis. Meanwhile, anguished screeches of cold fury could be heard from the trapped Maliskas and Vylnor knew Kalida would pursue him viciously until his demise for that slight, which only elicited a violent grin from his lips.

Sheathing his blades, Vylnor continued to run through the forest, skirting boulders and dodging ancient trees whose gnarled roots seemed intent on slowing him down, and paused only when he heard the familiar piercing howls of the Norags. Letting out an irritated growl, he inwardly hoped the Portalis was smart and had escaped while she could. Norags were savage creatures. Despite being blind, their enhanced sense of smell was unmatched and with a thick fur hide and saliva that could induce paralysis, they were not the easiest of opponents. So, bracing himself for his next challenge,

Vylnor switched weapons more suitable for long-range assaults and the fire spears that lit in his palms would do just that.

Senses on high alert, Vylnor's gaze darted across the twisted forest shadows for the three furred beasts that stalked his every step. He'd seen what a Norag's paralysis could do to its victims and Vylnor had no intention of being devoured alive.

Aria

After cautiously traversing the treetops, I watched on, emotions conflicted between terror and astonishment while Vylnor was pursued mercilessly by three huge beasts that I remembered from the attack at Port Framlington. Yet no fear marred the Lord of Oromos's features as he spun deftly and charged at the leading beast, fire spears in each hand.

The monster launched off its hind legs, an impressive feat considering its hulking size, and snapped its jaws wide, aiming for Vylnor's neck. Surprisingly, he dove underneath the first beast and forced the blade up and through its stomach. The fire spear carved easily through the thickened flesh, its innards falling to the earth in his wake, while the smell of scorched fur and rotten meat hit my nose. Vylnor meanwhile rolled to his feet and met his next opponent with confidence. At that point I noticed the streak of blood across his back and absently rubbed the spot of pain on my own, when all at once I was hit by an outrageous theory that sprung unwillingly to my mind. Forced to ignore the disturbing thought for the time being, given the current situation, I clung to my perch within a crooked oak tree. Having successfully traversed a few of the autumnal giants across the forest, I stared fixatedly through its thinning leaves while the remaining two beasts stalled their next attack, in favour of sniffing the air. Their large heads now pointed in the direction of their fallen pack member and they growled ferociously in unison, teeth bared and saliva drooling from their gums, no doubt in displeasure. Unruffled, Vylnor's composed form remained perfectly still as they encircled his body, while I could only hold my breath and uselessly wait until the next clash ensued. Simultaneously they charged towards him and in response, Vylnor vaulted at least twenty paces into the air. His relaxed body twisted effortlessly, the fire spear changing direction towards the earth and using the full force of his weight and gravity, he plunged it down onto one of the beasts and severed its spine. Light on his feet, the Oromos Lord dove away from the smouldering carcass and narrowly missed the attacking claws of the last remaining Norag. The wailing pain of its packmate caused the furred creature to halt its movements and allowed Vylnor the time to stagger unsteadily to his feet.

His breaths now became heavy with exertion and I worried when he failed to cast another weapon, instead choosing to draw his twin swords. The monster's nostrils flared and it growled menacingly, undoubtedly scenting the male's blood-saturated shirt.

With determined eyes that spoke of nothing other

than success, Vylnor braced his legs and readied his swords, before the mutated creature lunged once more. I winced at their brutal clash. Two powerful beings using little but their size and survival skills to ensure their own victory, when Vylnor was brought crashing to the ground. His twin blades were crossed and held in a defensive position above his head, the only protection he had from those vicious jaws while they snapped wildly at his face. I panicked. Realising the beast held the advantage, I knew I had to do *something* to help or I risked facing this monster alone. I could hide in the hopes it wouldn't find me, but as I witnessed Vylnor growing physically weaker before my eyes, so too did a sense of urgency grow within my chest. So pulling out the three throwing blades I had collected earlier, I cast my mind back to my training with Eron and, forcing my erratic heart to calm despite the anxiety-inducing danger below, I eyed the beast with intent. *Inhale. Exhale.* I drew the blade back and threw.

My elation as the dagger connected with its target soon turned to horror, when it merely bounced off its hide and Vylnor's dark eyes locked with my own from the forest floor. They were incredulous and I imagined the nasty words his eyes spat, *"Stupid girl, why did you not flee?"* Echoed by, *"That was pathetic."*

The beast halted its assault and sniffed the air while I held my breath and stilled, willing for it not to notice me when its head turned damningly in my direction. The Norag abruptly detached itself from Vylnor's blades and charged at the base of the oak.

"Great gaping bulls' bollocks!" I cursed, the force of its huge body and thick claws causing the aged bark to splinter under the brutal assault.

Vylnor rushed to his feet and followed the beast, slashing at its hide in an attempt to stop its progress, but the blow did little to deter it from its new target. Enraged further, it snapped its giant jaws at him, forcing Vylnor to retreat a few steps and slammed once more into the tree. The telling sound of snapping wood and crumbling bark caused my blood to turn cold and Vylnor roared, "*Move!*"

Desperate, I jumped to the nearest tree branch and as soon as my fingers took hold, I realised my dangerous mistake.

The snapping noise of the branch giving way burned my ears before I plummeted to the ground. Winded and gasping for breath after the fall, I struggled to my feet as the beast roared in my direction, but before it could launch towards me, Vylnor barrelled into its side to stop its advance.

"GO!" he bellowed and wrestled with the monster, their struggle violent, and before long it had him pinned beneath its hulking mass.

Claws and weight pressing into Vylnor's chest, he struggled to hold its muzzle at bay with nothing but his bare hands pressing it shut. His usually intimidating claws did little to puncture the thick hide and I knew his strength would soon fail. I could no longer watch the scene play out slowly, nor could I run and leave Vylnor to this fate, so I did not think and instead reacted.

Running towards them, I grabbed one of Vylnor's discarded blades and slashed it horizontally in the air. My magic formed an arch of light that erupted from the weapon and to my amazement, sliced the beast cleanly in two, but as I watched its demise my hands unexpectedly began to burn. I threw the offending weapon away, expecting to see burnt flesh in the place of my palms, when I was met with nothing but grazed and dirtied skin. My stunned eyes returned to Vylnor and I remained unmoving while he pushed the remaining parts of the dead beast off his form. The exertion caused the Oromos Lord to collapse amongst the long grass shortly after and he was left panting harshly. I rushed over when blood began to pool around his body from the aggravated wound on his shoulder, the male eyeing me with surprise and not the welcoming kind.

"At least you did not maim me as well. Why have you not left, you foolish girl?"

I tried and failed to hide my smirk. The male was still condescending, even when in pain, although he misread my smile.

"Glad to see you enjoy my suffering, I did not enjoy yours."

A little bewildered by that comment, I arched a brow and took in his features. I had hoped to find sincerity rather than deceit and swiftly acknowledged that there might be some unusual connection between us.

He frowned under my perusal and looked away while I continued to stare at him in his poor condition, wondering idly for a moment if he thought me sadistic.

Finally I gritted, "Will you be OK? What can I do?"

His head snapped to me disbelievingly. "You would *help* me?"

The question came out a whispered hiss and revealed there was much more to the Lord of Shadows beneath his calculating and cruel facade, but that one comment at least confirmed that his existence had been a lonely one. A harsh one. So with a sympathetic smile that was met by a pair of dubious eyes, I tentatively placed my hand on his chest and hoped I would not regret the searing pain that followed, which pulled me from the forest clearing and into a darkening abyss.

♦ 15 ♦

Aria

At first I felt nothing, just a persistent and timeless press of darkness all around me, until a blistering cold swathed my body and became almost suffocating. Did I finally find an end to the extent of my magic?

I remembered Vylnor lying on the ground, his wound dire and his magic verging on empty. Perhaps I should have left him there, but I knew I couldn't. I thought I could heal his wounds as I had Darnel's, or at least halt some of the bleeding enough to promote Vylnor's own healing. Was the volume of magic too substantial? Was my arbitrary effort wrong? Dangerous even? Vylnor was, after all, a superior immortal. Even if that were the case, it still didn't explain my current environment, when a small glow of light pierced through the imposing darkness and grabbed my attention. So with little other options, I decided to follow it.

Each step felt hollow and weightless and after a few moments of walking through nothing but a vast emptiness, a gasp left my lips upon finding the source of the glow. It was a stone. Nay, *the* stone from Anala's vision. I stilled and eyed it in wonder and horror. A shade of the deepest green which was all too familiar and a vision of Vylnor and his imposing eyes filled my mind. I shook my head and blinked rapidly to clear the image, only to inspect the stone further and it appeared, *damaged*. Veined in red, an eerie darkness was growing around the stone, its presence unnatural and pulsing with life. It was leeching away what remained of the stones light and had I but stumbled upon it at a different angle, I would not have seen it at all.

My magic stirred as though repulsed by the taint marring it and I reached out, surprised when a sinister voice rumbled, "You are lost, Portalisss." The hiss was uncomfortable. Like small needles scraping around the inside of my ears and I found myself covering them, in a vague attempt to alleviate some of the discomfort. Loathed for the voice to speak any more than necessary but my curiosity piqued, I replied carefully, "Who are you?"

"I would think that were obviousss, you aide my ssservant after all."

I stilled at its words, a cold realisation dawning of who it was that spoke to me.

"Your compasssion isss your weaknesss. These mortal attachmentsss a liability, Portalisss."

I shook uncontrollably and forced the uncomfortable feeling his words elicited away and added with a false bravado, "You speak of attachments as a weakness, but you are no more than a leech. Draining the life from our Three Realms."

A high-pitched grating noise caused me to double

over and I grabbed the sides of my head in agony, my teeth grinding through the pain. I was certain that blood began to spill from my nose, until the noise abruptly stopped and I gasped a sigh of relief, only wincing when more words ensued.

"Sssoon I will break that ssspirit Portalisss. You ssshall watch on, a prisoner, your own body the cage as you tear these worldsss asssunder in my name and all who dare oppose me."

His words infuriated and terrified me, but knowing the consequences should I fail only fuelled my resolve. My magic riled and pressed beneath my skin until it glowed and I could feel his oily presence retreating as I whispered, "Then I cannot lose."

I was jolted into consciousness and irritatingly so. I had yet to open my eyes, but could smell the fresh forest air and feel strong arms around my legs and waist, carrying me with haste. I was too weak to peer at my saviour, while the weight of my exhaustion pulled at my already heavy eyes. Instinctively I knew Vylnor was the one who carried me, but the speed at which we were running caused me great concern. Were we being pursued? I tried to talk, to see what was wrong and all that emerged was a mewling groan. The constant jostling was agony and my entire body felt bruised.

"Do not move!" Vylnor barked and my eyes burst open, startled, until I winced at the pressing sunlight that flashed through the forest canopy overhead. Seeing my reaction, Vylnor added more calmly, "Conserve your energy and I will get you to a healer, little Portalis."

"Still so bossy," I grumbled when he sprung forward and for a moment I felt weightless, comfortable, the sound of rushing water prominent until he landed back on the earth with an unpleasant jolt and I let out another wail of pain.

Vylnor cursed as I began to drift from consciousness once more and his colourful language started to fade. Concerned green eyes entered my blurred vision and I heard the words "Not much longer Aria" before I passed out completely.

I awoke irritable and in an unfamiliar room yet again. These fainting episodes were becoming rather tedious, although this room was much more agreeable than the criminal-infested establishment Vylnor had previously chosen.

The frilly, daffodil-yellow curtains and matching bedspread were not to my taste, but they did bring a sense of cheer and warmth to the room, which subsequently improved my otherwise gloomy mood. The door opposite my bed opened and I expected Vylnor to stride through, all brooding anger, and was left flabbergasted when Oriella stepped in, carrying pails of hot water and followed by two male elves with a tin bath.

She glanced at me in a way that implied she did not expect me to be conscious and stopped short as our eyes connected across the room.

"Aria!" she cried, dropping the buckets and sloshing water carelessly over the timber floor. Ignoring the mess, she ran to my side and grabbed my hands in earnest. "How do you feel? Oh your grandfather will be so relieved! We could not wake you, not like before and …"

"Slow down, Oriella," I interrupted, now clenching her hands with equal fervour. "What happened?"

"One moment," she stalled and turned to the two elves present. "Please send word to the First General and Jacoby Torvel."

The calm and composed warrior was now back in charge as the elves nodded and left quickly. She turned back to me, pale eyes intense. "We are in the village of Herringlea and arrived a day or so after you disappeared. The Elders wanted us to be in a strategic position, should the King call for aide. Also it was a likely place for Oromos to target, given that the town's merchant road connects unhindered to the Kingdom and the river Heron joins to the Bryn river, which flows just beyond the city's western borders."

"Yes, yes but how did *I* come to be here?" I knew I sounded dismissive, but I wanted to understand what happened to Vylnor.

"We would like to know that also," came the curious words from my favourite mage who hovered in the doorway, arms crossed and looking decidedly more harried than when I last saw him. He strode towards me with a smile. "I am glad to see you awake, Aria. You gave us a fright after your disappearance, but as it turned out, you are quite capable on your own."

He leaned over and kissed my forehead familiarly, adding, "Four healers were called in to wake you, including Oriella here, and yet you were as stubborn as an ox in winter."

"Indeed," Oriella confirmed, "apart from a few bumps, oh and a bruised rib ..." and she paused, arching a delicately winged brow suspiciously before continuing, "... we could find nothing amiss, apart from your strangely low magical reserves."

Monroe rubbed his stubbled chin in thought. "A message was also left with the innkeeper, Mrs Finley I believe, who notified us of your arrival in this room and naught else I might add."

He now stared at me closely and I wasn't sure where to begin my explanation. "Perhaps I should wait for Grandfather and Eron before I tell you what has happened?" I hedged. "But first," and I looked to the tin bath, "could I have a moment to bathe? I smell like a water possum's rear end."

Oriella chuckled before nodding at my request and thankfully went to retrieve another pail of hot water.

After an emotional greeting with Grandfather whereby a few tears were shed, I received an awkwardly prolonged embrace from Eron and was now lazily relaxing in my tin bath, enormously grateful to Oriella and the elves who had organised it. The water was deliciously warm, steam rising and the smell of honeyed lavender oils permeated the damp air around me. Sadly the luxurious experience failed to calm my otherwise frantic mind. I had managed to avoid any explanation thus far, citing uncleanliness, but how would I word the events following my abduction with Vylnor? Sighing, I closed my eyes and grasped the edges of the tin bath, when the sound of a clearing throat dissolved my momentary composure completely.

My eyes flashed open and I spotted Vylnor, lazily sitting on the window ledge, his shadowy form framed by the yellow curtains and I blurted, "Avert your gaze before I throw you out the window!"

My face was ablaze due to my rising embarrassment and frustratingly, my threat garnered little to no reaction when he huffed dismissively, "Calm down, Portalis, or we will be interrupted."

I scowled in his direction. Although he could not see my body due to the depth of the bath, I instinctually crossed my arms over my breasts and eyed him suspiciously. "Why did you bring me here? I thought I was your prisoner?" It was only then I noticed how well he looked. His deathly paleness from our last meeting had lifted and his dark eyes shone with clarity.

Those eyes soon turned vacant while he stared blankly about the room and uttered in a low voice, "I owed you for saving me, that is all."

"Well then, why not leave? Are you here to capture me again?" No reply. "Why are you here now?" I pushed, "other than to stare at me naked in the bath? Shall I add pervert to your list of transgressions also? Which is most ungentlemanly I'll have you know."

He smirked and I knew then I had successfully cracked his usually hard exterior.

"I'm no gentleman, as you are well aware," and

his gaze moved to the whipping scars across my back, eliciting an unexpected frown that I could not place. His next words however disappointed me. "My mission has not changed, Portalis, it has only been delayed." The immortal was now sounding cryptic and this annoyed me even further.

"Just be plain with me Vylnor, I am losing patience."

Jaw ticking he replied, "I will offer you a boon then. Ask me a question and I will answer honestly, we will then return to being enemies and I will drag you back to Oromos for my own self-serving purpose."

"Two," I bartered, "two questions."

Displeased he grumbled, "Fine, but make them count." He looked at me pointedly, before crossing his arms in front of his broad chest, the blood from his pervious injury no longer staining his dark leathers.

"Ramos has a war strategy, what is it?"

Vylnor tsked at my first question, seemingly disappointed and that damn blush returned. "Oromos is the foulest, most hatred-filled cess pit in the Three Realms and you think my Master and I have a general chit-chat about war strategy? My Master trusts no one and despises everyone, even his own servants. You just wasted your first question."

"Bollocks!" I cursed and splashed my fists into the water, forgetting I was naked in the gradually cooling bath. "Turn around so I can find a robe," I barked, and he countered, "Your nudity does not bother me."

Indignant I added, "Well it does me, you depraved prig, now avert your gaze!"

Rolling his eyes, Vylnor turned to look out at the clay-tiled village rooftops through the peeling window frame, while I ungraciously sloshed out of the water and rapidly donned a linen robe from the end of my bed.

"Well, don't you just look a picture of sunshine," the bastard mocked, while I stood in a disgustingly bright-yellow beacon of a bathrobe.

"Be quiet and let me think over my next question."

He moved further into the room and sat on a worn wooden chair in the corner of the chamber. His bulk appeared too big for the average piece of furniture, but still he crossed his legs, resting his ankle on his knee before sighing, "Do take your time, we have an abundance of it."

Ignoring his sarcasm, I thought back to my delirious experience when my magic attempted to heal him. "Shadow stones!" I blurted suddenly and his eyebrows almost met his hairline in surprise. "I would like to know what they are and how they work."

"Interesting," he replied and changed position on the chair. He now leant forward to rest his elbows on his knees and steepled his fingers. "Shadow stones can be generic or unique in a more powerful individual. Some are bewitched stalagmites from deep within the Oromos mountain, formed from the blood and sweat of my Master's slaves and victims, that are forcefully inserted into the chests of weaker willed servants. Those beings are almost immediately enslaved. However, ones with stronger wills go through a process called Agnicar." He held his hand up when I tried to interrupt and explained, "A soul stone spell, where the victim is usually tortured or coerced into agreeing to participate and trap their soul within a stone. This is to display loyalty to their one true Master. Should the servant betray the Master, the stone becomes corrupted. The process creates a shadow stone and turns the servant into a Hollow."

Rivetted and rather terrified I whispered, "What is a Hollow?"

"You have already met one."

And my eyes widened horrified, as I confirmed, "The healer in Oromos?"

"Yes, little Portalis, they are the ultimate servants. Magically possessed shells, to be used at the whim of our ruler."

I said nothing, alarmed to think of Vylnor's own soul stone and then understanding dawned. The darkness poisoning the green and Ramos's intrusion were all because of his Agnicar. My eyes whipped to Vylnor's in utter dismay, his answering gaze one of cold determination and now I understood why his mission was merely delayed. If he did not return with me to Oromos, he would become a Hollow for his failure. The weight of this new revelation threatened to drown me, when Vylnor abruptly rose to leave and in a desperate act of compassion, I rushed over to him and clasped his callous hand. I could not see nor determine his reaction, although his spine stiffened awkwardly at the contact. Slightly disappointed and beyond embarrassed, I released him quickly and weakly refused to meet his eyes as he silently walked to the window and disappeared into the night.

Vylnor

Vylnor was left confused about his odd encounter with the Portalis. His blatant lie about her nudity not affecting him sounded ridiculous, even to his own ears, but in her innocence she was duped by it. He thought her beautiful. The pale skin that he did see on display was dewy and slightly flushed by the warm water of her bath.

Clenching his fists on a tiled rooftop along the outskirts of the village, he thought over their conversation and was surprised she did not oust him as soon as she spotted him on the window ledge. She knew about the shadow stones, *his* soul stone to be exact. Why else would she have given him such a look of horror and grip his hand as she did. Vylnor was not used to such acts of kindness. His only interactions with the opposite sex being to sate his needs, with no emotional attachments involved, though even that had been some time ago. He struggled to remember a time when he had ever been so conflicted. This task was easy to accomplish and could have been over already. He had no loyalty to the Portalis after all. Of course she had saved his life, but that never stopped him from fulfilling his assignments before. Vylnor put himself first before all others in order to survive and over the centuries had developed this ingrained need to keep going, to keep *enduring* and for what purpose, he did not know. His memories were scarred with visions of torture, so achieving anything less than his Master's will would result in his swift demise and left Vylnor very much alone in this world.

He should end this quickly. Already he felt the negative effects of the soul stone's corruption due to his doubts, as the cold tirelessly deepened and grew within his chest. His willingness to endure fuelled his resolve and her sympathy he previously questioned was now viewed as an ending, to whatever comradery himself and the Portalis had formed. The girl would return to Oromos by his hand once more, however unsettling the thought was, and then his task would finally be complete.

Aria

Feeling forlorn, I stared out at the now empty window Vylnor had vacated mere moments before and did not turn when a gentle knock sounded at my door. Dismissively I called "Come in" and was dragged out of my reverie by a voice that had always brought me such comfort in my childhood.

"Hello Miss Aria."

"Wendy!" I cried and ran into her warm embrace. It took but a single look at her familiar face before I burst into tears, the weight of my woes having found an outlet in her comforting presence and I struggled to regain my composure.

"Now, now sweetie there is no need for that," she added gently, guiding me to the end of the bed where we took a seat, before she began to soothingly plait my wet hair.

"How are you here, Wendy? Are Berta and Geoffrey with you?" I sniffled. My tears had ceased for the moment and I wanted to hear that my friends were safe.

"We had always planned to travel to the Kingdom upon your departure from Great Barrington, however we stayed a few weeks longer to settle the farm's affairs and dismiss the farmhands for the time being." I meant to interrupt but she silenced me with a small tug on my braid, "And do not worry, they have been generously paid to last until at least next spring. Also, Geoffrey has escorted Berta and myself thus far and is currently enjoying an ale with your grandfather and Monroe in the bar."

I turned and beamed at her. "I am so glad you all arrived safely. I missed you."

She softly pinched my chin as she had when I was a child. "I missed you too, little one. Now, I would like to hear all about your travels. Your grandfather attempted to fill me in, but I hear you have your own version of events to tell."

I paused, debating what I should reveal. "Some of it you will not wish to hear," and I looked down, unable to meet her curious stare.

"I would hear it all, Aria. The good and the bad. Never be ashamed to admit the latter, as they are both a part of life and of learning."

After a moment or two's hesitation, I told Wendy of my adventures without restraint, even my most recent encounter with Vylnor. I did however omit the part where I was naked in the bath. She wouldn't care for that at all and might even smite the Oromos Lord if she ever saw him.

"Hmmm, this Vylnor is a riddle indeed, but I would not trust him, my dear. The servants of Oromos are conniving."

"I know I shouldn't feel responsible and yet I do. He saved me and is even closer to becoming one of those monsters because of it."

Wendy retorted sharply, "He is already a monster for choosing that path Aria."

I looked at her earnest blue eyes and offered a question that bothered me. "Did you not tell me before we left not to give up?"

Confusion entered her gaze. "Yes I did my darling and you have been so brave."

"And yet," I continued, "what is the difference? If I had stayed in that mountain, would I have been labelled a monster like Vylnor, if I chose to forgo the torture and accept a shadow stone? Which path would have meant my not giving up? How could I have avoided failure?"

Wendy sighed. "You have grown wise, my Aria, and I would say that you do whatever was necessary to survive and come back to us." My fatigue must have shown on my face because Wendy changed the subject. "Let us get you dressed. Eron tells me there are a couple of portals not far from here which must be secured and sealed."

"Another grandiose task that seems to have no end," I muttered, annoyance creeping into my tone.

"Crops are not sown and harvested in one day, young lady. These things are made up of many tasks, to be completed over time in order to reap the rewards."

I smiled at her reference to our farm and with her next chide, "Now enough of this self-pity, give me your robe, it is soaked and will need drying by the window."

I lowered the yellow monstrosity and frowned at her sudden gasp, shortly after realising my error. "Oh Aria!" Her hands moved to cover her mouth and, at a loss for words, I simply stood in mortified silence. Eventually I turned and moved my braid aside, offering Wendy a full view of my ruined back.

"These were not fully healed, like my ankle and wrists ... but they remind me that it was real. That it was not just in my head." I pulled the robe quickly over my shoulders and raised my palms to cover my eyes, trying to physically block out the memories, however useless the endeavour, when Wendy stopped me.

"No, my darling." And she walked over to gently lower my hands. "It is a reminder of what you *survived*. A reminder that you came back to us, and of your strength." She pulled me into a fierce hug while we cried quietly together, until the agony that had settled for so long in my chest, began to slowly lift and melt away.

♦ 16 ♦

Aria

Dressed once more in my leathers from Monroe, Wendy escorted me to the bar on the ground floor of the three-storeyed inn which was filled with not just regular patrons, but elves as well.

The inn was cosy and feminine, with more of the yellow furnishings that mirrored my room. It was then I discovered the name of the establishment, the *Heron Inn*. I thought over how appropriate yet unoriginal it was, given the river that was close by. It was remarkably opposite to the Bluffing Boar where we first took residence a few weeks ago and I was glad for it, for those patrons didn't display much in the way of manners.

There was a delicious smell of stewed vegetables in the air as I looked about the room, my eyes lighting at the familiar faces of Geoffrey and Berta, while they conversed animatedly with Grandfather and Monroe. I approached with Wendy in tow and greeted them both warmly with a firm hug.

"I am so glad to see you!"

Geoffrey harrumphed at the familiarity but Berta

patted my back gently before letting go to retake her seat at the rectangular table.

"You stole my own sentiments, Miss Aria, though I was just explaining to your grandfather here that you are in need of a constant chaperone, what with all these elven males skulking about." Dumbfounded by Berta's statement, I looked to see Monroe snickering and Grandfather's lips twitch in amusement as he replied, "Quite right, Berta. Perhaps you would care to inform the elven Generals of these sentiments, as your words are much more delicate than my own and less likely to impugn the entire elven race and their honour?"

"I think it unwise, Berta," chimed Geoffrey, which only fell on deaf ears as Berta persisted, "Well it's not appropriate I say!"

In that moment, Talos entered the inn, his authority noted by all who were present and their gazes strayed warily to the Third General who strolled quickly towards our party. His expression was hard and that of thunder, not too dissimilar from his mastered element, until he looked at me and his eyes softened.

"Aria, we are most relieved to see you back with us. The riding party is awaiting your arrival."

I nodded hurriedly and grabbed a bread roll from the table, my stomach growling when Monroe purred, "Ah General Talos, Berta here has a few ideas about Aria's safety she wished to run by you."

Berta was now beet-red and immediately dismissed Monroe. "Why of course not Monroe, they look to be doing a *fine* job," and ended her false statement with a flirtatious smile.

We exited the room, the howls of laughter from our group fading in our wake, which was swiftly followed by Berta's high-pitched scoldings. I looked to Talos and found it difficult to suppress my own chuckles when we approached Eron astride Argenti.

"Something funny, Aria?" His tone was laced with authority, so I decided not to let him in on the jest, until Talos chose the moment to wink at me as we mounted our horses and I was awash with laughter once more. Eron's confusion only added to the humour as we headed away from the inn with twenty elven warriors in tow and, to my delight, they included the riveting company of Oriella and Darnel.

The day was rather uneventful, but experiencing the village of Herringlea was a joy. The fisherman's cottages were, to my mind, a feat of engineering. Small and oddly shaped, as though they had been crammed into the undulating landscape rather than carved from it. The structures were linked together by a series of grey cobbled alleyways and meandered down gently to the small timber fishing docks in the centre of the village.

The village itself surrounded the river on both sides and was connected by one large stone bridge made to accommodate horses and carts, as well as people. It was by no means an ornate or impressive bridge, but how I longed to meander across its mild slope and enjoy the general splendour.

It was a clear day and there looked to be twice the

number of boats moored for their reflections were so incredibly clear in the crisp water. Many were worn, the purple and black colours of the Kingdom had begun to peel from their weathered surfaces, but still they floated proudly. Others, however, looked more appropriate for leisure activities, their boat rails tipped with lustrous gold paint and if circumstances were different, I would have requested a short voyage.

There were fish aplenty circulating around the docks and the smell was nearly overwhelming, had it not been for the sounds of whistling fisherman and haggling traders to distract one from the overpowering scent.

We had succeeded in locating two of the portals using the information garnered by Petriel, which thankfully had only taken till mid-afternoon to accomplish. Both were sealed without incident, but I failed to understand their odd placements. One was at the end of a woodcutter's track and the other in a most peculiar area obscured by tall water reeds on the edge of a bank, which turned out to be etched on a rather large pebble. After struggling to reach the runes, I discovered I could close the portals without uttering the spell '*sigillum*,' which both surprised and impressed my elven escorts. Even Eron had grumbled about informing Petriel of this new development, for there were no previous records of it within their historical scrolls. Rather than be alarmed, I preferred to infer the lack of information as a mere oversight, given the secretive ways of the first Portali. However, on our return, I gestured for Eron to ease the pace so I could ask him a question.

"I am aware there is little information on the runes and their placements, but is there anything you can tell me which might be of use? However small a detail?"

I think I surprised him with my question. He probably thought I meant to whine about the pace or my aching legs from riding most of the day, but he quickly masked this and replied, "The runes themselves are not a language. No two symbols are alike. They are sporadic and random. Petriel and others before him have spent many years studying them to find clues as to their magical origin and, disappointingly, there is little to show for it."

I sighed, disheartened. No answers and yet more questions.

"I suppose you could say the runes are as random as the selection process for the Portali that use them."

He looked speculatively into the distance and muttered, "Indeed," and then more loudly, "If I could take this moment to say, Aria," and my interest was immediately piqued, "please forgive me."

I blanched. "Now one moment, Eron!" But he continued nonetheless.

"I should have been more careful. Thinking you safe in my world left you vulnerable. I have arranged for an elven party of twenty to escort us in our search for portals and there are another two hundred or so warriors currently stationed around the area, should we require more force."

"Oh," I said bluntly, surprised by the number of elves as I had only spotted a few loitering around the inn.

Eron must have misread my words for he continued with a grimace, "Unfortunately strategies dictated we could not spare more, due to the irregular placement of the portals across the realms. Our forces are stretched rather thinly, until we can obtain more concrete information on where Oromos intends to strike next. I remember your nightmares and so wished to reassure you that you are safe with us."

I smiled gently at him. "You need not explain, Eron, we all have nightmares to bear, do we not? Any help you can give and have given so far is a comfort, I just hope the warriors are not needed too soon."

He looked relieved at my response, when his features turned irritated. "And should I meet that cretin Vylnor in battle, I will gladly remove his head from his shoulders on your behalf. After all …" and he grinned, "I did miss your constant whining whilst you were gone."

I couldn't help but smile back at his handsome face and playful nature, until my mind processed his words regarding Vylnor and my blood cooled. Alarmed by his declaration but unwilling to explain why, I blurted, "Darn that smile, it is nothing but a distraction!"

Realising what words I had carelessly spoken, I stiffened in my saddle and sat speechless as a faint redness grew across Eron's high cheekbones. Looking pointedly ahead to avoid his regard, my face warmed rapidly, so I hastily changed the subject and re-addressed his earlier words.

"Please understand, Eron, that I am no damsel in distress and will face dangers with or without your assistance. Do not burden yourself thinking you have failed me in anyway, besides ..." and I beamed an involuntary smile, "it's comforting to know that even someone your age still makes mistakes."

Winking at him, I drove my horse into a canter towards the Heron Inn and amusingly left the elven General gaping in my wake.

Eron had caught up to me shortly after my little getaway and we arrived back at the inn mid-afternoon to the sound of raised voices at the entrance. I was alarmed when those voices included Grandfather and Wendy, so I dismounted quickly and hurried towards the inn, when the slightly crooked front door burst open.

"That filth was in this building, Aria, and you did not call for aide! You let *Vylnor of Shadows* converse with you under our very noses!" He elongated Vylnor's rather unflattering title and I could feel Eron's eyes boring into my back. Wendy exited the inn shortly after and viciously scolded Grandfather.

"That was told to you in confidence with the understanding she would explain in more detail and you would keep a level head you buffoon!"

Grandfather studiously ignored her, his anger directed soundly towards only myself. "Well Aria, explain yourself?! Perhaps Berta was right, I should have you under escort if you are acting so rashly!"

I was hurt by his words and if they could have taken physical form, they would have struck me. I could see Eron in my periphery, face etched with irritation and arms now crossed over his chest. Our earlier comradery had been forgotten in the space of a breath and my hurt turned to anger. Did they trust me at all?

"You would judge me so quickly before asking what took place, before giving me the chance to explain ..."

Grandfather stopped me quickly. "You do not explain *after* the event young lady. That vile creature is naught but a danger to you, to all of us! Have you so quickly forgotten what happened in that mountain?! WHAT HE PUT YOU THROUGH?!" Grandfather bellowed his last words and I did not recognise this man. I could not reason with such fury and in my frustration, tears began to roll down my face.

Wendy strode over to my side and placed her hands around my shoulders when I spat, "You do not have the right to lecture me about withholding information. I *know* what he put me through, I see the scars of it every day!"

"Then why talk to him, it's not like you at all, Aria?" chimed Eron more calmly and I felt Wendy clench her hands in silent support as I admitted, "Because he saved my life and brought me here."

"He *what?*" Grandfather looked dumbfounded, as did a few of the other spectators which had gathered around our scene.

Monroe stepped forward and chose to add, "Well that shut you up my old friend. Perhaps you should have spoken to Aria privately as, despite your younger looks, your mind still seems to be going."

Grandfather turned to scowl at Monroe, who ignored him and moved past the throng to stand by my side.

"You let your fear get the better of you once more, Jacoby. Do not judge him too harshly, Aria, he worries like an old mother hen about you."

And with his lightened words, I was reminded that Grandfather had not understood what transpired between myself and Vylnor and so had acted in a blind panic.

Wendy huffed beside me, her hands now on her hips. "Well, if the stubborn man had just *listened* to me in the first place, he wouldn't have gone upsetting Aria and it will cost him a week's worth of good cooking when we get home I might add!"

I found myself grinning slightly. We were back to normality.

"Well I think that about settles it, although I would rather like to hear this tale Aria," Monroe added and gestured for us to enter the inn.

I paused before following, thinking back to the bridge over the river and decided it would be a good time for a walk to clear my head. "I will join you all shortly, I would very much like to take a walk across the stone bridge in the village."

With hunched shoulders, Grandfather replied, "May this old man escort you, my girl?"

I found it difficult to remain angry with him and sighed, "Of course" but the cut of his words still stung.

"I would ask that you take at least half our assignment of warriors with you, Aria," Eron ordered and, beyond aggravated, I pursed my lips and hissed, "That is ridiculous, we would cause a spectacle."

"It was not a request, I was being polite," he hit back and I rolled my eyes, praying to the Light for patience.

After a breath I decided to negotiate. "How about yourself and two warriors?"

"I would like to see some of the shops also," Wendy mused, probably excited to haggle a bargain.

Clicking his tongue, Eron reluctantly nodded his agreement and we set off on foot. The two warriors who joined us were Darnel, who gave me a sympathetic smile, and a new acquaintance, Wynona. She appeared a no-nonsense type in her warrior leathers and steel filigree armour plates, that to my mind, looked far too decorative to be used as battle garb. She was as appealing as the rest of the elves, but had a slightly stronger brow and nose, which, added to her ebony hair, only intensified her imposing exterior.

It didn't take long for us to reach the cobbled road adjacent to the bridge, a few of the villagers offering us wary glances as we walked past.

"There is an establishment that sells bath salts two doors up that I would like to visit," Wendy clapped excitedly before adding, "I won't be long!"

She attempted to leave but was halted by Eron's raised hand. "Darnel will escort you, Wendy."

She arched a brow at them both that implied it was unnecessary, but surprisingly did not argue and instead added politely, "If you are sure?"

"Quite sure," Eron nodded with finality, while Darnel offered Wendy his arm and accompanied her to the shops. The sound of her chattering voice grew fainter as they headed further away, while I on the other hand was left with a brooding grandfather, uptight soldier and a grumpy elven General. This walk was going to be an interesting stroll I thought and did not wait before moving towards the bridge.

I stared out across the river and leant against the bridge's stone wall, enjoying the freedom of the moment and inhaling the crisp autumn air. The sun was lowering in the sky, the orange and pinks shimmering over the water, and I felt more at peace than I had all day. Grandfather cleared his throat next to me and my eyes reluctantly moved to his face.

"I apologise, my girl. Monroe was right, I let my fear affect my judgement." He was looking at me with the utmost sincerity and held up his hands. "Now I cannot say I won't do it again, but I will try and learn to be more patient. This may come as a surprise but I too am flawed, my girl."

I feigned a look of disbelief at this statement and he chuckled before continuing in a more serious tone.

"You are my world, Aria, and these days I seem to be in constant fear for your safety and it has left me feeling …" and he begrudgingly spoke the word, "*vulnerable.*" He scrubbed his hands over his face and muttered almost inaudibly behind them, "Gosh, Monroe would have a field day if he heard this."

Warmed by his words and honesty, I moved over and hugged him. At first he stilled, probably not expecting my forgiveness so quickly, but it wasn't long before he returned the embrace gently. His warmth and the smell of pipe smoke reminded me that this was once the safest place in the world when I was a child and I decided to put the poor man out of his misery.

Stepping back, I said, "It is alright, Grandfather, and I love you too."

At this point Eron approached us. "Glad to see you two have made amends," he said, while Grandfather and I nodded in unison.

"So, my girl, mind telling us what happened whilst you were gone?" His question was tentative and I pursed my lips at him. "Yes, yes, I know, that should have been my *first* response after Wendy's announcement," he conceded, so I took pity and told him and Eron about what transpired between myself and Vylnor, while Wynona keenly scanned the surrounding area. Again, I left out the '*valore*' conversation and the part where I was bathing, as Grandfather could only handle so much information at once and I dreaded to think what Eron would say on the subject.

"You didn't owe him anything you know, Aria," was Eron's first remark to my story. "He put you in those dangerous situations and only kept you alive for his own gain."

I sighed and nodded, mostly to placate him, as I understood Vylnor had little choice in the matter.

"You must be careful, he will play on your sympathies as you are a good person, innocent of his wretched games," he warned again and I countered, "I am not completely naïve, Eron. I am fully aware of his selfish intentions, but given his scenario and being turned into a Hollow, I don't think he has much in the way of choices."

"Don't be so foolish Aria," he scolded. "The Agnicar ritual was a choice, the easier option. Rather than continue to fight the darkness, he chose to welcome it."

I retorted at his judgmental tone, "Your view of scenarios is so black and white, Eron, I do not think choosing subjugation rather than torture, was necessarily the easier option."

Grandfather was frowning. "You should have left him to those Norags, my girl, and what on earth possessed you to heal him, I don't know, but I will not scold you again. I am just relieved you are safe, those Maliskas sound horrific." He was rubbing his temples now, the tension clear in his frame. "You act with such kindness in a world that is not kind. If a choice like that ever presents itself again, please protect yourself."

I looked to the river, loathed to add to his worries but said honestly, "That is not who I am, Grandfather."

Eron's jaw tightened and Grandfather looked at me worriedly before surrendering, "I know, my girl, I know."

The sound of shattering glass from the shops below abruptly ended our conversation. Eron and Wynona responding by drawing their respective blades and the movement quickly spurred us all into action.

♦ 17 ♦

Aria

We dashed off the bridge just as Darnel was thrown through the shop window. Rapidly rolling to his feet, he stood, legs braced and with a broadsword in hand. Eron and Wynona took defensive positions in front of us, when the elven General ordered, "Take Aria back to the inn, Jacoby, and quickly, the warrior escort will protect her."

Grandfather grabbed my arm and began to pull me away from the scene, when I realised Wendy was missing.

"Wendy! Where is Wendy?!" I cried, fearful of the answer. "Darnel! *Where is Wendy?!*" I pleaded in his direction, his pale features apologetic but determined as his gaze swung back to the shop and I refused to move any further, despite Grandfather's lacklustre reassurances that Eron would ensure her safety. I knew he was as worried for her as I was, when I heard a smooth and sultry voice that turned my blood cold.

"Hello, little Portalis, did you miss us?" Kalida jumped through the shop window, twirling her curved machete as if were a mere toy, while Wendy was dragged roughly behind. She was held by a tall Maliska with braided black hair and bronze skin, her wicked short sword resting dangerously at Wendy's throat.

My mind stilled, whereas my body trembled violently with terror. I knew who these witches were, had seen what they could do and remembering the fate of the man in the forest left my magic riling beneath the surface of my skin.

"I will keep this simple, Portalis," Kalida added, ignoring Eron and the other elves and choosing to address only myself. "You will come to us willingly and without resistance, or we will be forced to slit this old dumpling's throat."

Anger surged through me and it must have shown on my face, as the Maliska holding Wendy pressed the blade even closer to her neck. I pushed the next ominous words out through gritted teeth. "If you harm her, it will be the last thing you ever do."

The witch merely smirked at my threat. "Perhaps you won't be a bore after all. Let us see what you can do," and the Maliska leader pulled a small orb from her pocket and launched it into the air. The stone burst in a sparkle of fine black shards that sent a cloud of smoke scattering into the atmosphere and Eron boomed, "Menrox!" The sky above began to shift with the promise of night and in response, Wynona retrieved a small horn from her belt and hastily blew. A rich, deep sound burst from the instrument, warming and yet intimidating. Soon I could hear the faint beat of elven armour in the distance, sparking a faint glimmer of hope within my chest which echoed, help was coming.

Kalida glared at the sound of the horn and spat a curse at Wynona. "Elven bitch!" The warrior remained composed and unbothered by the slur and simply drew her bow and arrow, pointing the weapon at the Maliska in response.

The witch's irritated gaze shot to me. "Choose, Portalis, our time is up. Come now or your precious Wendy dies."

"Don't you dare, Aria!" Wendy shrieked with some difficulty, a small trail of blood now running down her neck. I looked into her eyes which were conflicted and filled with fear, before she quickly closed them and her expression turned to one of pain. Without warning, they opened abruptly and cold determination poured forth.

"Leave Aria! *Leave me!*"

I stared stunned, full of disbelief and immediately rejected her words. My shock soon melded into anger and my heart raged as I refused to accept her death so easily. Knowing my actions would disappoint them all, I bolted towards Kalida and was sharply halted by Eron's firm grasp around my waist.

"Release me!" I screamed at him, only pausing my tirade when the black smog from the sky began to shift and take form.

An obscure shadow, humanoid in shape with no face and thick midnight armour veined in red stood before us at least three stories tall. Despite its billowing form, the armour solidified around its being and its weight alone began to crack the centuries old cobbles beneath its feet. Any movement faltered in the face of such an enemy and I could hear the villagers' cries of alarm surround us as they began to flee in haste.

"Head for the inn!" Eron roared, attempting to direct the chaos, while fear held me firmly gripped in its talons and I remained speechless, not knowing what I should do, but knowing that I must act.

I dragged my eyes away from the Menrox and clawed at Eron's leather-clad arm, determined to break free.

"You will cease your struggling, Aria, they cannot have you! Don't you see, they will kill Wendy either way!"

Tears streaked down my face as I took in Wendy's blue eyes and the malicious smiles of the Maliskas. "You cannot know that! I will get to her! I *must* get to her Eron!" I aimed an elbow at his face haphazardly, but he dodged the move easily and continued to drag me further away. In my desperation, I pleaded with Grandfather, "Do *something*! This is Wendy, *our Wendy*!" My words ended on a shriek while he remained unmoving, sword braced before him and his face filled with indecision.

"A shame," Kalida tutted, eyeing her nails as if bored before clicking her fingers. The Maliska's blade drew back and time slowed, Wendy's eyes clenching in agony when the cold steel was slid between her ribs and my world shattered.

The witch released her body which collapsed unmoving to the floor, blood pooling around her and I became nothing but a typhoon of grief and rage. My magic spilled from every pore of my body uncontrolled and I did nothing to stop it. Soon my distorted vision disappeared completely beneath hues of gold and were replaced by nothing but a vengeful hatred directed fully at the witches. And only when their eyes turned to concern and they held their weapons protectively at their fronts, did my magic twist into a state of madness and unleash itself in an explosion of wrath.

Eron

Eron knew his decision would end in her hatred of him, but he could not allow Aria to be taken again. She struggled against him viciously, screaming for Jacoby to intervene, but there was little the man could do in such a situation. He had to protect Aria from her naivety. They would kill Wendy either way, whether it be now or after they imprisoned her. Maliskas were cruel and conniving and he refused to see Aria in their grasp, but he did not anticipate what would happen next.

Suddenly thrown backwards by a surge of Aria's magic, Eron struggled to right himself and was not the only one. Both parties had been flung thirty paces or so from their original positions and Aria now had a clear path in front of her, with which to reach Wendy's fallen form.

Her eyes flashed gold as she vaulted towards Wendy, hands immediately drawn down to the wound and he could see the injured woman attempting to speak. Even with his enhanced hearing, Eron could barely discern her pained words.

"It's OK my darling," she uttered, the blood climbing her throat now hindering her speech, and he looked to Aria's face to gauge her reaction. It was devoid of emotion, her power surging through her form, unchecked and unrestrained, before her ethereal voice echoed in reply, "You will not leave me." A flash of light erupted from Aria, while glowing runes left her body in a rush and Eron found himself shielding his eyes from the piercing glare.

The Menrox screeched its anger at the intense glow and Eron bellowed his orders in the distraction. "Darnel to Aria! Wynona to me! We must halt the Menrox until reinforcements arrive!"

Calling *"mirorst!"* Eron's ice shield materialised along his left forearm, before he charged at the unnatural creature and drew its attention. From his knowledge, Eron knew that the Menrox were not particularly fast, but what they lacked in speed they made up for in strength. Their armour was notoriously tough, made from compressed Oromos bedrock and nearly unbreakable. In previous battles, it had taken at least two or three powerful elven warriors to crack, but once you were through, they merely disintegrated into a cluster of Skygge demons and became easier to dispatch.

If he and Wynona could hold off the Menrox until Havrel and Talos arrived with reinforcements, they would stand a better chance of dispatching it. Eron's thoughts turned to defensive manoeuvres, for he could not attack the creature head-on, not even to summon the river. Given the close quarters of the fleeing mortals and his companions, it was too great a risk to launch such a large-scaled assault with no guarantee of success, so instead he called, "*glacioterra!*"

The stone cobbles and earth around the Menrox's feet froze into a thick sheet of ice and Eron hoped the slippery surface would provide an opportunity to unbalance its bulk and force the giant to its knees. Sadly that didn't happen. The sheer weight of the Menrox ultimately broke through the ice and even the earth beneath. Eron's magic had no effect on its footing, while in the same dial Wynona's air propelled arrows, which would normally pierce mortal armour, failed to inflict any damage at all and aggravatingly just ricocheted off the creature's armoured exterior.

Each Menrox carried different weapons and this one's weapon of choice was an axe, which it swung in a wide berth, intending to hit both Eron and Wynona in a single strike. Using their immortal speed, they dodged quickly, the axe now chasing their forms and Eron cursed when he noticed that the Maliskas were now up and moving, two more having been added to their ranks. He could hear the howl of Norags in the distance and knew that when the sun disappeared completely below the horizon, the Skygge demons would also enter the fray.

Another portal must be close, one they remained clueless of. Cursing, Eron eyed Jacoby and Darnel who stood on opposite sides of Aria, still in her magic-infused trance while she gripped Wendy's wounded body. He trusted his warrior and Aria's elder to keep her safe until his kin arrived, so dodging another swing, he danced with the Menrox, conserving his energy, and waited patiently for the right moment to strike.

Aria

All I saw was Wendy. I could make out her clammy features and pale lips, but I could not feel my hands on her wound. There was so much blood and yet I watched on like an unfeeling spectator and had never experienced the like before.

My melodious voice was foreign and yet not. It was knowing and ancient, a part of me and yet separate and I struggled to find a way of understanding how to harness it. Symbols crossed through my vision, portal runes I realised, but uniquely altered and I knew instinctively they were my *own*.

I felt my consciousness fade into the background, my ability to take control over my own body almost non-existent and the experience was unsettling, perhaps frightening, but the consequences should I remain in such a state would be very dangerous indeed.

My family and friends were in peril. I could not sit by motionless and rely on my magic alone to save us, it was too volatile. My power flared demandingly, as if in response to my thoughts and I instinctively wrestled to suppress it, or to at least gain some measure of control. Instead it lashed out, my body at odds with itself and my back arched painfully under the onslaught. My bloodied hands gripped the sides of my head, nails scraping across my scalp in some vague attempt to halt the pain and I could not understand why this was happening.

My magic and I were one and the same, it would not benefit from hurting me. Perhaps fighting back only meant that I was hurting myself. It was a risk, but I had to try accepting my magic, it was the only route I could see through the agony. Wendy was counting on me and I refused to let her down. Thinking of the only mother figure I had ever known, memories began to swirl of her in my childhood. Tending to injuries, telling tales before I would slumber, the smell of my favourite apple pies baking in the kitchen and soon, my mind let go. With great trust, I embraced the deeply veiled root of my power as though an old friend and a warming beam of light spread from my core, to illuminate every vein.

My consciousness slammed violently back into my body, while my features began to shift and burn. Limbs began to stretch. Leaner and thinner and filled with a newfound strength and speed while my magic continued to struggle for an outlet as it hummed restlessly just below my skin, even through to the tips of my hair.

Wendy was now breathing gently beneath my hands, the blood now ceased its pouring and I sobbed in relief, innately knowing that there was nothing more to be done. The sounds of clashing blades and cursing reached my ears, while I moved my tender limbs cautiously to study my surroundings which now appeared crisper, sharper. Two more Maliskas charged towards Grandfather and Darnel, Kalida and the braided one poised on the outside of the fray, ready to kill at the first opportunity. I blinked my eyes rapidly, unnerved at the finer detail. Even the gritty remains of shadow drifting in the soft breeze were now highlighted by my sight, from what was previously just a dark cloud. The fine threads coming loose from the Maliska's braids were distinguishable and I turned my new focus onto the bitch who stabbed Wendy. As though she felt my gaze, her own dark eyes turned to me in challenge and I snarled, "You shall not go unpunished," before launching at Wendy's attacker with an unrestrained fury.

Vylnor

Vylnor held his position downwind behind a thick chimney stack and currently perched atop one of the river front cottages. The Scorgue stone housing the Menrox demon splintered into a cloud of shadow as it was released into the sky and he cursed Kalida. Always one to show off when speed and efficiency were more effective. That was why many Maliskas were not promoted into the Oromos ranks and stayed as merely followers, unable to see the bigger picture and wholly reliant on their Queen.

That dust was now a beacon for the elven reinforcements to follow before darkness completely fell and put added pressure on his mission to obtain the Portalis. Having previously convinced himself this was his next course of action, he hesitated. Instead choosing to assess the events unfolding before him. He could feel Aria's anger and her struggle, like a subtle beat in his subconscious. It was *wrong*, Vylnor thought, this connection he did not understand or expect between them. How could he feel this mortal's emotions and yet have barely any of his own? It vexed him fiercely, complicating matters which should be simple and interfering with his task. More pointedly, it risked his future, or what was left of it.

His eyes spied a rush of activity, when the elven oaf now tried to subdue an irate Aria, until Kalida unwisely ordered her subordinate to end the older woman's life.

"Kalida, you cretin, that was your best bargaining tool," Vylnor spat scornfully under his breath, when unexpectedly he was struck by a wave of Aria's all-consuming grief. The weight of emotion sent him staggering across the clay roof tiles, a clawed hand pressed to his chest while he tried and failed to dispel the horrid emotions. Thankfully it wasn't long before the unwelcomed feeling was cut short by a burst of power the Portalis released in retaliation and Vylnor righted himself once more, unnerved by his overly intimate connection to her.

Meanwhile the girl was now completely exposed, her focus limited merely to this Wendy with only a mediocre elf and the old man to protect her from four Maliskas. Not quite believing what he was about to do, Vylnor threw himself off the tiled roof and sprinted down the cobbled street towards the fight. Reaching an alleyway between the set of riverfront buildings and almost parallel to Kalida, Vylnor remained hidden and ready to intervene at a moment's notice. Just before he struck, he was halted by a shift he felt in the Portalis's power.

It was stunningly bright and he immediately clambered onto the nearest rooftop, intent on obtaining a better vantage point and reluctant to be caught off guard again. An unknown enemy was a dangerous enemy after all and when he reached the pitch of the roof, clay tiles rumbling in his haste, he was amazed to witness Aria's power changing, *moulding.*

It now flowed through her body unobstructed. Where once there was resistance, the magical barrier now melted away and her mortal shell with it. Leaner frame, unbound auburn hair set aflame with red and golden hues of light, her defined cheekbones and flawless features emphasised her now pointed ears.

"It cannot be," he hissed, stunned by what was occurring. Vylnor broke out into a cold sweat, nerves and excitement greeting him like an old memory, as understanding struck. He had heard the elven tales and dismissed them as folly, but now, awash with a euphoric sensation he had never felt before, he knew the stories to be true. Never for one moment did Vylnor expect to have a connection to anyone, let alone *the* connection that all elven kind craved. Him, a warped version of an elf with no memories and barely a soul, had found its other half. Aria was his mate and there was little else he could say to this revelation, other than, "*Shit.*"

Aria

I launched myself at the Maliska, but my movements were fast, *too* fast. Not only aided by my magic, I felt a change in my limbs and the speed I once needed magic to achieve was now naturally my own.

The Maliska clearly wasn't expecting this burst of speed either, for I barrelled into her before she had a chance to move her blade and we tumbled to the ground. Grappling one another, the Maliska rose on top of me, losing her blade in the chaos and began to punch me in the face. One shot, two, I was surprised at the dulled pain I felt, expecting the strikes to be more severe as I grabbed her fist after the third hit and stopped its course.

The look of disbelief on her face was priceless, before she added more pressure into her arm and the look soon morphed into nothing but contempt and disdain. I thrust my palm into her chest and with limbs that were now filled by a rush of magic, threw the witch off me. After jarringly rolling across the cobbles, she managed to spring to her feet a few paces away and threw herself back eagerly in my direction. Her target now obvious, I cursed myself for not bringing my blade on our little bridge excursion, as she flew across the street for her own that laid harmlessly on the floor. I may not be the best swordsman but fighting a blade with my bare hands did not seem like the best option. Remembering the battle at Port Framlington, I pondered whether I could create another arrow, but must have dallied too long when, before I knew it, the Maliska was swinging her short sword at my neck.

"Do not kill her, Marcia you fool!" Kalida growled as I ducked low and barely dodged the attack. My dread rose as the severity of the situation worsened, so with little else to do I thrust my magic into my palms and encouraged my limbs to become fluid and defensive. Swiping my hand at an approaching Marcia, she screeched and retreated back, with light bloodied claw marks slashed across her chest. Amazed, I looked down to see that instead of the blade I was aiming for, my nails had elongated into vicious claws, bright and deadly.

Marcia sneered, "I may have to keep you alive, but I will gladly tear your arms off with my teeth," and she rushed towards me.

We clashed head-on, both narrowly missing each other's weapons before she smashed the pommel of her short sword into my face. Pain exploded across my forehead and I crumpled to my knees, stunned, when the witch jumped onto my back. Using my claws, I imbedded them into her shoulders and flipped her over my head, before locking my forearm around her neck. Frustratingly, she held my left hand at bay and we stilled briefly, at a momentary impasse.

Clearly frustrated, Marcia spat, "Before we drag you back to the Master, I will make sure you watch while we devour that little dumpling before your eyes," and her jaws clamped around my arm.

I screamed a torturous sound as she began to shake her head from side to side, tearing at my flesh. I had to stop this and quickly, so did not consider my next move and just ripped my left arm free of her hold. With a vision blurred by tears, I stabbed my free hand under her top jaw to stop the assault and Marcia wailed. The sound so profound, I felt it tremble from my hand and up my arm.

My claws had torn and ripped out some of her teeth and I learnt quickly that a pained Maliska was an even more dangerous threat. In a vicious attempt to hasten her release, Marcia attacked in earnest and her left elbow began assaulting my exposed rib cage. With each bruising strike that landed, my determination solidified a bit more, thoughts of Wendy resurfacing and fuelling my fury until I sneered through the agony, "You will not get the chance, you stupid bitch."

Channelling my magic into my arm and hoping to rip the appendage free, I pulled my hand up, but to my horror, the top of her skull was pulled away with it. A wet crunching noise was the only sound that registered before her lifeless body fell to the ground and I stilled, mortified. *What had I done?*

♦ 18 ♦

Aria

Too much, it was too much magic and I began to retch at the sight of her decapitated head on the ground. Blood that was an unnaturally dark shade of red now coated my trembling and clawless hand like a glove, while my eyes darted about frantically, guiltily, until I saw Kalida eyeing me intensely just a few paces away. I was surprised that I saw no hatred or revenge in her gaze, but more disturbingly, challenge.

I staggered back a few steps, both arms hanging limply by my sides and I knew I was in trouble. Even without my injuries, it would have been nearly impossible to keep up with the leading Maliska. She strode forward and toed Marcia's head with disgust while I carefully retreated further.

"What a disappointment you are, Marcia, but no matter ..." and she grinned wickedly, "I will drag the Portalis back to Oromos myself," and the witch lunged.

I braced my trembling legs, preparing to dodge if that was at all possible, but before the assault could land, an arm gripped me around the waist and I was hauled out of her path.

"Drink this!" Vylnor barked, his arm like a vice around my middle as he thrust a vial in front of my face. Hesitantly I asked, "What is it?"

"Think I'd poison you, pretty girl?" he crooned and I didn't reply, still unsure of this immortal's motives, while he held me several inches off the ground and directly opposite to a seething Kalida. Impatient, he growled, "It's a healing potion, you fool," and thrust my body behind him, just as Kalida swiped at us with her machete.

Arms jolted, I cried out in pain and Vylnor cursed before calling "*infernous!*" and released a ball of fire at the witch, who dove out of its path with lethal grace before retreating back several steps. Vylnor turned to me, grabbed my hair roughly and pulled my head back to dump the vial's contents into my mouth.

"Drink the potion, you stubborn female!"

I spluttered, both at the awful taste but also in outrage at his treatment, when, in less than a dial, the painful throbbing in my hand and arm began to subside. I looked down to see the bite marks and slices in my flesh were still a garish red, but at least they had sealed.

Looking back to the scene before me, Vylnor and Kalida had halted their movements in favour of staring each other down, the witch jeering, "How much longer do you have, Vylnor? This treachery will not go unpunished as you well know, and I will enjoy seeing you act like a dog."

Vylnor's face however, remained impassive. "If that

is the case, then I will make sure you are not alive to witness it," and they slammed into one another. They hacked and parried, deadly wielders of forged steel and I quickly realised I had no stake in this fight, so hastily moved to a safer spot.

Eron, Wynona and the Menrox had relocated further up the river and I assumed the move was strategic, to distract the enemy until reinforcements could arrive, when Grandfather's alarmed voice drew me from my musings.

"Get out of here, Aria! Find Monroe!" He was breathing heavily, sword raised as he faced off against another Maliska, heavily aided by Darnel who was launching large cobbles and earth in their direction, keeping both of them at bay. Howls began to echo from the other side of the bridge. A bridge that mere hours ago I thought lovely, quickly morphed into a pathway that beckoned the darkness and its malice, just as the sun lowered behind the horizon and brought with it dusk. My anxious gaze watched the structure, while a gathering shadow began to thicken at its peak. A large group of Skygge demons had congregated and were now moving towards us, while the ground rumbled from the heavy footing of the Menrox. The gloomy atmosphere carried the promise of violence and despair and left an ominous mood in its wake, my only thought being, *where were the elves?*

"Having fun without me, Jacoby!" a familiar voice sung through the air and offered immediate relief as

Monroe jumped into the fight with relish and swiped at a Maliska with his glowing blade. Talos chose the same moment to appear, leading a company of elven warriors through the winding and abandoned streets. Worryingly, they all appeared rather battle worn and when the Third General's eyes locked onto the witches he called scathingly, "*aurasila!*" The magically summoned rush of air blasted both Maliskas across the cobbles, before his orders rang out across the space.

"Warriors to the bridge and halt the tide of demon filth!"

I sprinted in his direction and noticed his eyes glimmered with relief as he recognised me.

"Aria! Stay behind the elven line and only interfere if absolutely necessary."

But before he could issue any more ridiculous orders, I begged, "Please get Wendy out of here!" Her unconscious form remained where I had left her and was currently guarded by Grandfather, who had not left her side.

"Merrill!" Talos called and a female elf sporting a helm that covered most of her black hair stepped forward. "Take Wendy back to the Heron Inn, it is now secure and ask that Oriella see to her immediately."

She nodded and moved on swift feet towards Wendy, lifting her up with ease, before dashing away from the battle. I grabbed Talos's hand gratefully, his returning smile forced while he took in my appearance.

"What a surprise you are, Aria," he murmured, and I returned his look with one of confusion, when he suddenly ordered, "Darnel, form a perimeter, they must not reach the townsfolk!" Turning to me once more, Talos repeated firmly, "Stay behind the lines, Aria, myself and Erondriel will deal with the Menrox." The male rushed in Eron's direction and I hoped their combined power would be enough to destroy that monster.

Now satisfied that Wendy was safe, I drew my attention back to the growing number of Skygge demons on the bridge and noticed that Vylnor and Kalida had disappeared, along with the two other remaining Maliskas.

Soon after, Monroe and Grandfather ran to me, the mage's words suspicious, "Keep your eyes peeled. The Maliskas have gone into hiding, meaning one of two things, retreat or regroup. Let us hope it's the former and not the latter. We were lucky that only one leader was here," and my head turned sharply at this revelation.

"There is more than just Kalida?!"

"Ah, so that's her name, such a beauty, if not for that unnaturally huge mouth and sharp teeth. She'd talk your ears off and bite your ..."

"Monroe, focus!" Grandfather interrupted, though I could garner what the rest of Monroe's sentence would have been and chuckled.

"There are four leaders of the Maliskas. They each hold sway within the barren Oromos wastes. Trust me when I say, we don't want to be caught with them in a battle, without an army of soldiers at our backs. Now if you'll excuse me, my sword has a meeting with a few

Skygge demons." And the mage swiftly darted off in the direction of the bridge, twirling his luminescent sword as he ran.

"Aria?" I turned my attention from Monroe's shrinking back and met Grandfather's eyes. He was staring at my face with a mixture of confusion and awe.

"I never knew, or even thought?" I frowned, concerned by his stuttering. "What is it, Grandfather?" His actions baffled me and I feared the battle had taken its toll on him mentally as well as physically.

"You are elven."

His unbelievable statement startled me, even when he gestured to my appearance with his free hand, and I stammered, *"Wwhat?!"*

"Not that it makes any difference," he rushed to reassure me, while my hand absently felt for the newly pointed tips of my ears and I pulled them away sharply, when his claim had been confirmed.

"How?" I whispered, stunned and feeling slightly nauseous, until he steered my worries back to the present.

"There will be time enough to find out, for now you will head back to the Heron Inn and the healers." His voice had turned stern and I knew it would be difficult to argue, when a shout of alarm reached us and the word "Norags!" echoed from the elven party, sparking our attention.

Four of the beasts charged across the bridge and tore viciously into the elven lines, one having caught an unsuspecting elf by the arm and began to drag him across the cobbles. Shortly after, the elf went limp, his loose helm having fallen from his head during the clash and left his dark, unbound hair whipping in his wake.

"Ardon!" cried another warrior who immediately gave chase, and I knew I could not stand by and do nothing. Sprinting away from my protesting grandfather, I realised quickly that the Norags were fast, despite their bulk. I knew they were nimble on their feet from our last interaction with Vylnor, but with an open path ahead of it, its speed was incredible.

My elven comrade struggled to keep pace and fell behind, still desperately shouting, "*Ardon!*" Upon hearing his urgency, I channelled my magic into a burst of speed and in less than a dial, drew alongside the hulking beast. With no weapon to hand, I did the only think I could think of and rammed its flank with my shoulder to try and stop its course, only to stagger jarringly back. With gritted teeth, I ran towards it once more, my razor claws extending from my nails, and leapt with a silent prayer onto the Norag's back. Unsurprisingly, its pace didn't alter while it continued to drag its unconscious victim further away and I could see the blood as it poured from Ardon's ravaged arm, his body hanging loosely from it like a rag doll. Deciding quickly, I grabbed the Norag's thick, dark pelt and slashed frantically with my claws, aiming to startle it into releasing the elf. To my astonishment, my glowing claws carved through its neck like butter and the creature staggered, before falling sharply to the ground. The unexpected movement meant I was thrown roughly across the cobbled path, my shoulder first to hit the solid floor as I rolled and finally came to halt.

I lay dazed for a moment or two, winded and coughing before gingerly testing my abused body and struggling to my feet. A sharp pain burst from my left shoulder and I quickly realised it had been dislocated, for it draped uselessly beside me.

"Tis not my best day," I grumbled moodily to no one in particular, my throbbing head hissing in protest while I attempted to support my injured shoulder and stave off the resulting tears.

The elf who had been chasing Ardon arrived by his side and scooped him up protectively in his arms. The stark relief that lit across his pointed features only added to my own, while he repeated his thanks to myself and his Goddess Anala. Feeling uncomfortable at the receiving end of such gratitude but unwilling to cause offence, I held the elf's thankful gaze, when his eyes widened sharply and he bellowed, "Miss Aria, *move!*" I felt the rumble of earth beneath my feet first, before the whistling sound of a blade splitting air reached my ears and in the space of a breath, I was thrust from harm's way.

"Look where you are going, Portalis, I'm tired of rescuing you." I snorted at the arrogant boar who currently held me aloft in his arms and countered, "Is that what you did? Forgive me for thinking otherwise while we are chased by a giant demon harbouring an axe."

The male's lips twitched, his eyes lighting in challenge

when Eron boomed, "*Vylnor of Shadows!*" interrupting our petulant conversation. "Release her or feel the wrath of my blade!"

"Dramatic, interfering snowball," Vylnor growled, before taunting the elven General. "Shouldn't you be focusing on the enemy you have yet to defeat?" And he manoeuvred us out of the path of a second swing, yet still the Menrox continued to stalk our steps. Our next vault to avoid the axe jarred my shoulder and I cried out in pain.

"I'm out of healing potions in case you ask, girl. You seem to be incapable of avoiding injury, even with your newly acquired immortal strength."

I ground my teeth. "I do not recall asking in either instance and you could always let me go."

He scoffed, "And what, let you be in the hands of that simpleton General? I think not."

I peered at him, his answers were always so unexpected and confusing. Why did it matter if Eron was capable or not? And why wasn't he fleeing us towards Oromos?

"So what's the plan? Keep jolting me about for eternity? Some rescue."

"Depends how long those elven fools take to dispatch the Menrox. Unfortunately for you, the demons and Norags will follow you like a moth to flame, so as the bulk of elven forces are here, we shall remain until the opportune moment presents itself."

I looked at him, incredulous. "You would have us wait on the sidelines rather than help?"

Vylnor's eyes narrowed, his gaze pointed. "I am no

hero, pretty girl. Do not mistake me for one."

His words were disappointing, despite their honesty, and I pursed my lips in irritation, quickly noticing Vylnor's gaze had tracked the movement. Suddenly I was very aware of our close proximity, my cheeks growing warm under such perusal and yet neither of us were willing to break the stare. Eron's unexpected roar cut through the pounding in my ears, thankfully releasing us from the confounding moment.

"Talos now!" The Third General raised his arms to the sky and called "*lisulyn!*" when a bolt of lightning was unleashed from the encroaching clouds and struck the Menrox squarely in the chest, cracking its armour.

"Not bad," Vylnor muttered begrudgingly, and I ignored our oddly intimate encounter, in favour of berating him. "If you know how to kill it then do so, before other people get hurt, you stubborn old ass!"

He smirked. "Old?" And I could only whine in frustration. "*That* is all you took from my words!" His features quickly snapped back into the composed Vylnor I was accustomed to. "Need I remind you, Portalis, of our previous discussion? Helping is not really on my agenda."

Of *course*. How could I have forgotten the shadow stone corruption? I understood then that Vylnor *was* helping, in the limited way he could. I let out another pained curse, when the Oromos Lord none too gently rushed us out of the Menrox's path to land atop a cottage roof.

"Fix it!" I blurted. "Fix my arm!"

His response was sarcastic. "I don't recall receiving my healer's guild approval," when I growled, "Just do it! You can't dislocate it again and I know you can set it, no matter how much you protest otherwise."

He shifted me in his arms and scouted the area before jumping into a cottage's small courtyard and placed me on the floor. Impatiently he barked, "Sit up straight," and kneeled down to pick up my affected arm by the wrist. I tried not to wince as he moved it in line with my shoulder and pulled sharply forward. Pain burst from my shoulder and I wailed, slumping forward while Vylnor's hand remained at my collarbone and the only barrier keeping my body from toppling over completely.

Thankfully it didn't take long for the pain to dull to an acceptable ache and I begrudgingly thanked the Oromos Lord who swiftly moved away. I looked up to see his broad back and shoulders were unusually tense.

"This is where I leave you."

He hesitated briefly before retrieving an item from his person. "Think before you act, girl, and do not force me to interfere again."

Vylnor threw a blade to the floor, the sound of steel ringing against stone startled me, but it did not take long to register what the weapon was and its significance. It was Grandfather's gift and the one Vylnor had stolen from me those weeks ago in Oromos. My eyes widened in shock at seeing the small piece of elven steel and before I had the chance to interrogate him further, Vylnor launched himself over the courtyard wall and willingly left me alone.

Vylnor

Vylnor faced another infernal struggle as he left the Portalis, nay *Aria*, in the courtyard. Watching another's pain had never affected him before, but he worried for her and found himself seeking her out to ensure her safety. The unwanted feeling was bothersome and he now recognised the emotion he felt when he saw the scars across Aria's back at the inn. *Guilt.* It was guilt. How could he ever atone for hurting the female that turned out to be his mate? Maybe this was another form of torture these worlds intended to throw at him, for some heinous past transgression. He had already come to terms with his role in life as a servant to his Master, with no room in his psyche for any other possibilities. It had been that way for so long, that how his actions affected others meant very little to him. Vylnor thought very little of himself, truth be told. Unable to remember his past, any family or positive experiences, he was cold and unapproachable and even though his meetings with Aria had been few, she had managed to make him smile. To make him *feel* again.

He watched her from a distance as she stood and moved her arm slowly to test its limits, before walking unsteadily over to the blade. Picking it up, she perused it thoughtfully for a moment or two before leaping over the short courtyard wall and towards the General.

Vylnor's elven blood raged at seeing her care for that sorry excuse for an elf and despite his own rational thoughts on the subject, his protective instincts had already begun to leech out from within and the complete lack of control really ticked him off. He even pondered killing the elf in that moment, but thought better of it for he knew Aria would not be pleased. When had he begun to care for her opinion?

Vylnor shook his head, disgusted with himself and the mewling wretch he was becoming. It wouldn't be long before they destroyed the Menrox, so with any luck, Vylnor wouldn't need to get involved. After all, the darkness within him was spreading, his soul stone fading and every move was risky and would only quicken the process if he did not act wisely. Unfortunately for him, luck was not on his side as he caught sight of several shadows moving in from the north and heading towards his mate. Kalida had not scarpered as he suspected after their fight. Her actions were unsurprising, given that she was bloodthirsty and stubborn, only wishing to please her Queen. Vylnor would be forced to intervene and as there was no chance of Aria accepting him, he reasoned that perhaps this was as far as he was supposed to go. Circumstances had brought him to this point and if he became a Hollow to save her beautiful soul, then so be it.

♦ 19 ♦

Aria

After testing my tender shoulder for the extent of
movement, I walked over and picked up the blade.
My blade. I turned the light weapon over in my hands
and knew this unexpected action from Vylnor was
momentous, but with little time to ponder it, I placed
the elven dagger in my belt and headed towards Eron.
I knew I had to help defeat the Menrox even if they
wished that I avoid the danger, but more importantly,
Grandfather was within its midst and I couldn't risk him
being hurt, not after what happened to Wendy. Once
the Menrox was defeated, we could focus our collective
efforts on the Skygge demons and Norags. I wasn't so
naïve to think the tide of battle couldn't swiftly turn,
but a brief scan of the ongoing conflict showed that the
elven fighters were more than capable of handling their
enemies. A few of them unleashed small bursts of fire at
the Norags, while others channelled water from the river
to form shields and ice shards to be used as arrows. Their
skill and speed were impressive, as barrage after barrage
of ice arrows were released against their opponents and
held off almost all of the enemy's progress. If I looked

carefully, I could see glimpses of Monroe's lux sword dipping in and out of the Skygge demons' shadows. His movements were quick and sporadic, which led me to hope that the mage hadn't been injured at all. But we needed to end this and soon.

So moving cautiously towards the Menrox and being careful not to garner its attention, I halted when a gnawing feeling gripped my stomach. It felt as though a set of malicious eyes were burrowing into the back of my skull and I paused at the sickening feeling. Scanning the immediate area, my heart began to thunder when I noticed a shadow creeping out from one of the many alleyways. As it edged closer to the northern side of Eron and Talos, I spun nimbly on my feet and bolted towards my comrades before bellowing a desperate warning – *"AMBUSH!"*

My outburst garnered stares of concern from Eron and Wynona, who looked about anxiously, now on high alert. Talos and Grandfather, however, failed to respond and I feared they had not heard my warning when Kalida suddenly made her first move. She launched herself from a nearby rooftop and tackled Wynona to the ground. The sounds of the scuffle grew louder at my approach but I dared not interfere, as Wynona grunted *"gerus"* and blasted a jet of air at the witch, throwing her off successfully. But the Maliska was not so easily deterred as she drew four throwing knives and released them directly at the elven warrior who, to my relief, deflected with another gust of wind. Eron was currently dodging a swing from the Menrox, but after recognising his comrade was in trouble, soon re-directed his movements and headed straight towards Wynona, only to be intercepted by two more Maliskas. The first was stocky, with short grey hair and a stark tattoo lined across her face, while the other was a brunette sporting twin braids that would have lent her an innocent air, had she not been snarling with those vicious teeth. Both harboured short swords, which now pointed menacingly towards Eron. Their movements were slick and calculated as they eyed each other conspiratorially and reminded me of the snakes which hid in the long grasses back home.

Undeterred, Eron pushed forward and was now summoning ice blades and deflecting their assaults with his long sword, almost making the process look easy. I glanced back to see Kalida striking her machete repeatedly against Wynona's bow, but the elven warrior held her position, even as deep notches were being hacked out of the famously strong cedaris wood.

During her vicious advance, I soon realised that Kalida was herding Wynona backwards and towards the ever-encroaching Menrox. The witch leader was effectively cornering the elf and forcing her to fight on both fronts. I could see Wynona struggling. Her intent eyes so focused on keeping Kalida at bay, that she failed to notice the Menrox approaching, so wailed my alarm, "Wynona, *move!*"

But it was too late. Kalida deflected Wynona's lunge and kicked the female warrior violently backwards and into the demon's waiting axe.

"*MIRORST!*" roared Eron, as a path of jagged ice speared across the earth and arced into a shield at Wynona's back, but it was not enough. I saw the shock cross Wynona's beautiful face as the tainted steel was brought down, shattering through Eron's desperate barrier and split her torso from shoulder to hip, cutting her in two.

I screamed. Wanting to shut my eyes against such brutality. Against the harrowing sound of splintering ice that echoed Wynona's destroyed future, but found I could not look away. Even as the top half of her body fell to the iced cobblestones and her lower half followed. I would witness Wynona's valiant fall, even though it threatened to break me.

The brutality caused uncontrollable tremors to wrack my body and Eron's roar of grief only heightened my reaction. In a rush of irrepressible anger, I flung out my hand, power pushing sharply from my arm, and threw Kalida across the riverfront and into the once tranquil waters with a garbled splash. Regrettably, the Menrox behind her remained unmoving, while I could only reflect on my failings. Late, I was too *late*.

Internally I wept, screamed and scolded myself, my mind in a chaotic state, but it was all useless and futile. Wynona was dead and while I remained clueless as to the depths or scope of my powers, it meant that ultimately I was unreliable and unfit to help my comrades. I pushed aside the gnawing guilt and tried to stop the tears from falling down my cheeks. I had to gain some measure of control. Eron attacked the Maliskas with renewed vigour, his rage almost palpable while Grandfather attempted to distract the Menrox in whatever way he could. Sadly, he too was not equipped to deal with this opponent just as I was not, but still he *tried*. The Third General's face was contorted with rage, but his movements remained stilted and I wondered why, until I felt him gathering power, most likely for a second attack. It meant we were without Talos's aid for the time being so I trained my eyes on the Menrox as it twisted, its heavy movements vibrating the cobbles under my feet and I knew its next target.

Flinging myself forward, I glided over the ground and watched while the two Maliskas forced Eron closer to the demon, using the same vile tactic as Kalida to ensure their victory. I could not let that happen to Eron. I would *not* let that happen to Eron. But Eron was the First General of Elavon, he was no one's victim and held his ground. Upon realising this, the Maliskas looked to one another and a momentary madness entered their eyes. Suddenly, they threw their short swords directly at Elavon's General and charged him while he was busy deflecting the random assault. As they converged upon him, he struck the tattooed witch away with his shield before the second Maliska jumped and twisted her legs around his shoulders. Struggling for balance, Eron was brought down by the witch, the second jumping into the fray and they both grappled fiercely for his weapon. Using their combined weight to hold him to the floor, it was soon evident that it would not be enough. Eron heaved a great breath and threw them off his body. With little warning but the rumble of earth, the Menrox was now upon them and again brought down its wicked axe. Not breaking my stride, I grabbed the two fallen short swords and vaulted the remaining distance to my friend. Without much time to consider my next move, all I could do was cross the two blades above my head and channel as much magic into my body as I could muster.

The axe collided with my swords as though fuelled with the weight of the Ingoreen Mountains and forced me down. The ringing sound was stark and harsh to my ears, but I refused to move, even as the ground began to quake under my feet. I could see Eron in my periphery, his eyes momentarily wide before he shifted back into the First General and bellowed, "Stand your ground, Aria!"

Unbelievably, the Menrox applied even more pressure and my arms began to shake violently. I was trembling profusely and feared my already weakened arms would snap under the crushing weight.

"YOU SHALL NOT GIVE IN!" Eron roared once more and I was utterly determined to follow his instructions, despite the all-consuming terror of the axe as it slowly made its way towards my skull.

Ultimately, the pressure was too great and I was brought helplessly to my knees. I could hear Eron now on his feet and in a desperate attempt to loosen its hold, he hurled all manner of ice-forged weapons at the monster. And when the Menrox remained firmly in place, Eron released a desperate boom, "TALOS!" The

Third General once more raised his hands to the skies, his power gathering while he chanted for lightning. A charge zipped through the air and through the tips of my hair, the Third's magic building with it, but it was agonisingly slow and I knew I couldn't hold the Menrox at bay for much longer.

I heard Grandfather's muffled cries, but not one word broke through the fog of terror that blanketed my mind. So focused I was on not being sliced in two, that I didn't feel Vylnor's presence until he threw a barrage of dark magical energy at the Menrox and knocked the vile creature back. I gasped with relief as the pressure on my arms disappeared and collapsed to the ground, the borrowed blades dropping hastily from my hands.

Spinning on his feet, Vylnor charged and followed his assault with a fire spear, aimed at the shadowy creature's leg that toppled it to the ground and brought a couple of cottages with it for good measure. The sheer weight caused the earth in the vicinity to shake violently and I feared it would set off an earth tremor. Eventually the quakes subsided and I looked to see Vylnor now hunched over and panting. The Menrox was down but not slayed and he shouted irritably to Talos, "Finish it, you fool!"

Finally the bolt of lightning had been summoned and gloriously shattered its way through the Menrox's already damaged armour. A barrage of Skygge demons erupted violently from its fallen form and I shied away from the inky darkness which began to shift and writhe around us, when "*illumenti!*" was cried to my left.

The brightness following the spell was once more blinding and all I could so was turn my face away from the overwhelming glare. Once the glow faded, I blinked my eyes open to see Monroe now standing fifty paces away and looking utterly exhausted.

"Well done, my friend!" Grandfather called and a lacklustre wave was Monroe's only reply. Knowing they were outnumbered, the remaining Maliskas fled towards the nearest alleyways in search of escape, when Talos rallied for reinforcements and quickly set off to give chase.

"They cannot be allowed to escape!" he ordered and disappeared into the village with a consignment of elves. The immediate threat taken care of, I slowly rose and made my way towards Vylnor, but was soon intercepted by Eron who stood directly in my path. I could feel rather than see his face of disapproval and was surprised when Vylnor's gaze remained riveted to the floor.

His chest was heaving with exhaustion and I feared for what consequences his actions had wrought upon him, but it didn't take long for us to find out. I gasped in horror when he finally turned his pained eyes up to look at me and saw that they were veined in black. Sweat was beading on his pale forehead and he ignored Eron completely in favour of holding my gaze with an intense directness, that had my heart stuttering. After what felt like an eternity, Vylnor smiled, almost sincerely and winced, "You are welcome, pretty girl," before collapsing to the ground.

I intended to rush to his aid, but Eron clamped a

hand around my arm and stopped my advance.

"Are you mad, Aria?! You saw his eyes, it won't be long before he is a Hollow and an even greater danger to us!"

I struggled against him. "Release me Eron! Do not force my hand!"

Grandfather rushed over and gratingly repeated, "Calm down, my girl!" over and over again in some poor attempt to placate me, but I could feel my magic stirring with anger.

With a lowered tone I hissed at Eron, "Do not interfere!"

The elven General slowly exhaled as though defeated and added with a voice oddly filled with sadness, "Forgive me, Aria."

I frowned, not understanding his words or his tone, when something struck my temple and the world abruptly stopped.

I awoke to the glare of sunny yellow curtains and a pounding headache. I was back at the Heron Inn and vexed to say the least. I sat up cautiously and gently winced at the slight lump forming on my temple. Normally the healers would have seen to injuries like these, but after the battle I assumed they must still be tending to those with graver wounds and soon I was swiftly reminded of the reason behind the injury. *Eron.*

The elvish snowball struck me and stopped me from reaching Vylnor. Those pained, black-veined eyes caused my chest to ache, along with his final words,

'*You are welcome, pretty girl*'. His actions were always so contradicting and difficult to follow, but the most important message I took away from our encounter was that he *helped* me. Helped *us*. Despite the dire repercussions.

I looked down and saw I was still dressed in my dirty leathers. The blood-crusted surface felt disgusting and I could hear the subtle cracks when I began to rise from the cot. My face and hands remained itchy with the dried substance also, but, forgoing a quick wash, I remained intent on seeking out the Oromos Lord. Sadly, I was halted by a bout of nausea and clung weakly to the nearest side table and, waiting patiently for the feeling to pass, shortly left the room, determined to find out what had transpired and to check on Wendy's progress.

It was almost impossible to sneak into the main bar area, as the stair timbers were so uneven and creaky, so I strode in with purpose, unwilling to be questioned by anyone. The normally cheery room had now been turned into a large healing bay, the tables padded with blankets and cushions and arranged along each wall for the most severe patients. It upset me greatly, seeing the large number of injured elves currently occupying the makeshift beds, my thoughts drifting to Wynona and all the other lives that were lost because of one being's unrestrained cruelty and greed.

Very soon my eyes met Oriella's across the room while she tended to a warrior with deep claw marks down his forearm. I rushed over and embraced her, relieved to see she was well.

"Thank the Light you are OK, Oriella!"

"I mirror the sentiment entirely, Aria, I hear it was quite a fight." She eyed my face assessingly, her eyes sweeping my temple with a frown before turning towards my shredded sleeve and the angry teeth marks marring my skin. "Those look nasty, let me see to them."

I shook my head but smiled in gratitude. "Thank you but no. Please attend to those who need your immediate aide. Do you have word of Wendy's condition?"

She smiled and I let out the breath I had been holding. "She is fine, Aria. You did very well and I think she will enjoy waking up to a few less laughter lines on her face."

I rubbed the back of my head to hide the rush of fear that greeted me at remembering Wendy's precarious state and instead grimaced awkwardly. "I will admit, my skills need refinement," I muttered while Oriella chuckled good-naturedly, unaware of my inner turmoil.

"I would also welcome you as our kin, Aria. It is quite astonishing really, your transformation."

A small frown spread across her face and, curiosity piqued, I asked, "Why is that?"

"There will be time to discuss that later." Her reply was strangely evasive, but deciding not to press her further and having my own agenda to settle, I said, "All I know is that I will be in need of your training once more, Oriella. I charged straight into a Maliska unable to slow down."

She barked with laughter at that titbit of information and cheered, "And you lived to tell the tale, perhaps you are not so in need of my training after all." But her tone soon sobered. "Elven or not, I consider you a sister, Aria, and I would ask that you not run into anymore enemies if you can help it." She ended her light scold with an embrace and I turned to leave, but not before adding, "Now I have a certain First General to quiz and return this favour."

I gestured to my temple and she gaped in disbelief, before I stalked out the front door, foolishly unaware of the commotion I had walked into.

A battle had clearly been fought around the inn. The surrounding grounds were scorched, the cobbled paths tarnished with claws marks and blood, as well as being in a state of general disarray. I turned back to see the uneven timber-framed building remained mostly unscathed, but only just.

Elven warriors and villagers in varying states of exhaustion were currently clearing what debris they could from the large area in front of the inn and, with some difficulty, had begun removing a few hulking Norag bodies to undoubtedly be burned.

Oddly I received a few side glances from the other warriors, but quickly ignored their reactions when I heard the voice of my target. "I want a head count, all able-bodied warriors to me! Those of you who are wounded, take yourself to the healers!"

I saw Eron delivering his orders just outside the stables and stomped towards him, anger seeping from every pore.

"How dare you strike me! First General or not, I will return the favour and when you least expect it!" I ranted mercilessly, the expression of the elves in the immediate vicinity soon morphed into shock, when Monroe emerged from the stables.

"Tsk tsk, the First General hitting a female elf, how utterly despicable." I noticed the stares now turned to frowns on some of the warriors' faces, others even bold enough to outright scowl at Eron, who gritted quietly, "Do not judge my actions before you hear the reasoning."

He rumbled at our little crowd, "The rest of you, back to your duties!"

He grabbed my arm and attempted to pull me to one side but I shrugged him off, willing to stand my ground. "Where is he, Eron? Where is Vylnor?"

"You would ask after that traitor?!" he spat, incredulous.

"That traitor *saved* our lives!" I countered to no effect.

"Yes but that does not absolve him from a lifetime of heinous crimes! You saw his eyes as did I, he is nothing but a walking corpse."

I could tell Eron was struggling to keep his temper in check, but I cared little for his feelings in that moment or his opinions on Vylnor's condition. "Who are you to judge after you chose to let Wendy die!" I screamed in his face and was met with only silence.

Monroe walked to my side and squeezed my shoulder gently.

"They would have killed her anyway, Aria," Eron explained steadily, and I hissed, "It was *not* your call and you would do well to remember that I make my *own* decisions, especially when it concerns my family!"

Eron gave me a hard stare in return, his tone having turned lecturing. "You are young and naïve to the dance of war. Had you been taken, the Three Realms would have been lost. The risk was too great regardless of your feelings."

I snapped, "And don't you understand, had Wendy died, there would have been little left to lose in my eyes!"

Still stone-faced he countered, "Do not be so dramatic. I know loss. Have lived with it for many centuries. Know that when you risk yourself, you risk all of us."

Tears began to fall in my frustration, when I realised he would never see me as just Aria. I was the Portalis first and regardless of my feelings, he would act how he saw fit. "You would treat me as a pawn too then, Eron?"

His eyes widened a fraction. "That is not what I meant, Aria," and I held up my hand to halt his next words.

"What you say is of no consequence, for your actions speak much louder. Now where is Vylnor?"

Eron did not reply, his scowl had returned in full force at hearing the Oromos Lord's name once more and in the end, the information I craved was offered by Monroe.

"He has been taken to Elavon, to stand trial and certain execution for his crimes against the Mortal and

Elven Realms."

I stopped breathing and Eron sneered into the silence, "Consider the execution a mercy, Aria, for one who is not deserving of it." My heart thundered within my chest and I whispered, horrified, "When?"

It was Monroe who looked up, pity in his eyes as he uttered damningly, "On the morrow."

I reached the inn before I could burst into tears, refusing to let the elven prig see my obvious distress, and heard the tread of booted feet following from behind. Instinctually I knew it was Monroe and, reaching my chamber, opened the door to allow him entry. He gently closed it behind us and uttered, "*silentium*," and only then did I allow myself to cry.

"Now, now, Aria, there is no need for tears."

Despite his sympathetic words, I struggled to compose myself. Monroe thankfully remained a silent support throughout the ordeal and gave me the space to process my thoughts.

"I thought we agreed to be companions, partners even in this, Monroe? Yet why do some still feel the need to make my decisions for me? It's in moments like these that I feel trapped. Have I no freewill at all?"

The look he gave me was surprisingly, one of understanding. "You are in a unique and very rare position, Aria, one that not many will appreciate, especially not the old elven codgers."

"Even the warriors found me odd, Monroe. They have never given me such a look before. Are my actions … *wrong*?" I found it difficult to forget their stares, even before my little outburst with Eron. Did they think me a traitor, for how I tried to defend Vylnor?

"No Aria, that's not it," he replied, his hand now running across his stubbled chin in thought. "You are indeed of interest but not for those reasons. They look at your new form. I have never heard of a Portalis that is elven, nor one who began mortal. The pairings were always strictly between elves and of Anala's choosing. It may concern them to learn of your new form, for it will incite questions. Questions without answers, so we must tread carefully."

I balked at such a statement. "What can that *mean*, Monroe?" I asked and then more desperately, "Then what am I?"

He sighed and began pacing about the room. "I will not pretend to know the answers, but I believe these things have a way of revealing their truths when necessary. The important point to remember is that you have a choice. Your path is your own to forge, thus you are not without freewill, despite whatever motivations each of the Three Realms possess." Monroe always warmed me with his insight and I found his words calming. If I could not find the answers immediately, I would focus on what I could change now instead. Perhaps forging my own path would not be easy, but I was willing to fight for it.

I stilled, and settling on my next course of action uttered, "I will not let them execute Vylnor, Monroe." My resolve sharpened like a dagger with each word, regardless of my lingering doubts. There was no guarantee of him surviving the soul corruption and becoming even more of a danger to us all, but still I could not allow him to die, despite my general dislike of the male.

"Can I ask why?" Monroe's question startled me out of my dire musings. It was not accusatory, merely curious, so I answered honestly, "I have a feeling this is not the end of his journey."

"Hmmmm," he mumbled, brow furrowed and clearly deliberating, until I feared he would argue against my plan, when his face eventually morphed into a mischievous smile. "I've run into battles for decidedly poorer reasons than that!"

I beamed at him and he waggled his thick eyebrows in return, before crowing dramatically and raising a fist into the air.

"A rescue mission with impossible odds you say? Then I am with you, Aria my dear!"

I grinned from ear to ear, my mood decidedly lighter in the wake of his enthusiasm and a glint of challenge lit in his hazel eyes. "Let's go piss off some elves."

♦ COMING SOON ♦

The Locksnight Rises
Part Two of The Portalis Runes Trilogy

◆ ABOUT THE AUTHOR ◆

A.G. Brogan lives in the South of England with her husband, two children, and cocker spaniel. When she's not planning a walking holiday, the author is busy writing with a coffee in hand.

VISIT
www.agbrogan.com

MESSAGE
alice@agbrogan.com

FOLLOW
◎ @agbrogan

AUTHOR'S NOTE
This story began as a creative way to channel my anxiety. The more I wrote, the more it began to drift away, replaced by the thoughts and feelings of the characters on the page. I hope this book provides a temporary escape, even if it's just to one reader, and inspires people to pursue what they love.

CONTENT GUIDANCE

Please be aware this novel contains references relating to cannibalism, torture and violence, that might not be suitable to some readers.